SCORCH DRAGONS

ELEMENTALS:

SCORCH DRAGONS

BY
AMIE KAUFMAN

HARPER
An Imprint of HarperCollinsPublishers

ISBN 978-0-06-245801-8

Typography by Joe Merkel
Map by Virginia Allyn
19 20 21 22 23 PC/LSCH 10 9 8 7 6 5 4 3 2 1
❖
First Edition

For Michelle
My partner on many adventures
both past and still to come.

CHAPTER ONE

THE BATTLE BETWEEN THE DRAGONS AND THE
wolves was over.

Now, less than an hour later, Anders sat between his best friend, Lisabet, and his sister, Rayna, both of whom were on makeshift beds amid the bustle of the infirmary.

All the scorch dragons were in human form—the crowded cave was deep inside the mountain, not big enough for even one actual dragon. As it was, bodies were packed into every corner as medics hurried back and forth.

Anders's attention was abruptly yanked away from the flurry of activity when Lisabet groaned beside him. Her pale skin was whiter than usual right now, and even her freckles didn't look like themselves. She'd hit her head hard defending the dragons from the wolves she and Anders had accidentally led here.

"Are you okay?" He leaned in to get a better look at

her, but the answer came from his other side, in his twin's dry voice.

"She tried to knock her brains out. She's probably not."

He turned to look at Rayna, who was curled up under a huge pile of blankets, only her head visible. Her warm brown skin had turned a dangerous gray when she'd first been hit by a wolf's ice spear, and though it was slowly coming back to normal, her cheeks were still unnaturally pale, the color of ashes. *Cold damage*, the healer had said.

One of Anders's Ulfar Academy classmates had done that to her. He and Lisabet had come here to try and save Rayna, and his class had followed in pursuit. If *only* they hadn't followed, everybody would be safe right now.

During the long race to reach Drekhelm, Anders had been constantly afraid. Afraid Rayna was about to be sacrificed by the dragons. Afraid he wouldn't know how to save her even if he did make it. Afraid she wasn't his twin sister at all, since she could transform into a scorch dragon while he was an ice wolf, and everyone knew it was impossible to find both in the same family.

But instead of saving her, he'd found her settling in just fine. He'd brought danger right to her doorstep, and he'd made enemies of the wolves he'd just learned to think of as his pack. And now he was trapped at Drekhelm, the dragon stronghold.

"I'm okay." Lisabet's voice jolted him back to the present.

"The nurse said you'd have a headache," he told her quietly. "And you have to stay awake for a few hours more, in case there's any damage inside your head that they can't see."

"Rayna?" she whispered, and Anders and Lisabet both looked across at Anders's sister, who was still shivering.

"I'm fine," Rayna insisted. "It was just an ice spear, it'll wear off eventually. I'm lucky it only nicked me. I'll probably be walking around in an hour."

Anders felt a quick rush of affection, warming him from the inside out. That was Rayna, ready to get up and keep going, as she had been all their lives. He still couldn't quite believe he was by her side again.

But a nurse loomed up behind her, his hands on his hips. "You won't be going anywhere in an hour," he said firmly. "If you're lucky, you'll be discharged in the morning, and then it'll only be because we have others worse than you. As for you two"—and he nodded to Anders and Lisabet, his square-jawed face stern for the two wolves— "you can go to guest quarters. We've got an escort waiting to take you there. The Dragonmeet won't want to see you until the morning."

Anders followed his gaze and saw Ellukka, the blond

girl Rayna had said was her friend. She'd been anything but friendly at first, but right after the battle she'd seemed to feel a little differently. She'd seen Lisabet defending Leif, the head of the Dragonmeet.

Just now, she had her arms folded across her chest and was leaning against the wall by the infirmary door. She was bigger and broader than Anders, and with her arms crossed like that, she looked like she meant business all over again.

Anders turned back to Rayna. "I don't want to leave you here," he said, and his concern was *mostly* for his sister.

"They won't let me go until tomorrow," she said. "You know where to find me. Go and get some rest, I'll be okay."

His instincts still rebelled against leaving his twin, but he knew she was right. She had been safe up until now, and he did desperately need to rest. He'd run with the pack all yesterday across the plains, and overnight he'd crossed a river and climbed a mountain with Lisabet. It was late morning now, which meant he'd been on the move for more than a day straight.

"Tell them to call me if you get worse," he said to Rayna.

"If I were you," the nurse said to Anders, scowling, "I'd be more worried about myself right now. There are going to be a *lot* of questions for you tomorrow, and if you don't have answers the Dragonmeet likes, you can be sure they'll extract better ones."

"Leave him alone," Rayna snapped, pushing up on one elbow.

With one last significant look at all of them, the nurse stalked off to see to other patients, and Rayna turned her attention to Anders. "I'll make sure someone calls you if I get worse," she promised. "And let's deal with tomorrow when we get there. We'll make them understand."

Anders wasn't nearly as confident as she sounded—Rayna's version of talking their way out of things was what had started their transformation to wolf and dragon in the first place—but he knew there was nothing he could do today, not with his sister and his best friend both almost too weak to move.

So he helped Lisabet sit up, then stand, keeping an arm carefully around her. Ellukka pushed away from the doorway to lead them outside, but despite her improved opinion of Lisabet she didn't seem inclined to help keep her steady.

She led Anders and Lisabet down hallways carved into the dark stone of the mountain, all human-size rather than dragon-size. Anders wondered if, like the wolves, the dragons spent most of their time in human form.

The trio passed lamps that appeared to be made of solid metal, fixed to the wall by brackets. Whenever they came within a few steps of one, it began to glow softly, and when Anders looked behind him, the others had faded into darkness once more.

Lisabet was watching them as well. "That's actually happening, right?" she asked. "It's not just that I hit my head?"

"The lights?" Ellukka asked, looking over her shoulder. "Well of course. They're artifacts."

Now that Anders looked more closely, he could see the rows of runes engraved around the sconces. Those runes meant the lamps had been designed by wolves and forged by dragons—before the last great battle ten years before, no doubt.

Ellukka stopped by a cupboard built into the hallway, pulling out mismatched clothes for them in blues and greens and reds—the dragons seemed to prefer bright colors, and even in the short time he'd been here, Anders had noticed they all dressed differently. The wolves all wore the same uniform—a sign of their pack, their togetherness.

"This is the guest area," Ellukka said, in answer to his questioning glance. "There are spare rooms, spare clothes, things like that."

"Do you have a lot of visitors?" he asked, trying to

imagine who could possibly come all the way up a mountain. Trying to find a way toward friendly conversation with this girl who seemed to know his sister so well. He needed every bit of help he could get right now.

"Most dragon families and groups move around a lot," Ellukka said. "We live pretty spread out. There are aeries all up and down the Icespire mountain range—in mountains all over Vallen, actually—so we visit each other quite often. It's usually easier not to carry a lot of your stuff."

She stopped at a wooden door. Inside was a cozy bedroom with a bed on either side, each draped with a thick patchwork quilt. A rug covered the stone floor, and a glass-paned window peeked out onto the face of the mountain itself. There was another wooden door on the other side of the little room, and a water clock on the wall, a slow stream of liquid trickling through marked tubes to show the passing of time.

Good, Anders thought. They could use that to keep track of how long Lisabet needed to stay awake. And how far away morning was, and with it the Dragonmeet.

"It's warm in here," Lisabet said, and Anders thought immediately of the hot glow he'd seen deep inside the mountain as he'd flown above Drekhelm on Rayna's back. "And it was out in the hall too," she continued. "But there aren't any fireplaces. Do you use the lava?"

"What else?" Ellukka said, dumping the clothes on one of the beds and sorting them into two piles. "And some artifacts help with the temperature as well. There's a bath right through that door there, as much hot water as you want. I mean, I know wolves prefer cold, but I assume you don't want cold showers."

"Not when we're in human form," Lisabet agreed.

"Well, get clean," Ellukka said, folding her arms and backing up toward the door. "You smell like wet dog."

The door closed behind her, and Anders sank down onto one of the beds. Every muscle in his body ached, but he made himself lean over to unlace his boots, and then pull off socks wet from the snow outside.

He realized he was still wearing his sister's coat. He turned his head and inhaled, and found it held that scent that was uniquely Rayna's, though now there was a hint of spicy sweetness to it that hadn't been there before. And even though it wasn't quite the same, the familiarity of it made his eyes ache.

He had done it. He was here, with Rayna. Whatever came next, he'd find a way through it, because he was with his sister again.

"You have the first bath," he said to Lisabet. He needed a few minutes to pull himself together.

She disappeared through the door, and he flopped backward onto the bed, staring up at the ceiling. It was smooth stone, just like the walls. *Because this room is inside a mountain,* he reminded himself. *Because it's inside Drekhelm.*

What would the Dragonmeet say tomorrow? What answers did they want to extract?

How could he convince them to let him stay near Rayna, without betraying the wolves?

But despite the nurse's words and the fear they'd kindled, he also admitted to himself that the dragons weren't at all what he'd imagined. He didn't quite know what they *were* like yet, who they were, but the stories at Ulfar and in Holbard had always made them out to be bloodthirsty villains, living only to hurt those who weren't like them. And whatever the truth was, he now knew it was much more complicated than that. The dragons had friends here, family. They had rooms for guests and debates about the right thing to do.

Rayna had found a home here in a way he'd never imagined possible. He wasn't sure what that meant for him, or for Lisabet.

He was still lost in this thought when Lisabet came out of the bathroom. She was clad in a dragon shirt, tunic, and trousers, her black curls wet. There was color back in her face now, her skin a little less white and a little more pink beneath her freckles, but she was nibbling her lip in the way she did when she was worried.

"Anders," she said quietly. "What are we going to do?"

"I don't know what we *can* do," he admitted. "If the Dragonmeet has questions for us, and we can't answer them . . ."

"I know." Her words were barely audible. "But we can't go home. Somehow, I thought we'd be taking Rayna back with us, even though I suppose there was never really any chance that we'd manage to . . . I mean, the pack was always going to follow us. Professor Ennar would never let us go alone. And what would we have done with a dragon once we got back to Holbard?"

Anders felt another deep pang of guilt at the thought of Ennar, their combat teacher, who had put herself and all the class in danger, coming after them. If only, if *only* they hadn't followed.

"Rayna likes it here," he said, not quite knowing what he made of that fact.

"How can she?" asked Lisabet. Lisabet had always been the one to stand up for the dragons in class, to ask questions about how they could be as evil as their teachers claimed, when they'd once worked alongside wolves to produce the magical artifacts found all over Vallen. But now she looked small, and scared.

"She's had weeks," he said. "It doesn't sound like very long, but I was at Ulfar for the same amount of time. And we got to know each other pretty well."

"Of course," Lisabet said. "You're my best friend. She's had the same time to get to know the dragons, I suppose. She'll want to stay here."

"Well, besides the fact that she made friends here, the Wolf Guard tried to kill her last time she was in Holbard," he pointed out. "She'll want us to stay too." She'd want *him* to stay, at least—he'd make her see about Lisabet. "I don't know if it's safe, but we don't have anywhere else to go. We stole the chalice. Or at least I did, but they won't believe you had nothing to do with it. Not after the fight. They saw you defend Leif."

"I had to," she said helplessly, sinking down onto the bed opposite him. "If the head of the Dragonmeet had been killed, it would have started a war big enough to make the last great battle look like a game. Anyone can see that."

"Anyone can when you explain it," he agreed. "But you saw it straight away, and nobody else stopped to think at all." That was Lisabet, always clever, always solving puzzles. "What do you think would happen if we did try to go back?"

"Exile," she whispered. "Stealing the chalice and

fighting just now was a betrayal of the pack. They could put us on a ship out of Vallen, never to return."

They were both quiet, imagining that total loss of their home, that separation from everything they knew. In her own way, Lisabet had lost even more than he had.

Lisabet was the daughter of Sigrid, who was the Fyrstulf, the leader of Ulfar—of all the wolves. And though Sigrid was sometimes terrifying, usually overwhelming, and possibly less than honest, she was still Lisabet's mother. Anders knew firsthand what losing family was like, but he had Rayna back, at least for now. Lisabet's loss was only beginning.

Anders could picture the Fyrstulf's cold, pale stare as clearly as if she were right in front of him. The fact that Lisabet was her daughter wouldn't save them from her wrath, or from exile, if she got her hands on them. Lisabet had to deal not only with the loss of the pack, but with the knowledge that her own mother wouldn't allow her to return to it.

"Go and wash," she said eventually. "I promise I won't fall asleep while you're gone, I'll follow doctor's orders. You'll feel better once you're clean."

He gathered up his half of the fresh clothes, making his way back into the bathroom. It was a small room with a stout wooden tub, a rail laden with towels, and another window, though the view outside was hidden in mist or cloud. He discovered there was a showerhead above the tub and also a spout lower down, in case you wanted to fill the bath. He passed on the idea of standing under the shower and instead turned on the spout, peeling off the rest of his clothes and climbing in carefully once the water was most of the way up the sides of the bath.

The hot water came up to his chin, his fingers and toes tingling as they warmed up, his skin itching as it adjusted to the temperature. And then the heat was soaking into his exhausted bones, finally warming him up completely for the first time since he'd left the wolf camp at the cache. Back at Ulfar, even warm weather had made him feel woolly-headed and tired. Now, heat just felt good. That was strange. What had changed?

His thoughts swirled around like the hot water as he scrubbed himself clean, a mix of relief at knowing his sister was nearby again—that he could walk down the hallway to find her whenever he liked—and worry, and regret for his friends at Ulfar. He'd begun to find a home there, and now he'd never sit around the table in the dining hall with them again, watching Sakarias try to wheedle his way into everybody's spare dessert, while Viktoria quietly put vegetables on his plate while he wasn't looking. No more suffering through combat class with everyone else, running endless laps around the gym under Professor Ennar's watchful eye.

He *had* begun to find a home there, and now he'd lost it—and he had no idea if he could find a home here instead. He was an orphan, and he was used to making do wherever he had to, but would the Dragonmeet even consider it? What would happen if he couldn't—or wouldn't—answer their questions?

He leaned down to pull out the plug and slowly dried himself. The clothes Ellukka had grabbed for him were soft and well-made: a pair of dark-blue trousers, a light-blue shirt, and a dark-green tunic to go on over it. As practical as his wolf's clothing, though more casual.

He pushed open the door and found Lisabet sitting on her bed eating a bowl of thick stew.

"Ellukka came back with food," she informed him around a mouthful.

Anders's bowl was sitting on the small table by the door, and he picked it up, sinking down onto his own bed, the soft patchwork quilt giving beneath him. For the next few minutes everything was quiet as they dunked dark-brown bread in the thick gravy of the stew and chewed their way through beef and carrot and potato.

When they were done, Lisabet still had a couple of hours to stay awake, so they tipped their boots over to rest the leather against the warm stone floor, hoping they'd dry, and leaned back against their pillows. Anders was dying to crawl under the quilt and close his eyes—because he was exhausted, and because falling asleep would give him a break from the thoughts and questions racing around his head. But he made himself keep his eyes open.

"So," he said, trying the words out loud. "We're in Drekhelm."

"We're lying in their beds," Lisabet agreed. "Pack and paws, we couldn't be more in Drekhelm if we tried."

"I wish you hadn't come," Anders whispered. "Not that I don't want you here," he hurried on, when he heard her hurt intake of breath. "But now you can't go home. I'm used to moving to new places, to finding my feet wherever I go. But Ulfar's always been your home."

"We don't even know if they'll let us stay," she said quietly. "You heard that man in the infirmary."

"That's what's worrying me most," he admitted. "What if they want us to tell them things we can't?"

"We might not have a choice. And they're not just going to ask questions about Ulfar's secrets, they're going to have questions about your icefire as well."

"*I* have questions about my icefire," Anders said. "I don't know how I did it, but I can tell it's . . . gone. I don't think I could do it again, I don't know how."

15

"Maybe we can tell them that," Lisabet whispered. "They'll think we're less of a threat." She didn't sound very hopeful.

But the idea was starting to take root in Anders's mind. "We don't have to just wait around," he said quietly. "We've been talking about how we can't go back to Holbard, but maybe there's an option in between going there and staying here."

"What do you mean?"

"If Rayna's better in the morning, she could help us get somewhere else. Somewhere they can't find us, at least until we know what they've got planned for us," he suggested.

"Do you think she'll be well enough to move?" Lisabet's tone said she was already seriously considering the idea, which told Anders she'd been as worried as he was.

"I think we should go see her as soon as the sun comes up," he said. "And find out."

As the evening drew on, the only noise in their room was the slow trickling of the water in the clock, and the occasional soft click as a tube filled up completely, and the hands ticked on to show another quarter hour, draining out the water to start again.

Every so often he checked to make sure Lisabet was still awake, and she always was. Eventually the clock had counted off the hours they'd been told to wait, and it was late in the afternoon, almost a day and a half since they'd last woken up. They left the blinds open so the morning light would wake them, and each climbed under their quilts.

Anders waited for sleep to take him. The mattress was luxuriously soft, and the quiet trickle of the water lulled him. Against all the odds, and in defiance of every story he'd ever heard growing up, this was the most comfortable bed he'd ever slept in. Sleep tugged at his eyelids.

Whatever tomorrow held, he'd have to be ready to fight. If Rayna could hide them, that would buy them more time to learn the Dragonmeet's intentions and try to make a plan. If she couldn't, he'd have to face down the Dragonmeet and do something he'd never imagined he'd want to—he'd have to find a way to convince the council that he and Lisabet should be allowed to stay at Drekhelm.

CHAPTER TWO

ANDERS WOKE UP BECAUSE HE WAS *STARVING.* For a long moment he couldn't work out where he was, staring up at a smooth stone ceiling that looked nothing like his room at Ulfar. Then he realized he couldn't hear Sakarias mumbling in his sleep or the distant sounds of the city.

It came back to him in a flash: he was at Drekhelm.

He pushed upright, looking around the little room he was sharing with Lisabet, who was still a sleeping lump under her quilt. They were alone, and the room was far too bright. He shoved back his own quilt, hurrying over to the window and peering out.

Behind him, there was a bleary groan of protest from Lisabet as his movement woke her, but he barely heard it. The sun was much too far above the horizon, and his heart thumped an alarm—it was mid-morning. They'd slept much too long, and their chance of finding Rayna without running into anyone on the way was surely gone.

"Whatimesit?" Lisabet mumbled from under her blankets.

"Morning," he said, his head whirling. "*Late* morning." *Pack and paws.*

He crossed back to his bed, sitting down to pull on his boots, lacing them tight. They had to get moving, do something. They had to try and find a back way to Rayna, to figure out how to keep themselves out of the hands of the Dragonmeet and their threats.

"We'd better hurry," said Lisabet, pushing off her quilt and hurrying out of bed, over to the door so she could rest her ear against it, one hand on the doorknob.

"There must be more than one way to the infirmary," he said. "Rayna will . . ." But he trailed off, because Lisabet had the strangest expression on her face.

She stood with her hand on the doorknob, trying to turn it, then trying again. She shoved her shoulder against the door, rattled the knob one more time, and finally gave up, leaning against the door and looking back at him. "It's locked," she said. "They've locked us in."

Anders stared at her, a shiver going through him.

They were prisoners.

"We can't just wait here until they come for us," she said.

"Agreed. And Rayna would have come for us herself by now if she knew we were locked in. So she doesn't know, or else they haven't let her out of the infirmary yet."

He crossed over to Lisabet, dropping to a crouch beside her to take a good look at the lock. He could see a tiny sliver of the corridor beyond through the keyhole. This lock didn't look much harder to pick than Hayn's had been, but he didn't have so much as a hairpin to try with. He gazed at the metal, trying to think through what he knew of locks.

Neither he nor Lisabet were strong enough to break it, so they needed to trick it somehow. Lisabet pressed her fingers to it, pushing hard, though they both knew it wouldn't work. Seeing her gave Anders an idea, though.

"Could you freeze it?" he asked. "If you can blast metal with enough cold, it's not so hard to break afterward."

"I can try," she said, closing her eyes in concentration, then slipping down into her wolf form.

Anders stepped back, and Lisabet brought down her paws, casting a quick, thin ice spear straight at the lock.

It struck the keyhole, and the metal all around it turned white with frost.

Anders followed it up with the hardest kick he could muster, twisting to stomp the sole of his boot against the lock, driving his heel into it.

The lock cracked but held.

"Again," he said, and Lisabet cast a second spear, the air in the room turning freezingly, refreshingly cold.

Anders kicked once more with all his might, the shock of it traveling up his leg.

This time the lock came to pieces, and he pulled them free of the door, which swung open slowly.

Lisabet pushed herself back into human form, panting. "Transforming is much harder work than usual in this heat," she said, grabbing her boots and lacing them up quickly. Meanwhile, Anders stuck his head out into the hallway to check that the coast was clear.

"Let's try for the infirmary," he said. "I want to find out where Rayna is."

"The dragons are going to ask questions if they see us wandering around," Lisabet pointed out. "They locked us in."

"Most of them won't even know who we are," he replied. "We look just like them when we're in our human form. And we're wearing their clothes."

She hesitated, but he knew she was going to come around. Otherwise, she wouldn't have helped him break open the door. "Let's do it," she agreed.

They made their way quietly out into the hall, keeping on the balls of their feet, ready to move—ready to run—at the first sign of trouble.

They did their best to retrace the path they'd followed with Ellukka the day before, but it proved busy, and soon enough they were obliged to duck into lesser-used passageways, taking each new turn that seemed to lead them in the right direction—or so Anders hoped. The first few hallways they looked down were nothing special—they found more bedrooms, and then a small communal area with nobody in it. The common area had tables and chairs, some couches, some playing cards left out. On the bright side, it also had a bowl full of dark bread slices spread thickly with creamy butter, waiting for hungry dragons to come along. Anders and Lisabet both took a slice in each hand and kept on their way.

It wasn't until a few hallways later that they discovered the room of maps.

When Anders carefully poked his head through the doorway, the chamber waiting for him was much larger than any they'd been in so far, except for the Great Hall.

The walls were plastered with maps, showing everything from small sections of Vallen to the whole of the island—that map took up nearly an entire wall.

A big table ran the length of the chamber, with a dozen seats around it, all facing toward one end of the room.

At that end, a huge map—taller than Anders himself, taking up another whole wall—was pinned up.

It was a map of the city of Holbard, capital of Vallen and home to Ulfar Academy. Around the edges were marked the plains that surrounded the city on three sides, as well as the harbor that bordered it on the fourth.

"That's a map of home," Lisabet said, poking her head in beside his.

They both walked into the room, their footsteps audible on the stone as they made their way up to stare at the Holbard map.

"There's Ulfar," he said, pointing at the squares that outlined the adult barracks and the Academy. There was a large red cross marking it.

"Why do they need to look at it on a map?" she whispered, sounding as worried as he felt.

They walked along the base of the map, taking in all the landmarks they knew so well. By the docks, there was another place marked with a bold red cross. Anders peered, trying to determine exactly what it was. Suddenly, all the air went out of him. "Lisabet," he whispered.

She was at his side in a moment. "What is it?"

"Right here, this is where the fire was at the docks. This is the exact place, the exact buildings."

"Pack and paws," she whispered.

"Are you lost?" someone said from behind them, in a pointed tone. It was Ellukka's voice.

They both turned and found her standing beside Mikkel, the smirking boy they'd met on the mountainside the day before with Ellukka and Rayna. Mikkel dipped into a deep, sarcastic bow. "I see our honored guests have been exploring," he said.

"We've been looking all over for you," Ellukka added.

"You thought we'd be in our room, where you locked us in?" Anders asked pointedly.

Mikkel shrugged. "You're wolves," he said, as though that explained it.

Ellukka, despite her irritated expression, actually looked away. Maybe she wasn't quite as unapologetic as he was.

Lisabet cut across his thoughts. "Why is the site of the docks fire marked on your map?"

Ellukka frowned, walking into the room to stand by them and stare up at the map. After a moment, Mikkel followed. He was tall, with a shock of copper hair, long and curly on top, short on the sides, and had fair skin.

He looked a lot like Anders's wolf friend Sakarias, except that where Sakarias's eyes were blue and always full of laughter, Mikkel's were a dark brown—clever, intent, and maybe even unfriendly.

"Right there," Anders said, pointing. "That's where a huge fire started just a week ago. It was dragonsfire, I saw it myself."

"Look," said Mikkel. "I don't know what it was, but nobody would have lit a fire in the middle of Holbard. It's too dangerous." He sounded sure. "We'd know."

"Or perhaps they didn't tell you," said Lisabet, "because you're twelve."

"Maybe someone was investigating the fire," Ellukka said. "It's just a map of the city."

"It's more than that," Lisabet replied. "You know it doesn't look good."

"What, and you're looking good right now?" Mikkel snapped. "You just broke down your door and started snooping around Drekhelm."

Anders stared at him. "We broke out after you *locked us in*!"

"You're *wolves*!" Mikkel replied, voice rising to a shout.

"And?" Anders replied hotly. "That means what, exactly?"

"It means you're not to be trusted," Mikkel replied.

"And you proved it by prying into our business at the first opportunity you got."

Anders growled in the back of his throat. "You can't seriously be arguing that. We went looking for my sister after you *locked us in*, and can I remind you again that we found a map marked with your *attack plans* when we did?"

"Look," said Lisabet, holding up her hands. "I don't think anyone's looking good here. Are we really going to stand around debating things like whether locking us in or breaking out was the worse crime?"

Ellukka spoke up. "We came to get you because Leif is ready to see you. You should ask him what this map is if you're so sure it's evidence of something."

Anders's heart fell into his boots. They'd lost their chance to get away from the Dragonmeet. Now they'd have to face whatever the dragons had in store for them.

But Mikkel was still gazing up at the map, head to one side, as if he was trying to make sense of it too. "What's this?" he asked, pointing at Ulfarstrat. "The main street?"

Lisabet turned to see what he was looking at. "That's right," she said.

Mikkel was quiet for a little before he spoke again. "What's Holbard like?" He didn't sound angry or frustrated now. Mostly, he just sounded curious.

"Big," said Lisabet eventually. "Big stone walls around

the city, lots of cobbled streets, and colorful houses. They're mostly two or three stories high, and they're all painted pinks and blues and yellows and greens, you name it. The window frames are wood or white, and the rooftops are covered in grass—it keeps the cold out. In spring and summer, flowers grow up there, and it's almost like being out on the plains. And the city's on the harbor, so the ships' masts are like a forest of bare trees when the harbor's full. There are huge metal arches at the port, wind guards. Wolves and dragons made them together, to keep the ships safe."

"Artifacts so big a ship can sail under them?" Mikkel whistled, impressed.

"There are all kinds of people there," Lisabet continued. "From just about every country there is. They speak different languages, they look different, they sell different food and play different music, it's wonderful. The sea's right there beside the city, so whatever the weather is, we know about it. Sometimes the rain's so hard it seems like it wants to drive us into the ground, and sometimes you get a warm breeze that feels like it's come all the way across the ocean from some other country."

Mikkel and Lisabet seemed to have forgotten Anders and Ellukka were even there. In that moment, Mikkel could have been any of their fellow students at Ulfar.

At first, when Lisabet had said "big" and mentioned the walls, Anders had thought she was trying to make sure Mikkel understood how well-defended Holbard was. But that wasn't it at all. Lisabet had seen what Anders hadn't, or she'd suspected it. The young dragons were as curious about wolves as the wolves were about dragons. They probably had their own scary stories to match the ones Sakarias had told around the campfire, come to that.

It was Ellukka who broke the spell. "The Dragonmeet will be waiting," she said. "And when I left the infirmary, they were about to let Rayna out, so she should be there to meet us in the Great Hall."

"Good luck," said Mikkel, sounding like perhaps he even meant it a tiny bit. "I'm meeting Theo in the gardens. I'll see you later."

Anders swallowed, then nodded. He couldn't wait to see his twin, but he had to focus. Since they'd missed their chance to hide, he had to find a way to stay at Drekhelm without betraying the wolves. At least Mikkel's words made it sound like the young dragon maybe did expect him to stick around, but the cross on the map was a reminder that there was a lot Anders didn't know about the dragons.

He had to look after the people he cared about. That was what mattered.

Rayna was indeed waiting for them outside the door to the Great Hall, and as soon as she saw Anders, she hurried over to his side, slipping her hand into his, giving it a squeeze. Her touch was familiar, her skin warm.

Wolves didn't like hot weather—it made them weaker, made it harder to think clearly—any more than dragons liked the cold. But her warmth didn't bother him now, just as the bath hadn't the night before. It was very odd. Perhaps something had changed in the wake of the incredible, impossible silver icefire he'd thrown to end the battle the day before? It had been neither the ice of the wolves nor the fire of the dragons . . . but somehow both.

With Rayna on one side and Lisabet on the other, he followed Ellukka through the double doors into the Great Hall, where the Dragonmeet was waiting. It was a huge room with a high ceiling so smooth he wasn't sure if it had been carved or if some long-ago lava bubble had somehow created it. Enormous doors, big enough for a dragon to fly through, led out to the side of the mountain, though just now they were bolted closed. Below those, the human-size doors through which his classmates had come were also closed and bolted.

At the other end of the room was a long table occupied by the twenty-five members of the Dragonmeet. Leif, their leader—the Drekleid—was sitting at its head.

He had a shock of red hair and a neatly trimmed beard, and ruddy cheeks, as if he spent a lot of time outdoors. He was built on sturdy lines, and looked strong and capable. At the moment he wore a serious expression.

Anders had a better chance to study the rest of the Dragonmeet now than he'd had the day before—they were as mixed as the people of Holbard, their clothes practical and comfortable, brightly colored in most cases. Whereas the wolves of Ulfar all wore uniforms, if these people hadn't been sitting around a table together, Anders never would have known there was anything to connect them. They lacked a sense of . . . pack.

The two youngest looked no older than the final-year students at Ulfar, and they wore slightly friendlier expressions than the others. Anders also saw the man who looked like Ellukka again—he had a heavyset, broad-shouldered build with suntanned skin and a wheat-blond braid, and he was frowning. And beside him was the man who had been most suspicious of him the day before, hard eyes unfriendly beneath unruly black eyebrows, mouth hidden by a bushy beard. He was almost as big as his companion, and even more intimidating.

"Good morning," Leif said, and Anders stopped inspecting the others, turning his attention to the man who led them. "Anders, Lisabet, we all met briefly yesterday, but once again, these are the members of the Dragonmeet. We are chosen by election. We come together from all over Vallen to discuss the issues most important to dragons, and to decide what action, if any, we should take. I am the Drekleid, the leader of the Dragonmeet, but we are all equals here. I lead the discussion, but I do not make our decisions."

Anders nodded, fighting the urge to glance at Rayna or Lisabet, or even at Ellukka, who stood beside Rayna as if she were facing the Dragonmeet as well. He thought perhaps Leif was letting him know, with his quiet words, that Anders needed to find a way to appeal to all twenty-five people sitting in front of him, not just their leader.

"Thank you for letting us stay," he said, and Rayna eased a little closer, pressing her shoulder against his encouragingly—reminding him he wasn't alone.

"That's not decided yet," growled the man with the bushy beard.

Leif replied as if he hadn't spoken. "As you can imagine, we have many questions for you."

Anders's heart was thumping. How was he supposed to answer the dragons' questions—which would certainly be about the wolves—without being the traitor his friends and classmates already thought he was? It was one thing to hope he could find a home here in Drekhelm. It was another to cause harm or hurt to those back at Ulfar.

And what would happen if he couldn't? What exactly had the nurse in the infirmary meant when he'd talked about extracting answers?

Lisabet spoke beside him, her voice quiet, and he knew she had the same fear in her mind as he did. "We'll try and answer."

"The first," Leif said, "is how you found us. We have gone to great lengths to conceal Drekhelm—we were forced to move after the last great battle ten years ago, and we do not wish to do so again."

That, Anders thought he could answer, because there was a good chance the dragons would guess anyway. "We used Fylkir's chalice," he said, and a murmur went through some of the adults sitting up at the table.

"An artifact?" an older woman with a thin face asked. "How does it work?"

"You fill it with water," he explained. "And then float a special needle in it. It acts like a compass, only it points to the largest gathering of dragons in Vallen."

"And why have you wolves never used this to attack us before?" Bushy Beard demanded.

"We thought it was broken," said Lisabet. "It was just a week ago that anyone began to suspect that if you took it all the way out of the city, away from the people in

Holbard who might have traces of dragon blood, and used it at the equinox, when the magical essence in nature is strongest and when the dragons come together in greatest numbers to celebrate, it might work one more time. And it did."

"And we stole it," Anders concluded. "To try and find my sister."

There was another round of rumbling from the adults, most of whom, Anders knew from the day before, still didn't believe Rayna could be his sister, since he was a wolf and she was a dragon.

The man with the blond braid who might be Ellukka's father leaned forward. "And where is the chalice now?" he asked.

Anders and Lisabet exchanged a look—the dragons really weren't going to like this answer.

"We dropped it," Anders said. "When Rayna and Ellukka and Mikkel found us on the mountainside. We think our class was tracking us, so they probably found it."

"So you left a trail," Bushy Beard said, lifting a finger to point at them. "You showed them the way to attack us!"

"No!" Anders and Lisabet replied in unison. "Of course not!"

"Father," protested Ellukka from one side, in unexpected defense, but the big man with the blond braid shook his head at her, and she fell silent.

Leif lifted one hand to still the murmurs that were starting again. "If *I* were going to leave a trail for attackers," he said mildly, "I'm not sure I'd leave it for an army of twelve-year-olds, and luckily for us, that is what we got."

"This time," said a pallid, silver-haired woman farther up the table, her expression grim.

"What will the wolves do?" Leif asked Anders and Lisabet. "Will they be readying themselves for war?"

Anders was torn—how did he answer that? The truth was, he and Lisabet knew that Sigrid was doing exactly that. They'd overheard her talking about her animosity toward the dragons in her study, the need to find them. But if he admitted that, would the dragons just attack the wolves before the wolves could make the first move?

Lisabet answered quietly. "They don't know enough about you. It's easy to believe stories—you believe them about us, I can tell. And there have been fires and kidnappings in Holbard. Our class came to rescue us, not to fight. But like you said, we're twelve. The leaders of the wolves don't discuss their plans with us."

Her voice was calm and even. However upset she was about losing the only home she'd ever known, she was doing a good job now of explaining why they should be allowed to stay at Drekhelm.

34

Finally, one of the two youngest members of the Dragonmeet spoke, the girl. She had light-brown skin and curly blond hair tamed into a messy bun. Her mouth and her round cheeks looked as though they were made for smiling, which made it hard to be afraid of her. "It was only ten years ago, the last great battle," she said. "Don't the wolves remember how things were before it?"

"I don't," Lisabet replied. "We were only two years old when it happened. But the way I hear it, things weren't easy between dragons and wolves even then."

"This is true," Leif allowed.

Bushy Beard dismissed Lisabet's words with a flick of his fingers. "Can we get to the point? They've proven they're willing to attack us. They've proven they want a war."

"No," Anders insisted. They had to make the dragons see that the wolves weren't all bad, they weren't what the dragons thought of them. "We only came for my sister."

"If she's that," Bushy Beard scoffed.

"I believe she is," Leif said quietly.

Rayna slipped her hand into his, squeezing tightly, but the Drekleid didn't seem inclined to say any more, at least for now.

Ellukka's father spoke again. "Torsten"—that must be Bushy Beard's name, Anders realized—"is not talking about the arrival of these children's classmates. He is talking about the theft. Anders, Lisabet—the wolves who you say came to rescue you stole artifacts from us. One of them was the Snowstone."

Every face up and down the table was grave now. During the battle, Anders had seen his friends Mateo and Jai disappear into the depths of Drekhelm's caves, and when the pack had retreated, each of the two wolves had been carrying something in their mouths. Had one of those somethings been this Snowstone? The name sounded familiar, but Anders couldn't place it.

"What does the Snowstone do?" he asked.

"In the right hands, it can alter the weather," Leif said gravely.

Anders's heart thumped. He *had* heard of it before. He'd seen it in the Skraboks—the records of artifacts—mentioned beside the plate that brought rain. "It makes the weather cold," he said.

"Yes," Leif said. "It can cause blizzards, bring hail and snow. In the hands of the wolves, if they can make it work, it could bring cold to Drekhelm. To all of Vallen. That is why we have always kept it safe here. The Fyrstulf can take away the heat we need to transform, and weaken us until we are easily defeated."

As if the Snowstone were already at work, Anders felt

a chill go through him. Sigrid was easily ruthless enough to drive the dragons from Drekhelm, or from Vallen altogether. By now she'd know they had her daughter, and she would be more furious still. It was one thing to convince the dragons they weren't bad purely because they were wolves, it was another to convince anyone—including himself—that Sigrid wasn't a danger to the dragons.

Every dragon—including Rayna—would be in danger from the Snowstone. Her hand was warm in his, her presence beside him giving him strength as he answered these questions. He couldn't bear to think of her in danger again.

No wonder the dragons looked grim. With Professor Ennar back in Holbard, Sigrid would know where to find Drekhelm. She would know where to aim that cold, and where to attack.

"We have nowhere to go if the wolves drive us out of Vallen," said Torsten quietly. "No other country would welcome us, even if we survived the trip. There isn't a place in the world that isn't claimed by some kind of elemental as their territory."

"We're not going anywhere," Leif said, but he didn't sound as firm as usual.

And Anders didn't feel so certain either.

CHAPTER THREE

THE DRAGONMEET SEEMED ALMOST TO FORGET for a time that Anders, Lisabet, Rayna, and Ellukka were standing in front of them. The members broke off into quiet conversations, many of them arguing with one another. Anders was pretty sure he and Lisabet were both thinking the same thing—that Sigrid was bound to use the Snowstone if she thought it would give her an advantage against the dragons, but that saying as much would probably only provoke a fight sooner. So he stayed quiet, and she did too. For now, they just needed to be allowed to stay here. To find a way to keep the three of them—he, Lisabet, and Rayna—safe. Then he'd figure out his next steps.

It was Torsten who turned his attention back to them first, frowning at them over his bushy beard. "Who will you fight for, when the time comes?" He was looking at

Anders. "Your icefire stopped their ice spears as well as our flame. You could be the deciding factor."

Every pair of eyes in the room turned to focus on Anders, and Leif held up his hands. "He is a child," he protested. "Children will not be fighting at all."

"If it comes to it, every one of us will defend ourselves," Torsten replied. "And we've seen what he can do."

"He's right," said a man with a long nose and neatly combed white hair, a few seats along. "Are we just going to keep them here in our midst, when he could attack us at any moment?"

"Are we just going to throw them out to roam the mountains?" another asked. "At least we know where they are here. We should lock them up."

There was a flurry of argument, voices rising over one another, and finally Leif was reduced to thumping on the table for silence. "Anders," he said. "Do you plan to use the icefire to attack us?"

"As if he'd tell us if he was," a woman snorted.

Anders cleared his throat, nervous. "I don't even know how I made it," he admitted. "I've never even been able to make an ice spear before. Everyone at Ulfar knew I was hopeless."

Beside him Lisabet was nodding, and though he'd always winced at his own ineptitude before, now he was grateful for the confirmation. Rayna squeezed his hand a second time, and he knew she was holding herself back from the reply she always gave when he said he was hopeless at anything—a vehement denial, and quick, fierce support. But for once it was better that she let them believe it, and she clearly knew that.

"I was desperate when I threw the icefire," he went on, thinking of the instant in the middle of battle that he'd thrown the silver flame. Icefire, a thing of legend, meant to be impossible. "I don't know how to do it again. And I don't plan to do it again."

He could tell that at least half the Dragonmeet didn't believe him, and all of them were studying him closely. Except for Ellukka's father, who pointed at Rayna. "What about you?" he asked. "If you really are his sister, can't you do it?"

Rayna shook her head. "I can't even breathe a spark, Valerius," she said. "Leif's been trying to teach me."

Lisabet turned to look at her. "Maybe you will be able to do it too," she mused. "If you can't make flame, and Anders can't make ice, perhaps both of you are made to throw icefire instead."

"Perhaps you can both learn in time," Leif said. "We must try to teach you."

"So you want them to stay?" Torsten asked, throwing

up his hands as if Leif simply couldn't be reasoned with.

"We cannot throw them out," Leif said simply. "They will be attacked if they return to the wolves, and they will die on their own. And they cannot be prisoners here forever. That is not who we are."

Anders was pretty sure it *was* who some of them were, and a moment later, the hubbub around the table confirmed it.

"A vote," Ellukka's father, Valerius, suggested, his voice rising over the others. "We have spoken enough, let us put it to a vote."

There was a general rumble of agreement up and down the table, and Anders felt like his knees were going to give out. This vote was *not* going to go their way. No matter what Leif said, it was clear nearly all the Dragonmeet mistrusted them.

"All those who—" Valerius began, clearly intending on holding the vote then and there, but Leif cut him off.

"I invoke—" he began loudly.

"Raise your hand, all those—" Valerius tried again.

"Valerius, no," Leif snapped, finally raising his voice properly. He lowered it again, to speak over the shocked silence up and down the table. "By the power invested in me by the vote of my people, as Drekleid and as head of the Finskól, I declare the wolves Anders and Lisabet Finskólars.

41

I extend to them all the protections of the Finskól."

The table exploded.

"What's the Finskól?" Anders whispered to Rayna as the members of the Dragonmeet shouted at one another.

"It's a special school for gifted students," she whispered back. "The Drekleid runs it and chooses the students. If you're in his school, they're not allowed to throw you out *or* lock you up."

"Leif," protested Valerius. "They're wolves, you can't possibly think—"

"They're not just wolves, they're the wolves who led their pack to find us," Torsten pointed out, and plenty of others raised their voices to agree.

"Finskólars?" said the young woman with the messy blond bun. She and the young man beside her were the only two who seemed likely to vote with Leif.

"You and Mylestom have recently graduated," Leif said, nodding to the pair. "Anders and Lisabet will take the places you have vacated. The decision is mine alone, and it has been made."

Ellukka's father tried again. "Leif, the Finskól is an honor for dragons alone."

"Actually," said Ellukka, speaking up again from her spot by Rayna's side, "it's an honor for whomever Leif chooses."

"That's enough, Ellukka," he snapped, and she shot him a defiant glare.

"Your daughter is correct, Valerius," Leif said. "And today, I am choosing Anders and Lisabet."

"At least we'll know where they are," said the young man called Mylestom. He had short, dark-brown hair where the young woman beside him had messy blond curls, darker brown skin than hers, and a serious expression to match her smile. He studied the two wolves through wire-rimmed glasses.

"At least we'll know where they are?" Valerius repeated. "We don't even know *what* they are."

Torsten thumped the table in agreement with one of his big fists, drawing more murmurs. In some ways, the Dragonmeet reminded Anders of the flocks of birds he'd seen down by the docks—when one made a noise, all the others joined in with raucous agreement.

"Besides, you *would* agree," the woman next to Torsten said to Mylestom. "You were his student until last year."

"And he taught me how to think for myself," Mylestom shot back. "Saphira and I ask more questions and have more open minds than any of you, and that's exactly what the Dragonmeet needs. It's why we were elected—the younger dragons see it, even if you don't."

"Perhaps," said Leif, cutting across what was setting out to be a pretty magnificent argument, "we can conclude this conversation at another time. We have further matters to discuss. Anders, Lisabet, Rayna, please do not depart Drekhelm without permission. There are no lessons today, as we prepare for tonight's equinox celebrations. I will expect you in class tomorrow morning."

Just the day before, Anders had stood here believing those very equinox celebrations would include the sacrifice of his sister's life. That she and the other kidnapping victims from Holbard were part of some terrible dragon ritual. Now he knew it was simply a party, and that the kidnappings were only to rescue those children who would die if they weren't helped to make their transformation into dragons.

So, said the little voice in his head, *that's one problem out of about nine hundred and seventy-three solved, at this rate we'll be safe in no time.* He shushed the voice as Leif dismissed them.

* * *

Nobody spoke until they had closed the doors behind them and were out in the hallway.

"Well," said Ellukka. "Not exiled or locked up. That went better than expected."

44

"What?" Anders said, turning to face her. "You thought they were going to—"

"Never," said Rayna. "I mean, they might have tried, but we'd have argued with them, don't worry. And Leif's right. Even the ones who don't trust you will see that it's better to have you where they can see you."

"Great," Anders muttered, letting Rayna start him moving down the hallway again with a gentle push.

"Overall, I think it went quite well," Lisabet said. "As long as Leif's protecting us, we're safe, right?"

"You should be," Ellukka agreed. "But I wouldn't give anyone a reason to mistrust you, that's for sure. Leif's in charge, but he's still only one vote out of twenty-five."

The danger of their position hung over Anders's head as they walked down the hallway, but at least they had a chance to stay here at Drekhelm. They'd bought themselves some time—or rather, Leif had bought it for them.

Perhaps they could yet find a way to prove themselves to the dragons while keeping their pack safe. Perhaps the answer did lie with his icefire. If he could figure out how to create it again, could the threat of using it keep both the dragons and wolves from attacking each other? Would that give Rayna and him a safe place to live? He tucked that thought away for future consideration.

"Where are we going now?" he asked as they turned a corner.

"Mikkel and our friend Theo will be in the gardens," Ellukka said. "We'll go find them."

A question was nagging at Anders, but he wasn't sure how to voice it.

"Ellukka," he said, and she looked back over her shoulder without breaking her stride. "I didn't expect— Thank you for standing up for us in there." He could hear his voice tilting upward at the end, the question unspoken but clear enough—*But why did you do it?*

Ellukka shrugged, dismissing the thanks. "You're Rayna's brother," she said. "If they sent you away or locked you up, she'd do something stupid, and then I'd have to get involved in *that*, and I have better things to do than chase around after one of Rayna's plans."

Anders felt a faint smile tugging at the corner of his mouth, even as Rayna elbowed Ellukka in the side. He'd wondered for a moment the day before if Rayna had made friends as close as he had while they were apart.

But looking at the two of them side by side, he knew the answer. Outwardly, the two girls couldn't be more different. Rayna had warm brown skin and curly black hair constantly trying to escape from her braids. Ellukka was a full head taller than the other girl, and she had pink-cheeked creamy skin and blond hair pulled into perfectly neat plaits that fell down in front of her broad shoulders. She was wider, heavier, and stronger than Anders's sister. What they had in common was the same determined line to their mouths.

If Ellukka liked Rayna enough to know about all her harebrained schemes and still want to stand up for her, then the answer to his question was yes—Rayna had definitely found at least one friend here.

Perhaps he could too. He and Rayna had always found a way to live in Holbard, tucked into whatever attic or stable loft they could find, working together to keep themselves fed and warm. He'd managed at Ulfar, too, just as she had here. Now that they were together again, a team again, they could make another home.

He didn't have time to dwell on that, though, because Rayna was opening the door ahead of him, and he was catching an impossible glimpse of greenery.

The sight before him made him think he must still be asleep back in the guest room, and that everything that had happened that morning had been a dream.

He was in a large cave, with an opening leading out

of the mountain, and a view beyond the cave mouth of snowy crags and dark rock stretching into the distance. But that wasn't what caught his attention.

Inside the cave there was lush green grass underfoot, and plants sprouted from every inch of the walls and ceiling. Long fern fronds swayed faintly in the breeze; thick bushes with shiny, dark-green leaves crowded together; small purple flowers peeked shyly from the gaps in between. The air was as warm against his skin as a summer's day, and the whole cave was just as bright as one.

Mikkel stood over where the cave opened out onto the mountainside, his tousled copper head together with another boy's—perhaps this was Theo. He had the same light-brown skin as Viktoria—Anders felt a pang at the memory of his friend—and the same silky black hair pulled back into a ponytail. He was thin, but his slender frame seemed to hold a kind of barely contained energy, and he was bouncing on the balls of his feet as the two boys talked.

"Isn't this place incredible?" Rayna asked with a grin as Ellukka strode toward the others. "It's half mechanical invention, half artifact. There are artifact pumps that bring up heat from deep inside the mountain, and tucked in behind the plants are little tubes that carry water around, and those mirrors by the entrance relay the light in. A famous dragon created it all."

"Not all," Lisabet said. "Not if there are artifacts here. A wolf must have helped as well."

Rayna dismissed that with a shrug, and by then they'd reached the two boys.

"Made it through the Dragonmeet?" said Mikkel.

"Just," Ellukka told him.

He mimed wiping sweat from his brow. "Anders, Lisabet, this is Theo, kidnapping victim and dragon, all in one piece as you can see."

Theo pulled one hand from his pocket, wiggling his fingers in a slightly awkward wave of greeting.

"Were you scared?" Anders asked, wincing even as he said it. Of course Theo had been scared. But he probably didn't want to offend the dragons by saying so.

"Terrified," Theo replied cheerfully. "But I think my ma knew what was happening. I can't be sure, but she kind of looked at me when they grabbed me, and I just—I could see it in her eyes. I think she knew why the dragons were there, like maybe she knew something about our family, or suspected. And then she was kind of distracted by the fire in the stables."

"That was your house?" Now Anders's eyebrows were

up high. "Last equinox? Everyone heard about that when it burned down."

"That was an accident," Mikkel said straight away.

"It was," Theo agreed. "And everyone was safe, the dragons checked."

"It's a pretty serious accident," Lisabet pointed out.

Rayna, in that forceful way she spoke when she wanted to change the subject, changed the subject. "Mikkel studies history, he knows all about this garden."

Mikkel was diverted, immediately transferring his attention to the history of the place in a way that reminded Anders of Lisabet when she got her hands on a book about something interesting.

"It was created by a dragon called Flic," he said, turning to look out at the gardens. "At least five hundred years ago, maybe more. It's part invention, part artifact, part . . . genius. They say she had a special gift with plants, knowing exactly where they should go, or coaxing them to grow in the most unlikely places."

"There's a waterfall named for her over on the west coast," Ellukka said. "I went there with Leif and my father once, and I've studied her in class. There are all kinds of things growing there, and they say she had her workshop out that way, long ago."

"What kinds of classes do you all take?" Lisabet asked.

"They were talking about the Finskól just now, and it sounded like some kind of school."

"You're joining the Finskól?" Mikkel looked impressed, and Theo, pleased.

Ellukka nodded confirmation. "They were about to vote to throw them out or lock them up. Leif claimed them for the Finskól at the last second, it was all he could do."

"Sparks and scales," Theo murmured. "Pretty sure that didn't go down well."

"Not really," Ellukka agreed, turning to the two wolves. "There's twelve of us now, including you two. Rayna and I, Theo and Mikkel are all Finskólars. Leif's the teacher."

"The dragons don't have big schools like Ulfar Academy," Rayna explained. "Mostly their parents just teach them, and some dragons run small schools for groups of students they choose. They start schools because they're particularly good at something, usually. And of course the Drekleid always runs the Finskól. Saphira and Mylestom—you saw them on the Dragonmeet—they graduated from the Finskól last year, and the younger dragons worked together to elect them to the Dragonmeet. The Drekleid is the only person who can decide who's a Finskólar, and nobody can overrule him. Going to the Finskól is a sign you're going to really be somebody."

Anders's mouth felt dry. The last thing he wanted—the last thing he could imagine—was to be somebody. All he wanted was a safe place to live, and there was nothing safer than anonymity.

"Everyone in the Finskól chooses their own area to study," Rayna continued. "Or has their own reason for being there. Leif chose me because he said I was quick-thinking, and I'll have to choose what area to study in a little while, but right now I'm just working on my reading and writing."

"I'm learning storytelling," Ellukka said. "Stories are powerful. They can teach people, change their minds, make them laugh, or cry, or remember, or forget. So I'm learning about how to tell them, as well as learning as many stories as I can."

"I'm history," Mikkel said, with one of his smirks. "And there's plenty of that."

"I'm research," Theo added. "I'm only a few months in, but I've already learned so much. The records here are kind of a mess—for example, Mikkel and Ellukka aren't even sure how long ago Flic lived, and they can't easily look it up. Ellukka's father, Valerius, is an archivist, but he spends most of his time dealing with the Dragonmeet these days. So my focus is going to be on how to keep better records, which is basically how to keep track of what we actually know and what we don't. When the dragons moved here after the last great battle, everything got jumbled. There are whole storerooms full of artifacts in the archives that could hold anything."

Lisabet looked very approving of all these areas of study, but Anders felt a bit faint. He was terrible at reading and writing, and in his weeks at Ulfar he'd found every lesson a struggle. What was he going to do in a class for gifted students? He'd be found out as a fraud in no time. Then again, perhaps Leif already knew he wasn't suitable—he'd only brought him in to keep him safe. It made sense for Rayna to be there—as Leif had already noticed, she was quick-thinking, always ready with a plan or an idea. Frankly, it was better to have Rayna on your side, where you could see her, than off somewhere causing trouble. But Anders?

Still, he was in the safest place he could be, and he was grateful for that. If he wanted his icefire to show up again, if he wanted to protect himself and those he cared about, perhaps he could start by studying *himself* at the Finskól.

The young dragons—or at least Ellukka, Mikkel, and Theo—seemed willing enough to welcome him and Lisabet into Drekhelm, albeit a bit cautiously. Leif's approval evidently went a long way.

Lisabet's excitement at all there was to learn here was pushing her past her fear and worry, at least for now. But now that things were settled, Anders couldn't help thinking of the looks on the faces of their packmates as they ran, and the frowns of the Dragonmeet as they'd stared down the two wolves in their midst. Was it possible they could be safe here? What would happen when Sigrid started to use the Snowstone?

He'd been on a mission for weeks—first to get into Ulfar, then to figure out how to find Rayna, to get to her. He'd never really thought past making it to Drekhelm, and now he had a new challenge in making a home here. For now, he'd keep quiet and try to learn more about this place, and hope against hope a way forward presented itself.

They'd always found a way to survive. They would now too.

* * *

Anders and Lisabet didn't attend the dragons' equinox celebrations that night. It was one of the most important nights of the year for dragons, and for wolves. At the equinox, day and night were of equal length, and the magical essence found in nature—the essence that gave the wolves their ice spears and the scorch dragons their flame, that allowed both groups to make their transformations—was at its strongest. Lisabet had told Anders that the wolves celebrated the equinox quietly, with a night of reflection. The dragons, on the other hand, were famous for their parties.

Leif sent word that he felt it would be best if they kept to their room, with so many dragons still unsure about two wolves—even wolves who had saved them in battle—staying at Drekhelm. Lisabet was disappointed, as she said it was a lost opportunity for cultural observation, but Anders didn't mind. Leif was right—it was better to keep a low profile.

Rayna and Ellukka showed up at Anders and Lisabet's room just as the two wolves were starting to wonder about dinner, carrying plates laden with food from the feast: steaming fish spiced with chella, glossy buttered peas and orange and yellow carrots, dark-brown bread stacked on top of the vegetables. Rayna had little cakes as well, bright-yellow sponges made with sour cream, lavished with orange-flavored frosting.

Ellukka had red ribbons braided through her hair, and Rayna . . . Rayna's braids were gone. She'd cut her hair so it just brushed her shoulders, her curls springing free from their usual restraints.

"You like it?" she said, tossing her head this way and

that so Anders could look at it. "It was Ellukka's idea, for the party."

"I . . ." He wasn't sure what he thought. "It looks great," he said automatically. But a small part of him he didn't have time to examine felt strange about Rayna cutting her hair. She was different enough in her dragon's clothes, without changing the face he'd known for years. And because Ellukka had suggested it?

"Where do dragons get their food?" Lisabet asked around a mouthful, already eating. "You couldn't grow it up here in the mountains."

"We trade," Ellukka said, taking up position at the end of Lisabet's bed. Rayna came over to sit on Anders's bed with him. "The people we're trading with don't know we're dragons, obviously. And we have farms as well. Mostly run by people whose parents were dragons, but who didn't transform themselves. They don't mind living away from the mountains, but of course they shouldn't have to leave the community. They run farms in the Uplands, crew ships that sail out of Port Tylerd and Port Alcher. The oranges are grown in greenhouses near Port Baernor, in the southwest. Just like us, they follow the lives that call to them."

Anders ate his meal quickly, trying to make himself savor every bite, but so hungry he could barely slow down.

It was as if his body was still recovering after throwing the icefire yesterday. With a small smile, Rayna broke her orange cake in two, and put one half on his plate.

"Did the Dragonmeet talk all day?" Lisabet asked.

"All day," Ellukka confirmed. "Twenty-five people is a lot to have on a council, especially when you want everyone to have their say."

"And dragons always want *everyone* to have their say," Rayna interjected. "It takes forever."

"Even with the Snowstone out there, probably in the hands of the Fyrstulf by now, they can't hurry," Ellukka said. "They're trying to work out what she's thinking."

Anders and Lisabet exchanged a quick glance—they still hadn't admitted to anyone that Sigrid was Lisabet's mother, and Anders felt a guilty tug about that. After all, he'd been furious when Lisabet had kept that from him. But at the same time, they didn't need to give the dragons any more reason to doubt them than they already had. He was truly beginning to understand why Lisabet had lied about it.

"What's the party like?" he asked quickly, when he thought he saw Ellukka intercepting that glance.

Rayna and Ellukka looked at each other. Rayna raised her eyebrows, and Ellukka laughed. "Want to see?" she asked. "There's a secret spot where you can look down at the Great Hall, nobody will know. I go there sometimes to spy on them, when I'm trying to work out whether Father's ever going to be done talking. You can't tell anybody about it."

"We promise," said Anders, and Lisabet grinned.

Five minutes later they'd finished their meals, and they were in the hallways of Drekhelm, ducking off through a side door to climb a narrow, winding staircase carved into the rock. It was barely big enough for a twelve-year-old, so it was hard to imagine how an adult could ever get up there.

At the top was a little ledge. It looked as if it had just eough room for the four of them to pile in together like a pack of wolves settling down for the night, side by side and half on top of one another.

"I'll go first," Ellukka whispered, grinning. "I'm bigger than you, I'll squash you otherwise. Then Anders, he's next biggest."

She crawled into the nook, and Anders went next to lie beside her, with Rayna and then Lisabet cramming in after to lie on top of them. There was a hole in the rock that gave them a view down to the Great Hall, and it was covered by a thin metal grate.

"They think it's ventilation up here," Ellukka said.

"I wish," Rayna muttered, trying to get comfortable,

and making an apologetic noise when she drove an elbow into Anders's spine.

But he didn't mind. His gaze was fixed on the scene below. The huge double doors were flung open, the night sky visible beyond. In the Great Hall itself there was a bonfire, and musicians were standing on top of the Dragonmeet's long table, playing guitars and fiddles and drums for all they were worth.

The dragons were all in human form, and some were dancing around the fire, others talking in groups, eating and drinking. There was a kind of ferocity to the underlying energy of the room, as if their fear of the Snowstone, of the potential wolf attack, was driving them to greater, louder, more lively celebrations. Anders couldn't say why, but he felt a little as though the figures below him were shouting and singing and dancing all the more wildly to defy their fear.

In some ways, it was like the dancing he'd seen at year's end in the streets of Holbard. In others, from the mountain visible beyond the doors to the bright colors of the clothing below, the many red dresses and tunics and cloaks—a dragon color, one rarely seen in the city—it felt completely foreign.

But one thing was clear—just as the wolves were a pack, the dragons below him were connected to one another after all. This was their home, and together they were family. Their wild celebrations and their joined hands proclaimed it.

He felt a sad tug back toward Holbard, toward Ulfar, where his classmates would still be nursing their wounds. He wished there was a way to tell them he'd never meant for any of it to happen. That all he wanted was a safe place to be with his sister. But Rayna's body was warm against his, and though he didn't know if he could ever be part of the big family he saw dancing below, with her and Lisabet beside him, he hoped he could find his place here.

CHAPTER FOUR

THE NEXT MORNING RAYNA AND ELLUKKA came by to collect the two wolves for breakfast, leading them down the hallways with the lamps that slowly glowed to life as they approached and then faded out as they passed. Anders wondered if the meal would be in a dining hall like the one at Ulfar, with long tables of dragons. He was tense just imagining it.

He wished he had more chances to talk to Rayna. He'd expected they'd somehow end up in a room together, but she and Ellukka were sharing a room, and when he'd asked if he and Lisabet would stay in the guest room, the dragon bringing them more clothes and other supplies had said they would. Anders had got the distinct impression that although their door wouldn't be locked again, the dragons wanted to know where the two wolves were at all times.

It turned out breakfast was in a much smaller cavern

than at Ulfar, packed with little tables instead of long ones, the whole room occupied by perhaps twenty dragons, many of whom didn't seem to know that either Anders or Lisabet was anyone unusual. Ellukka sent the wolves to sit at a table with Rayna and plunged into the queue along one wall to find them breakfast.

"Dragons move around a lot," Rayna said as she thumped down onto a bench, then shuffled over to make room for Anders beside her. "Lots of them don't have what they'd really consider a home, they just have a lot of different places they stay. That's why there are cupboards full of spare clothes, guest bedrooms everywhere. There's usually about two hundred at Drekhelm, but there's lots more right now, because of the equinox, and because the whole Dragonmeet is here at once. Those of us in the Finskól are wherever Leif is, but he's almost always here at Drekhelm. He arranges our meals and our rooms."

Ellukka returned with the food, setting down a platter of buttered dark bread, slices of meat and cheese, and a jug of milk, then producing four mugs from where she'd stowed them precariously in her pockets. The four of them fell silent for a little as they ate and drank, and Anders listened to the worried hubbub around him. He caught only snatches of conversation—he heard the Snowstone mentioned, the Dragonmeet—and kept his head down.

"Today you'll probably discuss what you're going to study with Leif," Ellukka said. "And you'll meet the other six students. They're all older than we are."

"What are they like?" Anders asked.

"Some are nicer than others," Rayna replied, wrinkling her nose. "And we like Mikkel and Theo best. But they're all clever. You can see why he chose them." The nose wrinkle gave way to a quick, dimpled smile. "Same reason he chose us. We're brilliant."

The others laughed, and Anders did too, a moment later. He'd been caught looking at Rayna, finding his own face in hers. He had that same dimple, he wrinkled his nose just like she did. They were both holding their slices of bread exactly the same way in their right hands, come to that, their left hands curled around their mugs.

Leif had said he believed the two of them were related, however impossible Anders had always been taught that was, and Anders was determined to believe it. To learn more and *prove* it. This place felt nothing like home, but he had friends and family here, and he mustn't forget that.

He knew what he wanted to study at the Finskól—his heritage, his history, who he was. *What* he was, and what he could do. The more he knew, the better his chances of mastering his powers. Of protecting himself, Rayna, and Lisabet.

Mikkel and Theo showed up toward the end of breakfast to collect them, and the six of them made their way to class together, Rayna slinging her arm around Anders's shoulders, which was a little tricky, because he was taller than she was. Still, it felt better than good to have her at his side again, and he felt foolish for his reaction to her haircut the night before. It *did* look good, and just as he'd formed bonds to his pack, she'd formed bonds here. It didn't lessen their own. As she gave him a squeeze, he noticed once again that the heat radiating from her skin actually felt good. This newfound tolerance to—even enjoyment of—heat made him a little more certain that the clue to his icefire was to be found in his ties to both wolves and the dragon girl by his side.

"You've got to be kidding," Ellukka burst out behind them, causing Lisabet to laugh, and the others to turn around to check on her. "I'm not wearing any harness," she said, all indignation. "Just because dogs wear leashes, doesn't mean dragons wear . . ."

Anders was having trouble not laughing at the outrage in her expression, and Rayna, Theo, and Mikkel didn't bother trying to restrain themselves.

"Firstly," said Lisabet with dignity, though her mouth was still twitching to a smile, "'dog' isn't an insult like you think it is. We're wolves, not dogs, but dogs are tough, loyal, and intelligent. And secondly, isn't it just like wearing clothes?"

Ellukka snorted, turning her attention to the other dragons. "She wants me to wear a harness when I'm transformed, so she can ride me," she informed them. "And stop laughing. Would a little support kill you?"

"We're not allowed far from Drekhelm right now anyway," Rayna said, fighting to keep her face straight. "But it *would* be a safer way to all move together."

"Why would I want to do that?" Ellukka asked. "When I got there, I'd just have a wolf with me, what's the point?"

Rayna dissolved into giggles once more. "I'm sorry, you have to admit it's a clever idea. It can't be easy holding on otherwise. It might be useful for the people up here who don't transform, or for the children who haven't tried yet. Aren't you worried one of them will fall off one day?"

Ellukka pushed out her lower lip, considering, as Lisabet wisely remained silent. "I suppose," she said eventually. "Maybe."

The conversation broke off as they arrived in the classroom. It was a largish room already occupied by a few students seated at two long tables, both strewn with books and papers left there from previous lessons. There were bookshelves down either side, packed with books, boxes, and the occasional artifact, and a tall window with an arched top stood at the end of the room, looking out onto the mountains. It was sealed with thick glass, completely transparent in some places and a little opaque in others, thick strips of lead dividing it up into square panes. Anders was caught for a long moment, staring out at the peaks that stretched away to the northwest, growing higher and higher, flawlessly capped with white snow, until they vanished into the clouds altogether.

Then a voice yanked his attention back to the room. "Are these the wolves?"

The speaker was a short girl dressed all in black, unusual in a dragon—different from the others Anders had met so far. Her equally black hair was in two long braids down her back, and her skin was a deep brown, almost a match for her dress. She looked only a couple of years older than Anders, but she carried herself as though she was infinitely superior.

She sat next to a tall, thin boy with startlingly blue eyes in a white face, and a shock of black hair that flopped over his forehead. He was about the same age as she was, and he shared her sneer.

"Anders, Lisabet," said Ellukka, in the politest tone he'd heard from her so far—though also the frostiest—

66

"this is Krissin, who's studying sciences, and Nico, who's studying mathematics."

"Pleased to meet you," Anders said, and as Lisabet echoed his words, he almost sensed, rather than saw, Rayna rolling her eyes beside him.

"You can sit at the other table," Krissin told them, flipping one braid over her shoulder. Anders was only too happy to oblige.

"Yes," said one of the girls at the other table, pushing aside some books to make a clear space. "Come on over and sit here." She shuffled along the bench she was sitting on, her long sheet of jet-black hair, which hung down past her waist, rippling like water as she moved. She was athletically built, and looked like she had ancestors from Ohiro, like Theo did—and Viktoria, back at Ulfar. The boy opposite her had a broad grin that made it look like he'd already been up to mischief nobody knew about, tousled blond hair, and twinkling green eyes behind a pair of glasses.

"I'm Ferdie," he said. "I'm studying medicine."

"But really," the girl said wryly, "he's here because Leif realized he charms everyone he meets, so he thought someone better teach Ferdie how to lead, since he's bound to be in charge one day."

Ferdie simply laughed but didn't deny the charge.

"And this is Bryn," he said, pointing to his companion. "Languages. All of them, as far as I can tell." He pointed farther down the table at a girl with very pale skin, a tangle of curly brown hair, and a smudge of grease on her nose, who was bent over a small contraption, ignoring the rest of the group. "And that's Isabina, our mechanic."

Isabina lifted a hand to wave a greeting without looking up, carefully moving a cog into place with a pair of tweezers.

"And that's everyone," Ellukka said, settling down beside Ferdie, and hunting through the papers on the desk for the ones that presumably belonged to her. "Except Patrik, he'll be along at the last minute."

Rayna thumped down beside Ellukka, and after a moment, Anders and Lisabet took their places opposite the girls, leaving Krissin and Nico to have the whole other table to themselves. Mikkel and Theo located whatever they were working on farther down the table, near Isabina.

The final student of the twelve arrived just as Leif did, a solemn boy with long brown hair, trailing in behind the Drekleid. "Patrik, he studies art," Rayna supplied in a whisper as the boy sat down near Nico and Krissin. But with their teacher present, everyone was pulling out their projects, and Anders wasn't sure what to do. Lisabet was riffling through the papers in front of them, oohing and aahing over what she was finding.

"Anders," said Leif. "Please come join me at my desk, let's speak about your studies."

Anders rose from his chair, walking up to the front of the room, where Leif's desk was piled high with papers, artifacts, and other detritus. The Drekleid moved a pile of coats to the ground, revealing a second chair, and when Anders sat on it, the piles on the desk hid all the other students from view.

"Good morning," said Leif, running a hand through his red hair, getting himself settled. Though he had been more welcoming than most so far, he still made Anders nervous. Perhaps it was six years of living on the streets of Holbard that had made him automatically wary of authority figures. *Or*, his mind supplied, *perhaps it's the fact that he's all that's standing between you and being thrown out of Drekhelm as well as Ulfar.*

"Good morning," Anders said, trying to sound as studious as possible.

"Have the others explained how the Finskól works?" Leif asked.

"Yes," said Anders, deciding to plunge in. He needed to suggest his own course of study—an investigation into what he could do—before Leif set him to learning reading and writing, like Rayna. "I want to study—"

"Just a moment," Leif interrupted him. "There's no hurry. We'll begin with the basics, improving your reading and writing. We dragons take our time over important questions. We might be slow, but we reach the right decision."

Anders's heart sank. He was remembering what Ellukka had said the night before—that the Dragonmeet had talked all day, yet reached no agreement. Even with the danger of the Snowstone, they couldn't seem to hurry. The wolves were the opposite, of course—Sigrid made a decision, and then everyone did as they were told. That had its drawbacks too, but he wanted to know more about himself, to figure out more about what he could do, and why.

"I could do reading and writing alongside other studies," Anders suggested.

"The way of dragons has always served us," Leif replied.

"But I'm not a dragon, Leif," Anders said carefully.

"Even so."

Anders took a slow breath and kept trying, hoping a question might interest the Drekleid. "Leif, do you know what I am? I mean, who I am?"

"I must research the question before I can answer you properly," Leif replied gravely, and Anders's heart sank.

Theo's entire specialty at the Finskól was the dragons' records and research, because even a newcomer like Theo could tell it was impossible to find anything here.

Between the dragons' tendency to think things over forever and the impossibility of finding information, Anders had a horrible feeling he could wait years for Leif's conclusions. And all the while, the wolves would be preparing for war, and the dragons would be talking, talking, talking.

"I know you're impatient on many fronts," Leif said, reading his expression. "But you must apply yourself to your studies and let the Dragonmeet handle the question of what to do next, Anders."

Anders wanted badly to argue, but he couldn't see how. He wanted to rush the dragons, to explain how urgent things were, but when it came down to it, he was the one who'd brought matters to a head.

Professor Ennar would have used the chalice herself if he hadn't stolen it, so the wolves would still know broadly where the dragons were, but they might have spent months, or at least weeks, scouting the mountains for the exact location of Drekhelm. They certainly wouldn't have attacked already, and they wouldn't have stolen the Snowstone. Things would still be locked in the same tense stalemate, and that itself was a kind of peace.

On the other hand, the dragons wouldn't even know they were in danger without his warning about Fylkir's chalice, so there was an argument that Anders had done them a favor.

On the third hand—or paw, really, this was why you needed paws—the dragons didn't really seem to plan on actually doing anything about it, even though they *did* know.

He'd have to find out the answers on his own. But perhaps there was one thing Leif might know something about, or at least be able to include in his promised research into who or what Anders might be.

Anders told Leif what he'd noticed about his new tolerance for heat—that ever since the icefire, it didn't seem to bother him in the way it used to—the way it always bothered wolves. But the Drekleid only frowned thoughtfully and made a note on one of his dozens of files.

Ten minutes later it was Lisabet's turn to talk to Leif, and Anders found himself at the back of the classroom, sitting beside the window with a surprisingly patient Ellukka, whom Leif had asked to help him with his reading for the morning. She kept accidentally diverting into telling him stories—he could see why she was specializing in doing exactly that, because she was wonderful at it—and they spent more time quietly talking than looking at the reading primer she'd chosen.

It was a book of old stories, probably for small children, and in the front was a map showing where each of the tales took place. She had him read out each place-name one at a time, and then she'd describe it to him. She'd flown over all of them and knew how to bring them to life for him.

"This one's two words put together as one," she said, pointing to a spot in a high mountain range to the northwest of Drekhelm—one that almost formed a line between the dragon stronghold and the Flic Waterfall, where the dragon who'd been a genius with gardens had once kept her workshop.

Anders studied it for a moment, and the words clicked into place in his brain. "Cloudhaven," he said. "What story happened there?"

"There are lots of different versions," Ellukka said, looking out the window at the mountains that stretched away into the distance. "You see over there on the horizon, where the mountains lift up so high they disappear into the clouds? Beyond that is Cloudhaven. They say it's where the very first dragonsmiths discovered how to use their flame to forge artifacts. It's higher than any of the other mountains, and nobody's sure what's really at the top. The clouds never clear. But if the legends are true, then there's an abandoned workshop there, and who knows what kinds of secrets. It's forbidden to go there now."

Anders stared through the uneven glass of the window, studying the place where the mountains disappeared into the clouds. He wondered what the very first dragonsmiths had been like—he wondered what the very first wolf designers had been like. What kind of artifacts had they made together? Had they worked together to discover their gifts, or had they mistrusted each other as much as wolves and dragons did today, only coming together because they had no choice?

The lessons continued all day. For a couple of hours Leif taught the group, just as Anders's teachers at Ulfar had, but most of the time they studied independently, each reading or experimenting or learning about their own areas. Leif helped Bryn find an old text on Mositalan verbs, and walked Nico through a mathematical formula until he understood it. He seemed to know a little of everything, and was endlessly interested and patient.

Anders came away in the late afternoon feeling as if his brain was crammed full of facts and ideas, plus even more questions than he'd begun the day with.

Over the next few days, his lessons continued. Ellukka spent each morning with him, telling him stories and helping with his reading. Mikkel started to join them sometimes to help fill in the history, and Theo came to sit near them and listen—as a new dragon himself, he had a lot to learn. Rayna sometimes had reading lessons with Lisabet, and sometimes the two of them would join the others in the back of the classroom. Rayna and Theo left now and again for flying lessons—flying was mostly instinctive, but practice made perfect—returning with huge smiles every time.

Ferdie dropped through to see what Anders and the others were working on occasionally, just for fun. Bryn came by and showed them how words in different languages were sometimes the same as their own. Even Isabina looked up from her machines once in a while, though Krissin, Nico, and Patrik kept their distance. Always, Leif was there, sometimes teaching them himself, sometimes joining their conversation for a few minutes, guiding them toward a new idea or a new question.

There were times when Anders was so fascinated by the stories he heard and the new ideas that piled into his brain, and so absorbed in his lessons, that he forgot he was a wolf among dragons. He forgot that it was only Leif's invitation to the Finskól that was keeping him safe at all.

Nevertheless, he began to learn his way around, and to think that Drekhelm really might be a place he and

Rayna could live, if only they could fit in. The idea of he and his twin *living* anywhere—expecting their next meal without wondering where it would come from, putting on clean clothes every day—was still so strange he barely knew what to make of it.

But each time he was nearly comfortable, an older dragon would scowl at him as he walked down the hallway, or Nico and Krissin would whisper to each other, staring at him as they did.

Or Leif would leave the classroom to attend the Dragonmeet, and come back with a grim expression, or Anders would hear a murmur about the Snowstone. Most mornings Ellukka would show up at breakfast to report that her father said the Dragonmeet had met again the night before, talking and talking of what they might do about the possibility of wolf attack, without ever making any progress.

Sooner or later, Sigrid would make her move, and Anders wished he knew what to do to be ready. More and more, he saw he had to do something—because nobody else would.

* * *

One day nearly a week after his arrival at Drekhelm, Anders stayed back in the classroom at lunchtime to work on his latest lesson. Theo was on the other side of the table, trying to stop one of his giant stacks of records from falling over before he joined the others.

"What're you working on?" he asked Anders, experimentally letting go of his pile, and then grabbing it again when it started to topple.

"I'm . . ." Anders wasn't sure how to answer. "I'm trying to learn how to learn, I guess. I have so many questions."

"Hey, that's basically what I do," Theo said, lighting up with a grin, practically bouncing on the balls of his feet. Theo was *never* short on energy. "Research, archives, figuring out where and how to store information so we can find it again when we need it, or even just figure out what questions to ask. I'm going to be a dragon librarian eventually. They really need one here at Drekhelm. What are you trying to figure out right now?"

Anders looked across at the other boy, weighing his reply. Did he dare risk an honest answer? Perhaps he could—Theo might be happy at Drekhelm, but he had family back in Holbard, and surely he'd be worried about them.

"I'm trying to figure out ten things at once," Anders admitted. "I want badly to know what's happening in Holbard. What Sigrid's going to do with the Snowstone.

What they're all saying about Lisabet and me. I want to know who I am, and what I am." The words kept tumbling out, and he found he couldn't stop them. He didn't even know what he was going to say next, until he found himself saying it. "I want to know what I should do. About the wolves, and the Snowstone. Because I don't think the Dragonmeet's going to do anything."

Theo nodded slowly. "All they ever do is talk," he agreed quietly. "I've noticed too. And they don't seem to understand that just because it's the dragon way that doesn't mean there's time for it. If the wolves have the Snowstone and they know where we are, they're not going to wait around forever to attack."

"Exactly," Anders agreed. "But I have no idea what we can do, or what we should do. I thought maybe if I could figure out something about my icefire, I'd know how to protect us against it, but one wolf against an artifact that can affect the whole country?"

"Well," said Theo slowly. "I don't have an answer for that. But maybe I can help you with the other questions. Come with me."

They shored up Theo's stack of paper together and left the classroom, making their way through the hallways of Drekhelm toward the archives—the long series of caves filled with old files, records and books, artifacts and abandoned experiments, and creations left behind by generations long gone. The archives were a kind of combination library and storeroom, totally disorganized.

"How could you ever find anything in there?" Anders asked, looking through the doorway to the next cave. "Everything's everywhere."

"You're telling me," Theo agreed. "When they abandoned Old Drekhelm after the last great battle and moved here, they just hauled everything with them and dumped it, and I think everyone's been too intimidated to go through it ever since. I'm probably going to spend the rest of my life on it, but I bet I'll discover some amazing stuff. There are so many artifacts just lying around that nobody uses. I found one in the infirmary the other day being used as a paperweight! And it's supposed to be for keeping pots of tea warm. And look at Rayna's hairpins, they're the perfect example of an artifact doing a mundane job. I don't know what they're for, but I bet there's a record in here somewhere that would tell us, if we only knew where to look."

"Rayna's hairpins?" Anders was momentarily distracted from how overwhelming the collection of books, artifacts, and records was. "What do you mean?"

"Well, they've got runes on them," Theo pointed out. "And they're copper, right? They've got to be some kind of artifact."

Anders and Rayna had wondered that themselves, sometimes—they didn't know where Rayna had gotten them from, but they were the only thing that, no matter how desperate, the twins had never traded. And now a new thought struck Anders: if he and his sister really did have dragon blood in their veins, perhaps the hairpins had even come from family.

But Theo was climbing over a large, spindly artifact with lots of arms or legs or appendages of some sort, and pulling a huge book down from a shelf. It was the size of one of the giant Skraboks in the library back at Ulfar Academy.

"These are the old records," Theo said. "I'm still going through them, but there are lots of things in here that talk about ways to see what's happening somewhere else. And that would answer some of your questions about what's happening in Holbard. I don't know where most of the things in this book are, but if we at least know what we're looking for, we could come back here and search through the caves. I bet the others would help, or some of them, anyway."

Anders climbed in over the machine to look over Theo's shoulder as the other boy turned the pages. Theo could read more quickly than Anders, so he scanned each description and paused whenever he found one that talked about long-distance observation or communication. Some artifacts were marked down as lost or broken, and some were marked down as "intact."

"That means they're in here somewhere," Theo said, pulling his smooth black hair into a ponytail again, when it tried to fall into his eyes. "Someone's seen them and tested them and written it in here."

He turned the page again, and a jolt went through Anders at the illustration he saw. It was a large mirror, with dragons forged into the metal frame down one side of it, and a pack of wolves running down the other. He had no idea where he'd seen it before, but it looked familiar. "What's this one?" he asked, staring down at it.

"Communication mirror," Theo replied. "You can see and hear what's on the other end, and so can the person who has the matching one. They're relatively common, but most of them have one of the pair broken these days. And of course the other one has to be somewhere useful. This symbol here means it's intact, though, our mirror. Wherever it is."

Was the other one somewhere useful? Had Anders seen this design in the last few days here at Drekhelm, or was he remembering it from someplace in Holbard? And if so, where?

Suddenly a deep voice sounded from behind them.

"Can I help you?" It was Valerius, Ellukka's father, and he didn't look pleased to see them. His brows crowded together in a frown, a line forming between them. "What are the two of you up to?"

Theo promptly eased the big book closed. They both knew without saying a word that it wouldn't be a good idea to admit to a member of the Dragonmeet that they'd been looking up artifacts that might let them see—or even contact—people in Holbard. "I was showing Anders my work," Theo said, radiating innocence.

"Anders doesn't have permission to be in here," Valerius replied. "This is not an area for sightseeing tours, Theo."

"Apologies," Theo said politely. "It's time we were going to lunch anyway."

The two boys climbed out of the middle of the machine and walked out under Valerius's watchful eye. And as he followed Theo through the door, Anders racked his brain, trying in vain to think where he'd seen the matching mirror before.

* * *

Nearly everybody struggled to concentrate in class that afternoon. At first Anders didn't notice, he was so caught up in thinking about the mirror and wondering if it could give him a way to find out what was happening in Holbard, and what Sigrid was planning. But then Ellukka forgot the thread of her story three times, and quiet Isabina dropped her latest invention, sending pieces skittering across the classroom floor in every direction.

Rayna and Mikkel hunted for their books all over the classroom, lifting up everyone's sheaves of paper and disrupting all the other students, only to realize they'd left them on the table in front of their usual seats. Even Nico and Krissin didn't seem to be in the mood to snipe at anyone.

And when Leif noticed the disruption at all, he seemed to have been jolted from his own daydream, looking up at the chaos his students were creating and blinking in slow surprise.

"What's going on?" Lisabet asked plaintively, looking around her at the dragons in disarray.

"We all have bad days sometimes," Leif answered absently.

"This isn't a bad day," Krissin replied, irritable, which was unusual—normally she kept that tone for her fellow students, rather than her teacher. "This is everyone having a disaster afternoon at once."

"And I'm freezing," Nico said with a scowl, drawing grumbles of agreement from all around the room. Anders looked across at Rayna, and his heart thumped as he saw his sister's shoulders hunched over, her eyes dull as she hugged herself.

It was Lisabet who suddenly saw what was happening. "It's the weather," she said. "It *is* cold. I was feeling particularly good, the best I've felt since we've arrived. I feel like I can really concentrate for the first time. How about you, Anders?"

"I feel about normal," he confessed.

"There you have it, then," she said, with a snap of her fingers. "It's making me feel wonderful, everyone else feel rotten, and Anders isn't affected—just as the heat hasn't been affecting him."

Krissin, their science expert, stood up and stalked over to the instruments she kept by the window, tapping the glass on the barometer. "The pressure's dropping," she announced. "The wolf's right, it's getting colder."

Ferdie, whose constant good nature had been reduced to a quiet frown, looked up through his glasses, running his fingers through his blond hair. "Is that why I was having trouble transforming at lunch?" he asked.

"No doubt," said Lisabet. "I've found it really hard to transform ever since we got close to Drekhelm. But if the cold weather is outweighing the lava now . . ."

"Is it the Snowstone?" Bryn asked, hugging one of her languages textbooks against her chest, her voice quiet.

"Most likely," Leif agreed. "I should go and speak with the Dragonmeet. Please do your best to continue with your work."

Leif slipped away, and one by one the students at least pretended to get on with their studies, though most of them really couldn't concentrate. Anders exchanged a worried glance with Lisabet and tried to ignore the glares directed his way by Nico and Krissin, and even by Patrik, who didn't seem to particularly like them but was rarely outright nasty.

Their friends managed to stay at least moderately friendly, but everybody's tempers were a little short. After a time he went and sat with his twin, trying to warm her hands up between his and distracting her with quiet talk about anything he could think of.

As the afternoon went by, the temperature slowly began to ease back up again, but the damage had been done. At dinner, Anders and Lisabet were on the receiving end of scowls and glares from dragons who'd begun to get used to their presence. Everybody had seen what the Snowstone could do now, and as wolves, they were the closest thing available to blame.

Anders was preoccupied all the way to bed, the evening's conversation washing over him, endless questions fighting each other for room at the forefront of his mind.

It wasn't until he was actually lying in bed that night, listening to Lisabet's soft, even breathing on the other side of the room, that it suddenly came to him.

"Lisabet!" He sat bolt upright.

"Hmmmwhatsitnow?" she murmured, rolling over in bed and propping up on one elbow. He could only catch a glimpse of her in the moonlight through their window, black hair askew, pale face sleepy.

He pushed his covers back, hurrying over to turn on a light and pour her a glass of water from the pitcher by the door. "Wake up, I've remembered something," he said, and she obediently sat up, accepting the glass and taking a long gulp.

He told her about his lunchtime excursion with Theo—about the storage rooms and the endless books, records, and artifacts, pushing past the moment when her eyes lit up at the thought of exploring a place like that. He told her about the big record book they'd found, about the mirror and its description, and the symbol that said that somewhere in Drekhelm, the mirror was probably still working.

"And I know where I saw the other one," he finished, triumphant. "It was at Ulfar, in Hayn's workshop. Hayn showed it to us himself, Lisabet! He said that it used to be a big communication mirror, for speaking to Drekhelm. I can't believe I didn't remember!"

"I can't believe you're remembering now," she said. "It was just a few words, and weeks ago. And he said it *used to be*, that it was broken, right?"

"Yes," he admitted. "But what if he was wrong? What if the mirror on the other end wasn't broken, it was just put away? On purpose or by mistake, maybe it's in a dark, quiet room, and the wolves thought that meant it wasn't working."

She considered his words, nodding slowly. "If what you're saying about the way they store their records and artifacts is right, that could be what happened," she agreed slowly. "It might just have been stored somewhere, when they moved from Old Drekhelm. Or perhaps it *was* on purpose—they moved right after the battle, perhaps they didn't want the wolves to be able to contact them."

"We have to look for it," he said. "If we can find it, if we can see Hayn's office, perhaps we can find out something about what's happening at Ulfar."

"We can't let him know we're there," she said. "He told us Drifa, the dragonsmith, killed his brother. He must think we're traitors."

They were both quiet in the wake of those words. Hayn probably wasn't the only one who thought they were traitors. Their classmates—their friends—must all think the same. Were they wondering if Anders and Lisabet were all right? Did they hope they were, or they weren't?

"If we can't talk to him then we'll spy," said Anders. "Maybe enough will happen in his workshop that we can get some clue what the wolves are up to."

"I bet you're right," she said. "At least it's *something* we can do, instead of sitting around waiting for the Dragonmeet to finish discussing things. We'll be old by the time they're done, and my mother will attack before they ever decide anything. We'll start looking tomorrow. It's the only lead we have."

CHAPTER FIVE

THOUGH ANDERS HAD FALLEN ASLEEP FEELING confident about their plan, the next morning he had to admit that he didn't have any real idea about how they were going to find the Drekhelm mirror. As they got ready for school, he and Lisabet talked through their options.

"If we're going to use the mirror to spy on the wolves," he said, "we need to be careful who we tell about it. If the Dragonmeet uses it, they could find out something that would help them attack Ulfar. We want to keep us and Rayna safe, but we don't want to make things worse than they already are."

"Agreed," replied Lisabet. "It would be helpful if we could let Theo in on it, because he knows where all the records are. And he's come so recently from Holbard, I don't think he'd help the dragons attack it. His family is there. But Mikkel's his best friend already, and they're roomies, so we can't count on him not to tell Mikkel."

"And Mikkel's completely for the dragons," Anders replied. "I'm not sure about Rayna either. She's a dragon, so she's in danger from the Snowstone. And the wolves tried to kill her when she transformed. She has every reason to take anything we learn and use it against them. And she might tell Ellukka."

"So it's up to us," Lisabet said with a sigh. "We'll have to try and get into the archives."

But it turned out that was easier said than done too. They got out of class simply enough that morning, telling a distracted Leif they were having trouble concentrating and wanted to find a quiet place to read. They took books with them and headed straight for the archive caverns Theo had shown Anders, following the twisting and turning passages inside the mountain by memory.

When they made their way through the final door, they found none other than Valerius standing outside the main entrance to the storage rooms, talking to two other dragons. Anders and Lisabet ducked back inside the passageway and stood in the shadows, waiting to see whether the adults would leave or go inside.

But while Valerius departed after a few final words to the others, the other two took up a stance that Anders and

Lisabet recognized from seeing it thousands of times over back in Holbard, wherever the Wolf Guard went. The pair were standing watch, and they were in no mood for any trouble. Which meant that unauthorized wolf children had absolutely no chance of getting inside.

"Perhaps there'll be something in the books Theo has in the classroom," Anders suggested, not very hopefully, as they made their way back in defeat.

"Worth a try," Lisabet replied.

But as soon as they came back to the classroom, Leif looked up, his gaze lighting on the pair of them. "Anders," he said, rising from his seat. "Come with me, I want to talk to you. Rayna, you too."

Lisabet headed silently for the long tables, and Anders knew she'd see if Theo had anything in his books. For his part, he followed Leif out of the classroom, suppressing a sudden shiver of nerves. What did the Drekleid want? Had the dragons changed their minds about letting the two wolves stay? But in that case, it would be Lisabet by his side to hear the news, not Rayna. Wouldn't it?

Leif led them down the hallway and opened a stout door with his own name on it, engraved on a silver name-plate in curling script. Inside was a cozy office that in many ways reminded Anders of Hayn's workshop at Ulfar. It was crammed top to bottom with shelves down the left-hand side, and they were stuffed with books, artifacts, a few plants with green leaves trailing down the piles below, a teapot, a bag of apples, and what looked like a forgotten loaf of bread down near the floor. Down the right-hand side ran Leif's desk, equally crowded with his belongings. On the floor was a thick red rug to keep the cold of the stone away. At the other end of the narrow room was a floor-to-ceiling window like the one in the classroom, looking out toward the Icespire Mountains to the west. That was one way Hayn's workshop was different—it didn't have any windows, a fact that had forced Anders and Lisabet to pick the lock and break in only a few weeks before.

"Please, take a seat," Leif said, sinking down into his large, comfortable chair, and pulling two smaller stools out from where they were tucked in underneath the desk. Anders carefully removed a tiny mechanical model of a cow from one and sat down.

Leif took down a small, embroidered purse from the shelf, using a handkerchief so it wouldn't touch his skin. The fabric of the purse was red, and it was shot through with silver threads, which matched the silver clasp at the top. "This is an artifact," Leif said, "which after some considerable searching, I have managed to retrieve from our archives."

Anders was dying to hear what the purse had to do

with Rayna and him, but he couldn't pass up an opportunity to find out how Leif had managed to locate anything, let alone the thing he wanted, in the archive caverns.

"Theo showed me around in there," he said, making his eyes wide. "It looks like everything's all just piled up, one thing on top of another. How do you find what you want?"

"You probably shouldn't go into the archives," Leif said absently. "There are too many dragons still unhappy about your presence. Still, I suppose nobody told you not to yet. They certainly are disorganized, we need young Theo's work very badly. As for how I found it, there was a fair bit of undignified crawling around, but I also know that artifacts that served similar purposes used to be stored together at Old Drekhelm, and when they were picked up and carried here, they tended to stay together. So one might not know where exactly something is, but looking for things like it makes it easier to spot the group, and then it's just a matter of getting dusty."

Anders nodded, wondering if the mirror would be stored with other mirrors or other communication devices.

Leif shook his head. "My, but I get sidetracked by questions easily," he admitted.

"It's the dragon way," Rayna said, with an impressively straight face.

"True enough," he agreed. "Anyway, this artifact is going to serve a very useful purpose for us. It's a coin purse designed so that only members of the same family can open it. Now that we've found it, this is a very simple way for us to test whether you're related. We'll set it to recognize one of you, and if the other can open it, then you're family."

An unexpected shiver of pure apprehension went through Anders. On one hand, he was *positive* that he and Rayna were twins. He couldn't doubt that, not in his heart. He'd given up everything to be with Rayna, and it was worth it a hundred times over. On the other hand, that selfsame heart was thumping wildly at the prospect of this test, so hard he could feel it all over his body.

After everything they'd been through, the risk that Leif might tell him Rayna somehow wasn't his sister—might try to deny or take away that connection—made his mouth dry and his breath shake as he drew it in.

Rayna reached over and took his hand in hers, squeezing tight, and he knew without even looking at her that she was as nervous as he was, even if she'd try and bluster her way out of it.

He found himself speaking before he quite knew what he was going to say.

"Leif." His voice was surprisingly steady, given he was

pretty sure the rest of him was shaking. "We're family anyway. No matter what the purse says. Rayna will always be my sister."

"Yes," Rayna said, uncharacteristically brief, her voice a little rough, her hand squeezing hard. "No matter what, Leif."

The Drekleid inclined his head respectfully. "Of course," he agreed. "If you're prepared to try the artifact, I think it would be helpful for us to know whether you are sister and brother by blood, or simply by connection of the heart."

Anders looked across at Rayna, seeing his own doubt mirrored in her eyes.

"I think we should," she said eventually. "We both want to know who we are. What we are. And I hate that I can't make a spark, let alone a flame. If we know we're blood related, perhaps that means I can make icefire. Two's better than one, right?" Her smile was weak.

"Two's always better than one," he told her firmly, and they both knew he wasn't talking about icefire.

"Okay," she said to Leif, letting go of Anders's hand. "Let's try this purse, then."

Leif nodded. "I've released the previous bindings on the purse, which wasn't easy—I had to find a member of the family it used to belong to and get her to release it. It was the granddaughter, and she's living over in Port Alcher now. Quite a flight. She doesn't transform, but she has an inkling her grandmother did. Anyway, she—the granddaughter, I mean—runs a pie shop, and I had to buy a dozen pies before she made time for me." He paused, reflective. "They were delicious, though. And at any rate, now the purse is unattached, waiting for its new owner. It will bond to the next person who touches it. That's why I'm holding it with a handkerchief. Anders, would you do the honors? It will require just the smallest drop of your blood. Artifacts linked to family often do, among others. The blood of the most powerful wolves and dragons can achieve a great deal."

Anders took the purse from Leif's hand, cradling it in the palm of his own. He accepted a needle and pricked his fingertip, and with a quick sting a tiny drop of blood welled up, crimson against his brown skin. He pressed it to the silver of the clasp and his hand tingled briefly—a tickling, bubbly sensation that swept quickly up his arm and through his body in a wave. The purse itself seemed to glow for an instant, and then it looked normal once more.

"Done," said Leif. "Now, Rayna, if you would be so kind as to take the purse and attempt to open it, we'll have our answer. If it doesn't recognize you, it will scream an alarm. If it opens, that's all we need to see."

Rayna took a deep breath, and took the purse from Anders's hand, just as he'd taken it from Leif's a minute before. "Here goes," she said, and Anders knew she was trying to sound like her usual brave self, despite the tremor in her voice. She put her fingers to the little silver clasp on the purse and took a deep breath.

Then her fingers pressed against it.

It popped open, like it was waiting expectantly for someone to drop coins inside.

All three of them stared down at it, and then Rayna began to laugh in sheer relief. Anders's face stretched to a grin, and he threw both his arms around her, hugging her tight.

"Can you imagine?" she said. "If someone had come in, and we were all just sitting here, staring at the purse like it was going to start singing and dancing?" She was giggling, and Anders couldn't help but join in. Even Leif smiled, breathing out slowly as the tension dissipated. "Can I keep the purse?" Rayna asked.

"Yes," said Leif, still smiling. "Sparks and scales, you can keep the purse."

Anders had worried about the answer to the question of who he was, of *what* he was—ever since the moment of their transformation—but he hadn't realized just how much of an effect it was having on him until now. He felt so much lighter, he could have floated up to the ceiling.

"You may be the first confirmed elementals of mixed blood in Vallen," Leif told them, his voice quiet, thoughtful. "I mean, plenty of people have traces of wolf and dragon ancestry, and I suspect some transformed wolves and dragons even have traces of the other in their heritage. But there have only ever been stories about what might happen if two actual elementals—two people capable of transformation themselves—had a child. In you, we may have evidence that it's possible. We may have evidence that the old stories, which say that elementals of mixed blood have special powers, are true. This must be the reason for your icefire, Anders. And Rayna, it means you probably have a gift as well."

"There was an old story about a dragonsmith with special powers, wasn't there?" Anders asked, remembering Hayn's grim expression the day he'd told Anders and Lisabet about the dragon who'd killed his brother.

"That's right," Leif said, his smile dropping away. "Drifa, her name was. We attended the Finskól together as children. She grew up to be the greatest dragonsmith of our age. She was clever, inventive, creative, and daring, and the whispered rumor was that her father was a thunder lion from Mositala. They are elementals who control the wind and air. If she knew the truth about her parentage, she never told us, but the story was that her thunder lion heritage allowed her to control the winds around her forge and infuse them with essence. Then, when she worked with her own magical flame, she created truly incredible artifacts."

"That sounds amazing," Rayna breathed. "Why do you look so serious?"

Leif shook his head. "She died far too young. The wolves claimed she murdered one of their own, and afterward, nobody could find her. We searched as best we could, but we have no idea where she went, or whether she died too that day. It's been so long now that I'm sure she must be dead. Things were difficult between dragons and wolves before the day they say she killed a wolf, but afterward, they were impossible. The wolves refused to trust us, and their demands became more and more unreasonable, until eventually, they tried to keep dragons prisoner in the city of Holbard itself, to ensure we worked on the artifacts they needed. It was that wolf's death, and Drifa's disappearance, that led to the last great battle."

Both Anders and Rayna were silent, eyes wide. Anders knew this wasn't the story that was told about the battle in Holbard. He'd always heard that the dragons had attacked unprovoked, and the wolves had defended the city. But if the wolves had been holding dragons prisoner, that was a whole other story. Then again, if a dragon had killed a wolf . . . He didn't know what to make of it.

One thing he did know for sure, though, was that both sides would suffer if there was another battle. "Leif," he said, "has the Dragonmeet made any progress in deciding what to do about the Snowstone?"

The Drekleid shook his head slowly, regret in every line of his face. "We have been talking all week, and we remain deadlocked. Perhaps there is too much anger among the leadership on both sides of this fight."

"Then what will happen?" Rayna asked in a small voice. "War, again?"

"I hope not," Leif said gravely. "Perhaps . . ." He paused, then continued, looking directly at Anders. "Perhaps we need to come up with a new kind of solution. Perhaps someone will see a creative way out of this situation."

Anders felt quite sure in that moment that Leif meant him to listen carefully to those words. That Leif meant *him* to think about finding a way out of this.

On one hand, the task felt almost overwhelmingly large.

On the other, he wasn't the same boy who'd fled his own first transformation in terror. He'd found his way into Ulfar, to Fylkir's chalice, to Drekhelm itself. And now he was finding a way to get by, even to make a home at Drekhelm. Who knew what else he could do when those he loved were at risk?

As the three of them walked back to the classroom, Anders knew he had to tell Rayna about the mirror. He'd worried about whose side she might take in the wolf-dragon divide, but now she knew that she herself was born of both, things had to be different. They'd always worked together to solve problems in the past, and this one was going to need all the brains they could muster.

When they were back with the others, he quietly told Lisabet what had transpired in the Drekleid's office. He could see Rayna whispering the story to Ellukka as well. Lisabet's eyes went huge at the news.

"Pack and paws," she murmured. "You're . . . You two are a completely new kind of elemental, Anders. That's incredible."

"There's more," he said, leaning in close. He told her what else Leif had said—about the way the dragon had looked directly at him, as good as telling him to use his creativity to avert an all-out war, while the adults were tied up in endless, deadlocked discussions. "We have to tell Rayna," he finished, and Lisabet nodded.

"The others too," she said. "Ellukka goes where Rayna

goes, and we're going to need Mikkel's and Theo's help. We *have* to trust them. If the Dragonmeet is no closer to a solution, and we've seen what my mo—what Sigrid can do with the Snowstone, then this is urgent."

* * *

After dinner that night, Anders and Lisabet discreetly gathered up their friends and brought them back to their room. The dragons were all curious, but they came quietly, piling into the little guest room the wolves had made their own. Anders, Lisabet, and Theo sat on Anders's bed, and Rayna, Ellukka, and Mikkel took up Lisabet's.

"Well?" said Ellukka. "What's the big secret?"

Anders told them about his trip with Theo to the artifact storage caverns, and Theo joined in a little, confirming what Anders was saying, though he clearly didn't know why it was so important that they share this information right at this moment.

Then Lisabet took over from Theo, and together the wolves told the dragons about Hayn, and about the mirror they'd seen in his office—about their theory that perhaps the dragons' counterpart wasn't broken—especially since the symbol beside it in the book said otherwise—but instead simply locked up somewhere dark and quiet.

And finally, Anders told them what Leif had said

in his office that day—that to search for one artifact at Drekhelm, you looked for others like it, which at least gave them something of a hint as to how to narrow their search. And more important, that Leif had as good as told him to take action.

"What exactly does Leif want us to do?" Rayna asked, thoughtful. "What *can* we do?"

"We're twelve," Mikkel said, pale. "How can we be in charge of handling any part of this?"

"I'm thirteen," said Ellukka, and he elbowed her in the side. "Anyway," she continued, "we're Finskól students. We're there because we're all good at something special."

Anders nodded. "And if we do nothing, it's just going to get colder and colder. The Dragonmeet's talking forever and getting nothing done. We should try and find out what the wolves have planned."

"I agree," said Rayna. "We have to try and find the mirror, see what we can find out from watching this Hayn."

"Then do what?" Theo asked. "If we tell anyone where we got that information, we'll get in trouble for using an artifact like that without permission. Assuming they even believe us. And if they think we revealed to the wolves that the mirrors still work . . ."

"Then do whatever we can think of," Anders said, "to try and stop them using the Snowstone. To keep things the way they are, so the wolves can't attack."

Until now, it had been a matter of keeping himself, Rayna, and Lisabet safe. But now, looking around the room, he was realizing he had more to fight for than that. He needed to broaden his vision—he had friends on the wolf side *and* on the dragon side who would suffer if there was another battle.

"I think we should vote," said Lisabet. "It's a big risk for all of us. Anders and I could be thrown out of Drekhelm if we're caught using an artifact like that without permission, or risking the wolves using their mirror in return. Perhaps the rest of you could too, I don't know, if we got caught going behind the Dragonmeet's backs. Everyone needs to be in on this."

"Agreed," said Anders, his throat tight with nerves. What would they do if one of them didn't want to join in but already knew their plans? "Hands up, all who think we should try and find the mirror."

He raised his own hand, and beside him, Lisabet raised hers as well. Rayna did at the same time, backing him without hesitation.

Ellukka looked sideways at Rayna, and then raised her own hand, and with a soft, worried sound, Theo raised his.

Mikkel looked around at them all, biting his lip, considering.

"I think they really would throw us out," he said quietly. "Out of the Finskól for sure. Leif couldn't defend us. We might be exiled from every dragon community in Vallen, if they think we've shown the wolves a way to spy on us, or they think we were trying to talk to them."

Anders nodded slowly. "That could all happen," he admitted. "But if we do nothing . . ."

Mikkel held still for an agonizingly long moment. And then, finally, he raised his hand too.

"All right," said Rayna quietly, much more serious than usual. "Good. Should we go hunt for it?"

"What, right now?" Mikkel asked.

"Why wait?"

"It's not that easy," Anders replied. "There are guards outside the storage rooms, and Valerius already caught me in there once."

All eyes turned to Ellukka, who raised both her hands defensively. "Sparks and scales, don't look at me," she said. "You think I can get my father to do what I want? Try being raised by him, he's strict!"

"I can see how he really crushed your spirit," Lisabet replied dryly, and Rayna giggled, breaking the tension that had gathered around them.

Remembering Rayna's mistrust of Lisabet the day they'd arrived, Anders could scarcely believe they'd come so far in just a week. But then again, Rayna was quick and clever, and if she'd been watching Lisabet, she'd have seen the other girl was the same, and a friend worth having.

They talked for a while about the best way to sneak past the guards, and in the end, they decided that an old-fashioned diversion was their best hope.

"It'll have to be me," Ellukka said, with a resigned huff. "My father's their boss, they'll come running to see what's up with me, and that'll give you a chance to get inside. If they're back at their posts by the time you need to leave, we might need to get creative, but there's no way of predicting how long you'll need to hunt, so there's not much use in planning how to get you out."

"And nighttime is best," said Theo, who spent more time than anyone in the storage caverns. "During the day there's often someone looking for something or working with the books. Like Rayna said, there's no reason to wait, and this is the best chance to avoid running into anyone."

"I think I know what Ellukka can do," Rayna said, tapping her chin thoughtfully. "Anders and Lisabet, you've seen one of these mirrors, so you'll have to look for it, and you'll need Theo to help you search. If I can have Ellukka and Mikkel, I can . . . Anders, do you remember that time at the fish market?"

Anders's eyes widened. "Oh no," he said, lifting one hand to cover his mouth.

"Oh yes," said Rayna, grinning.

* * *

Half an hour later, Anders crouched in the shadows with Theo and Lisabet, watching the two guards standing outside the artifact storage caverns. Ellukka had wandered by a few minutes earlier to ask the two men a question, and while they were distracted with that, Rayna and Mikkel had silently crept along one of the tunnels approaching the guards. There, they'd carefully turned the dials that controlled the nearest wall lamps, dimming them to almost nothing.

That made a dark spot where Anders and his two companions could hide, giving them a clear view of the guards, so they could creep past them as soon as the watchful dragons left their posts. The students were only about thirty feet away, and they could make the run in a few heartbeats once Rayna gave them the chance.

And Anders was very certain Rayna was going to give them the chance. The fish market fiasco had been one of her finest hours, a chaotic plot that had fed half the street children of Holbard for a week. It had been one of the only times they'd teamed up with others, and Rayna had been fearsome in command.

"What's she going to do?" Theo whispered, sounding a tiny bit worried.

"You'll see in a minute," Anders promised. "Just don't worry if you hear any screaming."

"Screaming?" Lisabet echoed, shifting beside him, and he put his hand on her arm to stop her from standing up.

And then it began.

There was a faint scuffling noise up the wide passageway to the left of the guards, which descended toward the right on a gentle slope. You barely even noticed the angle when you were walking, but for Rayna's present purposes, it was perfect.

The scuffling stopped, and then a loud, banging, scraping noise began, the sound of wood thumping against rock, and Ellukka started screaming, the sound somehow both muffled and echoing all at once.

"What the—" Lisabet began, but she got no further.

A barrel went rolling by the guards at top speed, Ellukka's blond braids whipping wildly at one end—she was wedged tightly inside, turning over and over as the barrel flew along the hallway down the slope.

A second later Mikkel started yelling, and his barrel flew down in hot pursuit, with Rayna bringing up the rear, waving her hands in the air gleefully. "Barrel race!" she shouted to the startled guards, who stared, then took off after her at a run.

"Quick," said Anders, springing up like he was starting his own race and sprinting down the hallway to the cavern doors. He hauled them open, hurrying inside, with Lisabet and Theo right behind him.

"Barrel races?" Theo said, pushing the doors shut. "Seriously?"

The first time Rayna had tried this, Anders had been inside one of the barrels, Rayna in the other, and they'd gone straight through the middle of Holbard's busy fish market. Fish had gone flying in every direction, and by the time the angry stallholders had retrieved the twins and heard Rayna's dramatic, tearful version of their story—that older children had forced them into the barrels, that she'd been afraid for her life, that oh, her poor, weak brother might have died of fright!—the rest of Holbard's street children had made off with as much fish as they could carry.

Anders had still been dizzy when they'd met up later to collect their share of the spoils, but he had to admit they'd eaten very well that week. And their cat, Kess, had been amazed, her eyes going so round he thought she'd forgotten how to blink.

He hadn't seen Kess since shortly after his transformation, and he hoped desperately that she'd found someone else to sleep next to, and a safe place to be. He wished he could find her, but she'd run from him, smelling the wolf on him even in human form.

For now, he had other problems to solve. "This way to the mirrors," Theo said, hurrying along a jumbled pathway that had been cleared through the piles of old artifacts, and just plain junk. Outside, Rayna was probably giving a speech about the amazing benefits of barrel racing by now, and more than likely halfway to convincing the horrified guards that the dragons should take it up as a winter sport.

"I've seen mirrors before," Theo told him, pausing by a desk to pick up an artifact lantern, which was glowing dimly. He turned a knob to bring the light up to full strength, and then handed two more to Anders and Lisabet. "First place to check is whether it's with those."

They made their way through two more caverns, where stacks of books and crates, spindly-armed artifacts and piles of spare parts cast long, eerie shadows, the rooms growing dustier each time they made their way through a new doorway.

The third cavern they passed through held a huge wall of hammers—small and shiny, big, blunt, and black, they were hanging on hooks set into the rock. In the middle of the room stood a collection of anvils of all sizes. Anders had seen an anvil before, at a blacksmith's in Holbard, but there were dozens here.

"They must have belonged to the dragonsmiths," Lisabet whispered.

"No use for them anymore," Theo said, leading them onward.

No use now, Anders thought. *But once there was.*

When they came through the next doorway, Anders pulled up short—his lantern was reflected back at him in dozens of different mirrors, each showing a shadowed picture of a frightened boy, the glow of the lantern making his brown face pale yellow.

"Let's split up and search the room," Lisabet said. "It's not that big, we should be able to see one another, or at least hear if somebody calls out."

None of them were particularly enthusiastic about being on their own, but the urgency of their task pushed them on, and they parted ways, climbing through the piles of junk and stacks of files, checking the frame of each mirror, looking for the pack of wolves running down one side of it, the dragons snaking their way down the other.

But though Theo called Anders or Lisabet over a couple of times to check mirrors he'd found, and after a while they began to hunt in places the others had already been, they had no luck. "It has to be here," Anders said, desperate. "We have to find a way to see what's happening at Ulfar somehow."

"Perhaps it's hidden somewhere else?" Lisabet asked, not sounding very hopeful.

Anders closed his eyes, picturing the mirror he'd seen back in Hayn's workshop. "It . . . it has to be somewhere dark. Otherwise, Hayn would have seen or heard someone in it by now if it's working. Is there somewhere near here that's dark and quiet?"

Theo frowned. "Maybe? There are a lot more caverns. I've been in most of them, though, and I'm sure I'm not the only one."

"What's this?" asked Lisabet, from behind a stack of mirrors. They hurried around to join her, dozens of reflected lanterns jangling as the real ones swung back and forth in the boys' hands. Lisabet was looking at a heavy wooden doorway, sealed tightly shut in the stone.

"It could be somewhere dark and quiet," Anders said. Hoping against hope it wasn't just another room, he tugged on the handle, then leaned back, putting his whole weight on it. Slowly, the door started to open. He pressed one eye to the crack, and gasped.

He could barely make out the frame of the mirror on the other side of the door, set in the middle of a tiny room, but he could clearly see what was reflected in it.

Hayn's workshop.

The shelves crammed full of unrepaired artifacts, the desk full of Skraboks, the strings of lights along the walls— they were all there. And then Hayn walked into view, straight across the mirror's line of sight, disappearing on the other side. It was impossible to mistake him—he was a tall, broad-shouldered man with dark-brown skin, a black beard, and black, square-rimmed glasses, standing at least half a head above almost everyone at Ulfar.

Anders hurriedly shut the door, blinking at the other two. "We found it," he whispered. "He's right there."

Lisabet made an excited little squeak, and Theo jumped up and down on the spot.

"Let's put the lanterns out," Anders suggested. "If we close the door behind us quickly and sit in the dark, and if we keep quiet, there's no reason he'll even know we're there."

They turned all their lanterns down until their glows became faint, and then extinguished, and slowly, carefully, Anders opened the door. One by one they slipped inside, and Theo pulled the door closed after them. There wasn't much space in the tiny room, and the three of them had to bunch up together. They crouched on the floor in silence, watching the workshop and waiting to see if Hayn would appear again, or if he had company.

It was only a few minutes before their patience was rewarded. Hayn reappeared, opening one of the huge Skraboks sitting on his desk and slowly turning the pages. He was frowning at what he found there when the sound of the door opening interrupted his concentration. He looked across, almost right at the mirror—because of course, in his workshop, the other mirror stood beside the door.

"Sigrid," he said, and beside Anders, Lisabet gave a little gasp, then clapped her hands over her mouth to muffle it, though too late.

For an instant, Anders could have sworn Hayn's gaze flickered toward the mirror. But if it did, then the next instant it was back on the Fyrstulf again.

"Hayn," she said, her voice grim. Anders, Lisabet, and Theo held perfectly still as the Fyrstulf—Lisabet's mother—strode into the workshop. "Well?" she said, her back to the mirror, her arms folded. "Any luck?"

"None so far," Hayn said, glancing down at the book on his desk, then back up at the pale blond woman standing before him. "This is an incredibly delicate procedure, Sigrid. You have to understand it's going to take time."

"It worked the other day," she snapped. "Why can't you do it again?"

"Because it worked for about an hour, and then the augmenter melted," he said calmly. "So obviously I can't use that one again. It was too old, I still can't believe I got it to work even for a little. I'm scouring the Skraboks for something else I can use, but there's a reason we haven't done this in over a decade. There are a lot of risks, Sigrid, and I'm not sure—"

"I don't want to hear excuses," she said, her voice crisp. "I'll be back tomorrow, and I want better news."

Anders caught a glimpse of her face as she turned to stride for the door—her skin was always very pale, almost the same color as her white-blond hair, and the shadows beneath her eyes stood out like bruises. And then she was gone, the door closing behind her in a slam.

What was an augmenter? Why did Sigrid want it so badly? And why did Hayn sound so hesitant about it?

All was silent for a heartbeat, then two, then three, both in the workshop and in the tiny room where Anders, Lisabet, and Theo were crammed in side by side. Hayn stood staring at the door. And then his gaze turned once more toward the mirror.

This time he walked toward it, approaching until he was almost nose-to-glass, staring at what Anders knew must be a perfectly black surface on his end. Anders held his breath, lest the sound give him away, and the trio of spies were so silent that he was sure Lisabet and Theo must be doing the same on either side of him.

Then Hayn spoke. "Is somebody there?" He was squinting at the dark.

None of the children replied.

"I . . . I can't see anything," Hayn said quietly. "But I thought I heard something, just now. If you can hear me, please, I just want to know if our students are all right. Anders and Lisabet are only first years, and whatever they've done, they didn't mean to hurt anyone. They're good children."

Anders's heart was thumping so loudly in his ears he felt sure Hayn must be able to hear it. He stayed silent. He'd never imagined Hayn being anything but furious at what he'd see as Anders's and Lisabet's betrayal.

Hayn sighed. "If anyone's there, please pass on word that I need to speak to Anders. I need to speak to him urgently. I . . ." He paused, and glanced at the door again, before lowering his voice, and continuing in almost a whisper. "I have to tell him something that might be the difference between peace and the next great battle."

Anders felt like he'd been struck over the head, the shock reverberating through him. Hayn had something to tell *him* that might be the difference between war and peace?

He'd always liked the big wolf—Hayn had been kind the first day Anders had transformed, and he'd been kind when Anders and Lisabet had come chasing information. But they weren't exactly friends.

Anders scrambled for the right decision. He should check with the others before he revealed himself, since that had never been part of the plan—they'd only agreed to help him spy. Making contact with the wolves might be more than any of the dragons were willing to do.

But he might not get back in here again, and if he did, there was no guarantee Hayn would be in his office.

He had to take his chance while he had it. And as he reached his decision, Lisabet reached over to squeeze his arm in silence. He hoped that meant *you should say something*, because he was about to.

"Hayn?" His voice came out as nearly a squeak, and he cleared his throat and tried again. "Hayn, it's Anders."

Hayn had been halfway through turning away, but he whirled back, gaze fixed on the mirror. "Anders?" His voice was somewhere between fear and hope. "Are you all right? Who else is there?"

Anders felt movement by his side, and Theo turned the dial on his lantern until it came dimly to life, the essence captured within it powering its soft glow. "Lisabet," Anders said. "And this is our friend Theo."

"Hi, Hayn," said Lisabet quietly, and Theo lifted a hand in greeting.

"Pack and paws, I was so worried you were dead," Hayn breathed, reaching out to grip either side of the mirror. "Anders, I need to see you as soon as I can. Do you have any way to get to Holbard?"

Anders's eyes went wide. They were forbidden from leaving Drekhelm, let alone waltzing off to the wolves' stronghold. "I—I don't think so," he said.

"Are you prisoners?"

"Not exactly," Anders said. "But the wolves don't want us in Holbard, do they? Sigrid must be so angry."

"Sigrid's angry," Hayn conceded, with an apologetic glance at Lisabet. "But of course she's worried."

"Worried enough to forgive us if we came home?" Lisabet pressed.

The answer was in Hayn's expression, and after a moment he slowly shook his head. "Tell me," he said quietly. "Did you deliberately try to hurt your classmates? Or Ennar?"

"No!" Anders's answer came quick, bursting out of him. "We didn't want to, but they were attacking the dragons. It would have been the start of the next great battle if they'd killed one. We never even meant for them to follow us, Hayn."

Hayn nodded. "That's what Ennar and I thought," he said, to Anders's surprise. "Though she's still less forgiving than I am." He paused, and then pressed on. "Ennar said that you were claiming one of the dragons was your sister, Anders."

Anders nodded slowly. "She is."

Hayn didn't look surprised, which was odd. Just worried. "Anders, I must speak to you," he said again. "And your sister. Is there any way you can get here? I mean it when I say this might be the only chance to stop a war. It has to be in person. And it has to be soon. Tomorrow, even. One of your classmates stole an important artifact while they were at Drekhelm. It's called the Snowstone."

"We know," Anders said.

Lisabet spoke beside him. "And we know Sigrid will use it to freeze the dragons if she can."

Hayn nodded slowly. "Yes. But I think I have a way to counter its effects."

"Why do you want to do that?" Theo asked, finally speaking up. As the only dragon present, he sounded cynical.

"Because I don't want a battle," Hayn said. "Everybody will be hurt. And . . . for more personal reasons. Which I'd prefer to give Anders *in person*."

Anders exchanged a three-way glance with Lisabet

and Theo. He saw the doubt in their eyes, but Lisabet nodded a fraction, and after a moment, so did Theo. He turned back to Hayn. "I'll try my best," he said. "Where should we meet you?"

"In the port square," Hayn said. "In the southeast corner, by the water." The port square was where the wolves held their monthly Trial of the Staff. It was where Anders and Rayna had first transformed, and it was where Anders had watched helplessly as the wolves battled a deadly white-and-gold dragonsfire that took hold of the buildings all along the waterfront.

The port was also busy and bustling all day long, full of Vallenite buyers and sellers, hawkers and passersby, not to mention the visitors from faraway places, the crews of mercher vessels docked from all over the world.

It was a good place to meet because there was always a crowd to blend into. But the square gave Anders nightmares—memories of smoke and screaming, from that hazy place where all his earliest memories lived. He sometimes thought they might be memories of the last great battle. He had only been two years old when it happened, and he and Rayna had come out of it orphans, their parents unknown and forgotten.

"In the port square," he agreed. "If we get away after

breakfast, and if Rayna can fly that far, we can probably be there by mid-morning."

"Be careful," said Hayn. "You might be recognized."

Anders could hardly imagine anyone in Holbard would ever recognize him, beyond a few of his Ulfar classmates, but he nodded. "We will," he promised. "If we can get away, we'll be there." Getting away would require a lot to go right—the others would have to agree to the meeting, Rayna would have to be able to cover the distance, Leif would have to agree to let them out of class again. But he'd do his best.

"We should go," said Lisabet. "Nobody knows we're here."

Hayn nodded. "I'll see you tomorrow," he said, his gaze on Anders's face. "Be careful."

* * *

Getting out of the archives proved to be easier than expected—some ways up the hallway a kerfuffle was still underway, and several adult dragons, including the guards, were lecturing Rayna, Mikkel, and Ellukka about the perils of barrel racing, the irresponsibility of doing it in a hallway where anybody might be walking along, and the expectation that students of the Finskól would know better than to undertake such shenanigans.

Anders, Lisabet, and Theo snuck out of the storage caverns and took off in the opposite direction, hurrying back to Anders and Lisabet's room to wait for the barrel racers to return. Eventually, they did, their eyes dancing with mirth.

"We should try that again sometime," Ellukka said, gleeful, as she thumped down onto Lisabet's bed.

"You *would* say that, you won," Mikkel complained. "I was nearly sick." Even he looked pleased, though.

"Of course you were," Ellukka replied airily. "You rattled around in your barrel like dice in a cup. I was wedged firmly into mine, so I didn't move around. Much easier. You shouldn't be so skinny."

Mikkel made a grumbling noise, but he climbed onto the bed next to her anyway.

"Well?" said Rayna. "Did you find it?"

"Did we ever," said Anders.

They told the others everything that had happened, and their eyes grew wider and wider with each new detail.

"So you want to go to Holbard?" Ellukka said, in the end. "Do you know how much trouble we'd be in if the Dragonmeet found out? Or how much danger we'd be in if the wolves did?"

"I know," Anders agreed. "But if he really does have a way to stop the Snowstone bringing down the temperature, we have to try and find out. Otherwise it's just a matter of time until the wolves attack."

"Perhaps we should tell the Dragonmeet," Mikkel said, though he didn't sound very convinced.

"And what?" Rayna said, rolling her eyes. "Sit around while they debate it for the next month? This Hayn person said it's urgent. He said it needs to be tomorrow. We can't afford to wait. I vote we should go. I'll fly there, Anders, and take you."

"I think I should go too," Lisabet said. "I know more about the wolves' history than any of us. I'll know if Hayn's telling the truth." Anders glanced across at her, wondering if that was her real reason, or whether she simply wanted to be close to Ulfar, to see her home again, even if she couldn't return to it. He hadn't forgotten that they'd just seen her mother in the mirror too.

"If Rayna's going, I'm going," said Ellukka promptly. "But Mikkel, Theo, you'll have to stay here. Somebody has to cover for us. I have a plan that'll get us out of Drekhelm all right, but if we're not back by dark, you'll have to come up with some kind of excuse, or better yet, make sure nobody knows."

Mikkel and Theo nodded. Neither of them looked as sure about the plan, but Anders could see that neither of them had any other ideas either.

And so it was decided. For better or worse, they'd be going to Holbard in the morning. They'd just have to hope Hayn was true to his word—and that they were flying toward an ally, rather than a trap.

CHAPTER SIX

ANDERS DIDN'T GET TO FIND OUT WHAT ELLUK-ka's plan was that night—there was a knocking on the door before the conversation could continue, and her father, Valerius, was outside, looking supremely unimpressed.

"Ellukka, it's well past time you were in bed," he said, peering into the room, his burly frame filling up most of the doorway. "And the rest of you. Come on, get moving."

Nobody wanted to argue with a member of the Dragonmeet, though Ellukka scowled as she climbed off Lisabet's bed and trooped out into the hallway with the others. She'd said before that she couldn't afford to give her father a reason to stop her rooming with Rayna now, and insist she live with him in family quarters as she had when she was small, not when the Finskól students had so much to do.

As the dragons all headed off down the hallway, Anders could hear Valerius's voice drifting back. "I've just heard a story about barrel racing, and I'm not—"

Lisabet shut the door firmly behind them, turning her back on it and leaning against it, as if she could keep all the Dragonmeet—and all their troubles—on the outside. "Remember when our biggest worry was surviving Professor Ennar's combat class?" she said, rueful.

The two wolves got ready for bed in silence, both lost in their own thoughts. The same question kept nagging at Anders, but he didn't dare voice it aloud to his friend: *How far is Sigrid prepared to go?*

Hayn had looked deadly serious. Would Sigrid push the temperature down so far she killed the dragons? Killed his sister? Would the dragons talk and debate, hearing every voice and considering every view, until they were frozen solid? Would the wolves of Ulfar stand by and watch, as their Fyrstulf killed the enemy one by one?

He was afraid he knew the answer. He knew the stories the wolves told about the dragons. What they believed. Even his friends believed the worst of the dragons, and now of him too, he had no doubt.

But for all the questions whirling around in his head, there was nothing to do but drift into a troubled sleep and wait for morning.

* * *

The next day, Ellukka tackled Leif at breakfast. The Drekleid was eating alone, reading from a small book, blinking sleepily as he spooned up his porridge. Definitely not a morning person, but that only made him more susceptible to Ellukka's tactics.

"I want to take Anders and Lisabet on a cultural excursion," she told him, taking a seat at his table. "Rayna's going to help me. She needs to learn more dragon stories too."

"A what?" he said, blinking. "Where will this excursion go, exactly? You know you're not supposed to leave Drekhelm."

"We won't go far," she promised. "But I need to practice my storytelling. I thought we could visit some landmarks—just here in the Icespire Mountains nearby—and I'd tell them the stories that go with them. Lene's Pass, maybe."

Leif didn't look so sure, and Anders leaned down beside Ellukka. "We're also working on a design project," he said. "We want to design a special harness for dragons to wear when wolves or people are riding them. Something we could connect ourselves to, so we don't fall off." Remembering what Rayna had said the first time they'd discussed the idea, he added, "There are people here at Drekhelm who don't transform or are too young. It would be useful for them too."

Ellukka made a spluttering noise of protest, but Leif was nodding. "I do like to encourage innovation," he conceded. "And as you say, many dragons have human family members who might benefit from such an invention. You'll need to be home well before dark."

"We will," they chorused.

"And don't go far," he continued. "Make sure nobody from any of the villages sees you. Don't go too near Little Dalven, or High Rikkel. And don't forget there are farmers who live outside both of them."

"We'll be careful," Ellukka said, rising to her feet. Anders recognized this as an old tactic of Rayna's. *As soon as they start to say yes, run away before it turns into a no.*

"Well, then," Leif said, and Anders and Ellukka fled.

Mikkel and Theo saw them off, both looking worried, though Mikkel was trying to cover it up with his usual smirk.

"Be careful," Theo said, pushing his hair out of his eyes as he always did, shifting his weight from foot to foot. "And if you're late, we'll try to cover it up for as long as we can."

"And when that doesn't work," added Mikkel, "we'll go through your things and take all the good stuff."

Rayna poked her tongue out at him, and then walked over to the middle of the Great Hall, where Ellukka had already transformed. Ellukka's scales were the color of a sunrise, orange and peach, her wings a deep gold, shot through with hints of a reddish pink.

Rayna dropped to a three-point crouch, both feet and the fingertips of one hand resting on the floor, and bowed her head. An instant later she was swelling faster than Anders's eyes could follow, her brown skin glimmering, her shape morphing. Within two heartbeats she was her dragon self, her scales a dark red, streaks of gold and copper winding through them, gleaming in the early morning light.

All his life, Anders had been taught to fear dragons— to run for his life if he saw one—and he still couldn't tamp down the faint nervousness he felt when he was so close to a dragon, even if she was his sister. But he could also see how beautiful the colors in her scales were, how delicate the stretches of her wings.

He and Lisabet were putting on layers upon layers of clothing. They couldn't afford to wear their Ulfar cloaks to Holbard, in case someone wondered why students were entering the city from the outside, or walking about the city in a pair, instead of the compulsory foursome. So they'd found coats and cloaks in the cupboards full of clothes set aside for visitors to Holbard. Anders wore a pair of thick blue trousers tucked into brown boots, and a bright-blue tunic over the top, a green shirt beneath it. He had on a padded brown jacket, a cloak pulled over it for extra warmth, gloves, a scarf wrapped around his neck, and a leather hat lined with wool pulled down over his ears. It was one thing to enjoy the cold mountain air in a wolfish kind of way. It was quite another to freeze solid, flying at altitude.

Once Rayna was ready, he approached her. It was only the second time he'd seen her as a dragon, though he'd now been at Drekhelm for over a week. And what a difference a week had made. Last time he'd stood beside his sister as a dragon, he'd been terrified, Mikkel and Ellukka looking on suspiciously. Now Mikkel was standing beside him, weaving his hands together to boost Anders up his sister's side, which was much easier than climbing her leg. Her scales radiated a fierce heat, and they weren't as hard as they looked from the outside. There was a little give to them when he pressed his hand against one.

"Good luck," said Mikkel quietly, as Anders wedged himself into place between two of the ridges that ran the length of her back. "No pressure or anything, but the fate of all dragonkind's probably resting on you. Find out what he knows, and how we can stop them freezing us all, and whatever you do, don't let the wolves catch you."

"Easy," said Anders, with a weak smile. Then Mikkel was stepping back, Anders was curling his arms around the ridge in front of him—they seriously needed to talk about harnesses, this was a *terrible* idea—and before he knew it, Rayna was taking a dozen quick steps and spreading her wings. They were aloft!

They cleared the huge dragon doors of the great cavern with room to spare, and Rayna tipped down her left wing to wheel around and follow the curve of the mountainside, then snapped her wings wide open to soar. She trumpeted her pleasure at being in the air, and Anders heard a reply from right behind them—Ellukka and Lisabet must be close.

They flew for a couple of hours, their course taking them through the Icespire Mountains and over the Great Forest of Mists. The countryside below them seemed just like one of the maps Anders studied in class. In the crisp cool of the morning, mists were gathered not just around the forest, but in every gully and valley, as though they were white water that had drained down to the lowest points in the land. The fierce black rock of the mountains, cut through with pure white snow, slowly gave way first to the rich, dark-green treetops of the Great Forest, and after that to the familiar green-gold of the plains.

Anders knew the rivers below him were rushing, tumbling, fierce beasts, ready to grab at the unwary and drag them away, but from here they looked like blue and silver string, winding their way in endless curves through the countryside.

The sun caught the dew-wet plains, and they glinted at him like fields of diamonds, dotted here and there with outcroppings of jet-black rock, with the small shadows that meant a hill or someone's home. With so many of the village houses sporting grassed-over roofs, it was often difficult to tell the difference.

The view was mesmerizing, and up here it felt almost possible to forget all his worries and his fears. Up here, everything felt small and distant, like pieces on a game board to be moved—when he was down on the ground, he felt like he was in a dangerous game, where one wrong move could bring down an avalanche on him and his friends.

He felt a pang of disappointment as Rayna finally started to angle downward, coming to rest in a gully near the banks of the Sudrain River, following Ellukka into their landing spot. Their goal was to land some way outside Holbard and approach the city on foot, coming in through the west gate, which was often the busiest.

When he tried to climb down he found he'd stiffened into place, quick pain shooting along his limbs as he hauled his left leg over Rayna's back to slide down her side.

Lisabet was stumbling to the ground nearby, and without a word she half-ran, half-staggered toward the river's edge. Ellukka was transforming the moment Lisabet was clear of her, and she hurried after the other girl. Anders tried to make his tired arms and legs follow, and by the time he caught up, Lisabet was kneeling by the edge of the river, scooping up cold water and splashing it on her face. Ellukka was holding on to Lisabet's cloak with both hands to make sure she didn't fall in.

"What happened?" he asked. "Did she get sick?"

Ellukka simply shrugged and held on. "We don't exactly talk while we're up there," she pointed out. "Search me."

Rayna appeared beside Anders, her own transformation to human complete, and the three of them waited until Lisabet could lift her head. "Sorry," she said, her pale skin even paler than usual, her cheeks bright pink from the cold of the river. "It was the heat. I was all right for most of it, but I started to feel horrible toward the end. The dragons are so *hot* when they're, well, dragons."

Anders, with his strange new immunity to the heat, hadn't even noticed.

Ellukka, who might ordinarily have a wisecrack for Lisabet, instead produced a couple of cookies from her pockets. "Eat something," she said. "Usually helps me, if I've gotten cold."

"How did you get cookies to transform with you?" Rayna asked, indignant. "I had a sandwich with me last week, and it just vanished. Leif says nobody knows where things like that go, which I'd think would be quite an important mystery to solve, but apparently not."

"Size," Ellukka said. "If what you pack is small enough, and you can tuck it in your pockets, then I suppose your charm thinks it's part of your clothing." She fished out a necklace from beneath her tunic, which sported an amulet that looked a lot like the ones wolves wore to keep their clothes in place when they transformed.

"Just like ours," Lisabet said, echoing Anders's thoughts. "More evidence that wolves and dragons used to work together."

"*We're* evidence that wolves and dragons used to get along," Ellukka pointed out. "If we can now, they could then." Her lips quirked, and she pointed at Anders and Rayna. "And we know at least one dragon and one wolf liked each other, or they wouldn't be here."

"I wish we knew who they were," Anders said, and Rayna murmured agreement by his side. But that wasn't what they were here to think about, and after Lisabet splashed a little more cold water on her face, the four of them set off, walking down to the road that led into town. It stretched between a ford across the Sudrain River and the walls of Holbard itself, and was the way almost all of the farmers from the southern farmlands made their way into Holbard with their produce for market.

It was easy enough to wait for a gap in the people and wagons to dart down to the road, and once they were there, the four of them simply slowed their pace and let themselves be swallowed up in a slow-moving crowd of farmers and traders. It wasn't quick, but it was safe.

Anders could hear the farmers talking quietly, and he kept his head down, his cloak wrapped tight around him.

"We're halfway through spring," a man was saying, tugging his scarf more tightly around his neck. "Everything should be in bloom, putting out green shoots and coming to life, and instead it's still half-frozen in the ground."

"It's like the winter never ended," a second man agreed.

"Still," said the woman beside them. "If it's hard for us, it's worse for those dragons. I heard half the port burned down, the last fire they lit."

The first man clucked his tongue in worry. "I heard we'll have a battle before the year's out. I only hope we're not there when it happens, makes you want to stay out on the farm where it's safe, even if nothing's growing."

"The wolves are strong," the second man said. "Surely they'll defend us again."

"They'd better," the woman replied, with a snort that sounded a lot like Rayna's when she got indignant. "Wolf Guard on every corner, constantly stopping you and asking your business. And they take plenty of money from the city's coffers. The Fyrstulf offers protection, and that's valuable, but you bet your boots she knows how valuable it is."

"Don't say things like that," the man said, lowering his voice. "People might think the wrong thing."

Anders glanced across at his own companions—Lisabet's lips were pressed together in a tight line, and she was staring straight ahead. She'd grown up with stories of duty and honor, and it must be hard for her to hear what people thought of the wolves. Rayna was barely listening to them, busy glancing up and down the stream of travelers, calculating the best spot to be when they reached the gate. She looked cold too, her cloak drawn tightly around her.

And Ellukka, who had never been near Holbard before, was staring at everything with wide eyes, her hood pushed back so she could get the best possible view, blond braids gleaming in the sun.

Eventually the city gate reared up ahead. The black stone walls were high, and wide enough that the wolves could walk patrol along their tops—Anders could see two gray-cloaked figures making their rounds, if he squinted. The gates were a hardened, flame-proofed wood, thrown open just now so the people and wagons could make their way in through the wide arch. With any luck, plenty of these people would head straight to the port square where Anders and Rayna were meeting Hayn, and the children could mingle with them all the way.

Anders was just beginning to feel relaxed about the plan when the crowd ahead started to bunch up, slowing as it reached the gates. He craned his neck and felt a chill go through him as he spotted wolves up ahead, standing atop packing crates and surveying the crowd.

"Wanted," one called, holding up a large poster. "These children are wanted. Please look at their faces and report any sightings to the Wolf Guard immediately. Wanted!"

The poster held a fair portrait of Anders and Lisabet, and a less good one of Rayna—the wolves had even arranged to have them made in color, the twins' brown faces, brown eyes, and black, curling hair sitting alongside Lisabet's white, freckled face, green eyes, and black curls.

"Pack and paws," he whispered, a chill running through him that had nothing to do with the temperature. There was no way they could slip away at this late stage—they had to find a way to hide *within* the crowd approaching the gate.

He glanced sideways at Lisabet, who flipped her cloak's hood up over her head and slowed her pace, bending over as she did, until she was shuffling along like a very old woman, almost bent double. Because she did it gradually, no one person saw much of her transformation, and certainly not enough to be alarmed. She started to fall behind, but with any luck she was well hidden.

Rayna ducked around the side of a cart and dove beneath it—Anders caught a glimpse of her cloak as she crawled along below it, but nothing more.

Ellukka's face was unknown, so that left only Anders to hide. In a flash, it came to him. "Lift up your cloak," he whispered to Ellukka. Her brow creased in confusion, and then she understood. Without missing a beat she took hold of the edge of her cloak, swirling it around so it fluttered as the air caught it, smacking one of her neighbors in the face.

"Hey!" the man cried. Nobody noticed Anders

138

sneaking in underneath the cloak, staying as close as he could to Ellukka, hidden by the billowing folds.

"Sorry!" Ellukka said cheerfully. "I was feeling dramatic there for a moment."

The man grumbled but subsided, and Ellukka and Anders walked along carefully together, making their way through the gates. Anders could hear the guards above him still calling out their message.

"Wanted, these children are wanted. Please look at their faces and report any sightings to the Wolf Guard immediately. Wanted!"

Holbard had always been his home, and now he was a wanted criminal. Wanted badly enough that the wolves were prepared to stand by the gates each day and spread the word.

He wrapped an arm around Ellukka's waist, steering her along the main road from memory—he'd been to the west gate plenty of times, and he was sure there was a little side alley less than half a block in on their left. She understood what he was doing, and as soon as they reached it, she peeled away from the crowd to make her way down the narrow laneway.

Rayna picked her moment and darted out from beneath the cart, scrambling in to join them where they waited in an alcove, and after a little, Lisabet shuffled along in her old-woman disguise, waiting until she reached the alcove to abandon the pretense and move in to join them. Now all four of them were safe in the little alleyway.

"Wanted posters," she said, her voice shaking. "I mean, I knew—but I didn't think . . ."

"I knew the wolves would be looking out for us," Anders said quietly. "But I didn't think it would be like this."

"And someone must have described me from the Trial of the Staff," Rayna said. "Or else someone who knows us from the street recognized me when it happened and told." She scowled at the very idea of such betrayal, but Anders knew she was trying to cover a greater shock.

"Holbard is so big," said Ellukka, her voice smaller than Anders had ever heard it. "I've seen pictures, but I never imagined—I've never been anywhere like this. There are so many *people*." She was nibbling on the end of one of her plaits, clearly close to overwhelmed. Anders had never seen Ellukka anything but bold before, and he wasn't sure what to say.

Rayna wrapped an arm around her, though, and squeezed her tight. "You'll be used to it in no time," she said. "You'll forget all about how big it is. Anders, there's only one way we're going to get to the port, if they're looking for us."

"Agreed," said Anders. "It has to be over the roofs."

"The what?" said Ellukka.

Anders was the tallest, so as always, he boosted Rayna up until she could grab the gutter and scramble onto the roof—buildings crowded in on either side of the alleyway, blocking out most of the sky above them.

Then Rayna leaned down and grabbed Lisabet's hands as Anders boosted her. Lisabet disappeared for a moment, and Rayna turned her head in the direction she'd gone. "Stop sightseeing and come help!"

Finally Anders boosted up Ellukka, who was heavier than the other two, but she had Rayna and Lisabet to pull, and it worked out fine. Glad he was taller than the others, since there was nobody to push him up from below, he jumped until he could catch hold of the gutter, and all three girls pulled until he was scrambling onto the grass beside them. It really was colder here in Holbard—his hands were chilled, knuckles aching from the effort of gripping the gutter.

But then he looked around and forgot all about his discomfort for a moment. Something in his heart felt like it was unfurling at such a familiar sight, like a flower's petals turning to the sun first thing in the morning.

The rooftops of Holbard were all joined together on each block, sown with grass and flowers, so that a meadow stretched away across most of the city, gently undulating with roofs and hills. Instead of streams breaking it up, as they did on the plains outside the city, in Holbard streets provided the divisions. The city's clever street children had bridged the narrowest of those streets and alleyways with bridges made of planks, which meant that if you knew where to navigate, you could find a path almost the whole way across the city without touching the ground.

They saw a few other children in the distance, but they were too far away to make out who they were, so Anders and his friends simply waved, and set off. "There are four of us," Rayna said, "so it won't occur to them that we're the three they want."

Ellukka and Lisabet were amazed by the rooftop meadows, trying to look all around them as they hurried after the twins. Lisabet had only seen them once or twice before, training with the wolves. For Ellukka, it was calmingly like being out on the plains. The four of them only had to head down into a street once, darting across it and into an alleyway on the far side to climb up once more.

By the time they reached the port, Ellukka was wearing yellow-and-white flameflowers and red fentills tucked into her hair, and Lisabet was mumbling something about researching the historical use of the rooftop highways.

Anders and Rayna were strategizing.

"The port is a smart place to meet us," Anders said, even though he hated the place. "There are more visitors to the city there than anywhere else, and the guards are less likely to be keeping a lookout for us that far into town."

"Agreed," said Rayna. "Still, we need a better disguise than we've got. Now that we're past the entrance, it would be best if we looked like we weren't from Holbard at all."

So they found an inn where visiting sailors and merchants stayed, and climbed down into the courtyard, liberating clothes from Mositala and Halotan from the washing line. "Sorry, visitors," Rayna whispered. "Welcome to Holbard. It's not personal."

Ellukka was well-disguised just by being herself, since nobody knew her face, but Lisabet borrowed the dragon's cloak, which was bigger than her own, and concealed her face when she kept the hood up. "It looks a little suspicious," Rayna conceded, "but you might just be shy."

Rayna and Anders added the stolen clothing to their own—he carried his cloak and wore a bright pink-and-gold vest from Halotan, letting his jacket hang open to show it off. She tied a green-and-gold Mositalan shawl on over her skirts, twirling so it shimmered in the light.

"People will think we're traders' children," Anders

explained to the others. "If they notice one thing about you, like how bright your clothes are, most of the time they don't notice anything else."

Rayna shot a quick glance at him, brows lifted. When they'd both lived in Holbard—which felt like a lifetime ago, even though it had only been weeks—she'd been the one to say things like that. He thought perhaps she was surprised to hear he knew it too. Then she grinned, and he realized she wasn't surprised—she was just impressed.

The twins adjusted their outfits, and finally, they were ready to make their way out into the port square to meet Hayn.

Rayna, Lisabet, and Ellukka hadn't seen the place where the fire had been set—Ellukka hadn't even seen the port square, of course—and the three of them sucked in quick breaths when they saw the aftermath. Even Anders was taken aback, and he'd seen it at full blaze. The bottom stories of the homes along the port's edge were gutted, and the scorch marks reached all the way up to the roof, where he'd rescued Jerro and the others. If he hadn't, it was clear they'd have been scorched too, or worse.

"They're saying this was dragons?" Ellukka whispered, her cheeks pink. "We'd never! And in the middle of Holbard? Nobody could keep that kind of thing quiet even if they did do it."

"It would be *very* hard to transform into a dragon, light a fire, and transform back again without anyone seeing," Rayna said, dubious.

"They're saying it was definitely dragonsfire," Lisabet said, sounding almost apologetic. "Pure white, gold sparks. It's very distinctive. You never see that kind of flame anywhere else."

A sudden thought jolted Anders at her words. He *had* seen the fire somewhere else. Just the day before the Trial of the Staff and his first transformation, in fact. He and Rayna had watched a puppet show, and when the tiny dragons had appeared, the puppeteers had created a tiny dragon's flame. He'd even talked about it with Rayna— they'd used a kind of salt to make the flame white, and iron filings for the gold sparks.

But it was one thing to produce a handful of flame for a puppet show, and quite another to change enough of it to burn down whole buildings. Surely that was impossible? He tucked the question away for later, because they were reaching the southeast corner and the water's edge, and it was time to look for Hayn.

They were very near the easternmost pier, ships pulled up on either side of it, mooring ropes strung between them and the wooden structure like intricate spiders' webs, sailors jumping from ship to pier and back again with the nimble agility of long practice. Near the end of the pier was a series of makeshift food stalls, with tables made of half-barrels and chairs from packing crates.

And there, sitting on the edge of it, was Hayn. He was so big he practically dwarfed the packing crate he was sitting on, his knees up around his ribs, and he was watching the square anxiously. He started to rise to his feet when he saw Anders and the others, and then sank back down again, lest he draw attention.

They hurried over, and Anders and Lisabet took the packing crates nearest him. Rayna and Ellukka exchanged a glance, and then Ellukka settled down on her packing crate facing out toward the square. Her face was the least recognizable, and she would keep watch as the others spoke to the big wolf.

Hayn's face lit up as they joined him. "You're here," he said, relief all over his features.

"This is Rayna," Anders said, resting his hand on his twin's.

"Yes," Hayn said. "Yes, your sister."

There was no dismissal in his tone, and Anders was surprised to hear the big wolf speak as though he had no doubt Rayna was his sister. "Yes," he agreed. "And this is—"

"Someone else," Ellukka said, without turning her

head, cutting him off before he could give her name or explain who she was.

"Pleased to meet you," Hayn said diplomatically.

"Hayn," Lisabet said, breaking in. "What's been happening at Ulfar?"

The designer pushed his glasses up his nose, taking a deep breath. "They believe the dragons are preparing to attack," he said. "Suspicions are running at fever pitch."

"But the wolves are the ones who have the Snowstone!" Anders said, spluttering. "They're the ones about to attack."

"I know," Hayn said. "But most don't. Most wolves don't know about the Snowstone, and they don't know what happened to you and Lisabet. There are rumors you were kidnapped, and some that you betrayed us." He looked at Lisabet. "Your—"

"Leader," she said, cutting him off before he could say "mother" in front of Rayna and Ellukka. "The Fyrstulf, what is she doing?"

Hayn inclined his head, accepting the warning not to mention the connection. "Everything she can to make sure the wolves and people of Holbard understand she thinks an attack is necessary."

Lisabet flinched, though the news couldn't be a

surprise. She turned her head, glancing across the city to where the Ulfar Academy gates were hidden behind streets and buildings, and Anders wondered if a part of her had somehow imagined going . . . well, *home*, despite everything that had happened.

"It looks like the wolves and people of Holbard are believing her," Anders said quietly. "Do you?"

"I think I have things to tell you," Hayn said. "And that I'd better just do it, and then we'll see what's what."

"All right," Anders said, exchanging a glance with Lisabet and Rayna. "Go on, then."

"For a start," Hayn said, his tone solemn, "I believe that you and your sister are wolf and dragon born. You have mixed blood."

"Yes," said Rayna. "We know that."

Hayn's jaw dropped. "How could you possibly know?" he asked. "Everyone thinks it's impossible."

"Leif, the Drekleid, told us," Rayna said.

Hayn nodded slowly. "And was he able to tell you who your parents were? Because I believe I can."

Rayna gasped, and a thrill went through Anders. "N-no," he stammered. "He didn't know."

"Or he didn't say," Lisabet put in.

"I will," Hayn said quietly. "Anders, Lisabet, I've told you before that my brother, Felix, and I used to work with the dragonsmith Drifa. We designed artifacts, she forged them. The three of us were close. We worked together for years. The story is that Drifa murdered Felix and then fled. That was what reignited the feud between dragons and wolves, and ultimately led to the last great battle. I believed it when I was told—after all, he was dead, and she was seen fleeing, and after that she vanished. It came out of the blue—they'd always seemed to like each other, even care for each other—but I could see no other explanation. But deep down . . ." He sighed, looking out at the moored ships, pensive. "Deep down, I've always wondered."

Anders could barely breathe. "What do you think now?" he whispered.

Hayn swallowed and looked back at Anders, and then at Rayna. "Now, I wonder if he was killed by someone else. I wonder if Drifa and Felix did more than care for each other. I wonder if they were *both* attacked, and if she ran because she was pregnant. If she had to protect herself."

"So, you mean . . ." Anders could barely say the words.

"Yes," said Hayn quietly. "I believe you and your sister might be the children of Drifa and of my brother—my *twin* brother—Felix. That you might be my niece and nephew. You're exactly the right age."

"But, but . . ."

Anders had never heard Rayna at a loss for words

before. For his part, he was staring at Hayn, suddenly seeing a sadness etched in the man's face that he'd never noticed before. Anders couldn't imagine what it would be like to lose Rayna. He could see how Hayn might have believed the worst all these years.

Lisabet broke the silence. "So you're their uncle?"

A new wave of shock hit Anders. *An uncle.* He'd spent his whole life longing to know his parents, and now he had someone right here in front of him, someone he liked, even admired . . . a member of his family.

Perhaps he and Rayna weren't alone anymore.

Abruptly Rayna fumbled inside her coat. "We can find out," she said hurriedly. Her hands were shaking, and it took her three tries, but she yanked the little red-and-silver purse Leif had given her free of her pocket and held it out to Hayn. "Here, open this."

Hayn took it in one big hand, turning it over. "It's an artifact," he said, impressed. "Excellent workmanship. I think this was Eliot, I'd know his work anywhere. Now, what does it . . ." He studied the tiny runes engraved along the clasp, and then understanding lit his face. "It recognizes family," he said. He hesitated, then cleared his throat softly. Anders couldn't help but wonder if Hayn was as nervous as he was. And then Hayn's thick fingers pushed at the little silver clasp.

And the purse popped open.

They all stared at it—even Ellukka craned her neck to see what had happened—and Hayn's mouth curved to a slow smile as he handed the purse back to Rayna. "Well," he said softly, and then he had to push up his glasses and use one finger to carefully wipe the moisture from his eyes. "Well. I wonder if Felix knew. I hope he did. Drifa must have hidden you with someone in the city—the wolves were hunting her, and whoever killed Felix would have been doing the same to stop her from telling the truth—but I know she would have meant to come back for you. And I think she would have meant for me to meet you."

"You found us anyway," Anders said softly. "How?"

"Ennar and her class came back with a story about you telling them all your sister was a dragon," Hayn said. "And after that I spent a lot of time thinking. The first time I met you, I thought how much you looked like my brother at the same age, and that stuck with me. In fact, it was why out of all the wolves in this square that day, I led the pursuit when you ran for it, Anders. I'd been staring while you were on the dais, even though I knew there was no way you could actually be Felix's son."

"Except he was," Lisabet murmured.

Hayn nodded. "Twins run in the family, and after I heard word you were claiming to have a sister, I thought back twelve or thirteen years. I knew all the dragons that came into the city to work with wolf designers. There weren't an endless number of candidates."

"Gosh, maybe you're going to grow up as big as Uncle Hayn," Rayna said with a giggle, elbowing Anders. He knew, though he was sure the others didn't, that she was trying out the title, looking for an excuse to say it out loud.

"I thought I was alone in the world," Hayn said quietly. "And now I have the two of you. Anders, Rayna, you two are why I want so badly to prevent another battle between wolves and dragons, which is what will happen if we use the Snowstone for an attack. I have to protect you, and we don't have much time. Sigrid has me hunting for augmenters, artifacts that can be used to amplify the effects of the Snowstone. I've been able to stall so far, but that won't last forever."

Anders heard Lisabet draw a shaky breath beside him, and he silently squeezed her hand. Scary as it was to hear of Sigrid's plans, it must be even worse knowing it was your own mother planning it. He was about to speak again when there was a sudden outcry farther along the docks, voices raised in screams and cries.

He, Lisabet, and Rayna twisted around quickly, peering past Ellukka, who leaned forward, ready to spring to her feet if the attention turned their way.

But nobody was looking at them. A woman came shoving her way through the crowd, sending everyone in her path flying as she pushed them out of the way, her narrow face a mask of panic. She had light-brown skin and distinctive reddish-brown, wavy hair, whipping in the wind as she ran.

In a flash, Anders recognized her. Once he had thought of her as "the woman in the green dress," a dragon spy who'd followed him around Holbard the day of the fire, showing him Rayna's hairpin in an attempt to make contact. Perhaps she had been here today to spy as well.

She ran by not ten yards from them, pushing a sailor so hard he stumbled, arms windmilling madly for a moment before he fell into the harbor with a splash. The woman sprinted out along the arm of the pier, and when she was halfway to the end a pack of wolves suddenly burst through the crowd after her.

Snarling, they tore along the pier, and Ellukka let out a cry, then clapped her hand to her mouth, coming to her feet as though she meant to try and help the woman. Lisabet grabbed her by her coat, yanking her back down again with a thump. There was nothing one girl could do against fully grown Wolf Guards.

The dragon was nearly at the end of the pier, and

Anders's heart was in his mouth. She couldn't possibly dive into the icy waters—the cold might kill her. But at the last possible moment she doubled over, one hand brushing the ground, and vaulted herself into dragon form. She spread her wings, and as the crowd on the docks screamed, she was suddenly aloft, circling out over the harbor to safety.

The guards pulled up at the end of the pier, hurling ice spears after her, so powerful that a thin film of ice spread out across the water around them, and a chill swept through the air around the docks.

But she was gone, a rapidly shrinking shape in the sky, well out to sea and whirling around to head inland, no doubt toward Drekhelm.

The wolves came pacing down the pier, snarling their frustration, and all around the dock were shouts and cries, as those who had seen the chase told those who had missed it everything that had happened. Anders and the others bowed their heads as the wolves passed by, all silent. They were so big, so powerful. If they'd been chasing any of the children, there was no doubt they'd have caught them, as they'd nearly caught the dragon spy.

Hayn was the one who finally spoke. "I can't avoid finding an augmenter forever," he said quietly. "We have to do something, before her guards are strong enough to attack Drekhelm itself, and win."

"We want to stop a battle too," Anders said softly. He could barely remember how it had felt to worry only about protecting himself, his twin, and his best friend. It wasn't even just about his wolf and dragon friends, or his uncle, anymore. It was about every person in Holbard, all the innocent people who'd suffer in the cold or the heat, who'd be in danger if another battle came.

"We do," Rayna said. "But we don't know how. Isn't there a way to find the Snowstone? Take it back?"

"I have no idea where Sigrid's hiding it," Hayn said. "Believe me, I've tried to find out. She's the only one who knows, and she's not telling. But I think I have a way to level the playing field. If we can't get the Snowstone back, maybe we can make her think twice about using it."

They all leaned in. "How do we do that?" Anders asked.

"Drifa left a map, showing where she hid all her most valuable artifacts," his uncle replied. "I saw her use it more than once back when we worked together, and she didn't exactly have time to gather up her things, the day . . ." He paused there and shook his head. The day his brother— the twins' father—had died. He cleared his throat, then pressed on. "It's been useless until now, because like this purse, it's locked to all but family members. And until today we thought she hadn't left any of those."

"But now we can use the map," Lisabet said slowly. "And you think it can lead us to an artifact that can help?"

"Yes," said Hayn. "I believe you'll be able to use the map to find the Sun Scepter. I don't know much about how it works, but I believe it will counter the Snowstone."

"We have to find it," said Anders, Rayna, Lisabet, and Ellukka at exactly the same time.

"Agreed," Hayn said. "I don't think it will be easy, but if we can't find the Snowstone, it's the best plan I can think of. The map will challenge you—it will require knowledge of both the wolf and dragon worlds, because Drifa would have expected to raise her children learning about the histories of both their mother and their father. And knowing her as I did, I expect it will require daring and intelligence, but I know you have plenty of both."

Anders wasn't used to anyone saying anything like that about him, but Lisabet simply reached over and squeezed his hand, as he had hers a minute before.

"I'm going to steal the map from where it's stored in the library today," Hayn said. "I'll meet you with it tonight. I didn't want to risk it until I was sure my theory about you was right, because I'm being watched. I think perhaps Sigrid knows I'm not working as fast as I could at finding an augmenter. I'm sure she doesn't know about my connection to you, or she'd never have let me leave

Ulfar, but times are tense, and if she's ever suspected Felix was a traitor . . ."

"We can hide during the day," Rayna said. "But it would be better if we could meet you by the western gate to get the map. That way we can get out and on our way more quickly. We're expected back at Drekhelm." And, though nobody said it out loud, the closer the children were to a gate they could use to escape, the better.

Anders thought of their curfew with a wince—Mikkel and Theo were in for an interesting time, since the four of them certainly wouldn't get back by dinnertime. He hoped the boys were up to the challenge.

"I'll do my best to hurry—I'll aim to be there an hour before sunset," Hayn promised. He paused, then reached out, laying one hand on Anders's, the other on Rayna's. Looking up at him, Anders found he really could see himself there—Hayn smiled suddenly, and there were his and Rayna's dimples. He shared Rayna's jawline, and Anders's long limbs. "I'm so glad I found you," said Hayn softly. "I'll do everything I can to keep both of you safe."

Anders didn't know what to say in return, and it seemed that neither did Rayna, for they were both quiet. "We're glad too," he said eventually.

Ellukka leaned back to press her shoulder against Rayna's. "I don't want to break up the party, but we've been out in the open for a while now. I'd be more comfortable back up on the rooftops."

"Agreed," said Hayn. "Go. I'll see you soon."

* * *

They parted ways, and a few minutes later Anders was boosting everyone back up onto the rooftops again. The four of them made their way across the meadows in thoughtful silence, all of them shaken by everything they'd just seen and learned.

Anders saw the Wily Wolf in the distance—the tavern that stood at the highest point in Holbard. He and Rayna had slept there more than anywhere else, tucked into the space under a little hatch beneath the grass, curled up with Kess the cat. He'd told Lisabet about the hiding place, and Lisabet had told Sigrid—which had been the subject of Anders and Lisabet's first and only fight—and though he wished they could hide there now, Professor Ennar had told them that the wolves were now using it as a lookout point. Guards were no doubt scanning the skies for dragons right this very moment, not knowing that two of them were walking across the rooftops not far away.

"I know we just had some really big revelations," said Lisabet, "but I'm starving. And it's going to be a long day."

"Me too," Rayna said. "We should buy something to eat."

"What she said," added Ellukka, who had taken her cloak back from Lisabet now that they were on the rooftops again, and had it wrapped tightly around herself, shoulders hunched against the cold.

"I agree," said Anders, looking across at Rayna. "I don't suppose while we were walking into town, or across the square . . . ?"

Rayna pulled out the little red-and-silver purse once again, and when she shook it, coins jingled inside. Anders had a pretty good idea where his pickpocket sister had gotten them, but for once he wasn't in the mood to worry about it. He and the others were trying to save the world, and he figured the world owed them lunch.

Once upon a time he would have felt bad that Rayna had thought to find them some money when the thought hadn't crossed his mind. He didn't now. He was contributing, and he knew it. Just in different ways.

"It would be better if Ellukka went down," he suggested. "Nobody knows her face." He knew as he said it that everyone was thinking of the dragon they'd just seen fleeing from the port, but Ellukka simply nodded.

"I've never been here before," she said. "I won't be recognized."

They made their way across to Dreibaum Square, one of their favorite haunts, and lowered her down into a nearby alleyway with clear instructions on how much to pay for what she wanted.

"I wish I had my fishing line," said Rayna wistfully, as they watched her go. "I really feel like a sausage."

"A what?" said Lisabet, confused. But Anders shook his head—it would sound ridiculous if he tried to explain what the two things had to do with each other. That was a story from their time out here on the streets of Holbard.

They sat in silence for a little, waiting for Ellukka, a gentle breeze blowing across the rooftops. "So," Rayna said eventually. "We have an uncle."

"He's a great choice," Lisabet said. "He's one of the nicest people I know. And he's smart too."

"You know much about him?" Rayna asked, instantly curious.

"He's friends with my mother," Lisabet settled on. "Anders has met him too."

"He's the one who found me, the day we transformed," Anders said. "And I met him after, at Ulfar. He was always kind to me. I think if I could have chosen any of the adults I met at Ulfar, I'd have chosen Hayn."

It wasn't long before Ellukka arrived, bearing a bag full of hot pastries with fish and creamy sauce inside, and a bottle of milk with a cork stopper in the top for all of them to share. "There are so many *people* down there," she said, her eyes wide. "And so much noise, and they're selling—you should see all the things they're selling!"

"We know," Rayna pointed out, but that didn't stop Ellukka. She kept on, as they ate their pastries, and made their way across the rooftop meadows to the meeting point. She listed all the things for sale at the stalls, talked about the colored doors on the houses, the horse-drawn wagons, and the musicians she'd seen on one corner. Through Ellukka's eyes, everything that was normal to Anders was new again. It was strange that she was so accustomed to extraordinary things like the dragonsmith Flic gardens up at Drekhelm, but so amazed by something as simple as a shop selling candles and imported bales of cloth.

But there was something else about the city that Anders was noticing through Ellukka's eyes, and he was sure Rayna and Lisabet had noticed it too.

Everywhere he looked, he saw the Wolf Guard. He'd grown up with patrols, and even a couple of months ago, in the weeks before his transformation, he'd gotten used to seeing more guards on the street than usual. But now there seemed to be a pair on every corner, some in their gray uniforms, some in wolf form. They were out in force, looking for spies, for dragons, and for Anders, Rayna, and Lisabet.

The Wolf Guard stepped in front of anyone they wanted to question, looming over them, pushing for answers from humans wrapped up in coats and cloaks against the cold. He wanted to insist that this wasn't who the wolves were—that they were loyal, protective, that they cared about the people of Holbard. But it was hard to sound convincing just now, and he stayed silent.

They found a good spot to pass the rest of their time in the lee of a rooftop, settling in amid the flowers to wait, talking through the earlier meeting at the port square. Anders and Rayna kept coming back to the little details, trying to accustom themselves to the idea that they finally had another member of their family, after spending all their lives thinking they'd never know who their parents were, let alone discover a living uncle.

But eventually they had a different question to worry about. With a little more than an hour left before sunset, they started keeping watch for Hayn, taking turns sitting at the edge of the roof in pairs and watching the swirling crowd for the distinctive figure of the big wolf.

But the appointed time came and went, and the sun sank down until it kissed the horizon, and still he was nowhere to be seen. Eventually the city grew dark and still, and Hayn had not come.

"What do we do?" Lisabet asked quietly. "Do we give up?"

"Well, we know it wasn't a trap," Rayna said. "If it had been, he wouldn't have shown, but instead there'd be a dozen of the Wolf Guard up here to grab us. He heard Ellukka say we were heading for the rooftops. Something must have delayed him."

"Still, we can't wait all night," said Ellukka. "Perhaps we should try and come back tomorrow. It'll be hard to convince Leif a second day in a row, though. He's going to be mad we're back so late."

"We have to hold on a little longer," said Anders, desperately watching the street. "He'll come, I know it."

CHAPTER SEVEN

ANDERS STAYED WHERE HE WAS, SITTING AT THE edge of the roof, and suddenly he spotted a pair of figures that were much smaller than Hayn, but even more familiar.

"Lisabet," he said quietly. "Lis, come over here. Does that look like Sakarias and Viktoria to you?"

"After dark?" she said, but she crawled over obediently.

Below in the street were two children in what looked, even in the shadows, like gray Ulfar Academy cloaks, trimmed with white. One had long, black, shiny hair, and the other a face that looked pale in the moonlight. They were standing to one side of the crowd flowing in and out of the western gate, and if it *was* them, then Sakarias was talking quickly—which only confirmed Anders's suspicions that these were his friends—while Viktoria turned in a slow circle, studying their surroundings. Her head was angled back, looking up at the rooftops, though Anders knew she wouldn't be able to see him in the dark.

"Friends of yours?" Rayna asked, settling in beside him.

"Our roomies at Ulfar," he said. "Our friends. And they're not allowed out after dark. It can't be a coincidence they're here. They've snuck out to find us, it's the only explanation. I'm going to go down and find out why. We shouldn't risk all of us being seen."

The others lowered him down into a dark alleyway, their hands warm in his. "Be careful," Lisabet whispered.

"If they get you somehow, we'll get you back," Rayna promised.

"Don't trust them too much," Ellukka advised.

Anders was tingling with anticipation, his heart thumping. Sakarias had been injured in the battle between the wolves and the dragons, and Viktoria had dragged him free, helping him escape. Anders had been losing sleep over what his friends must be thinking about him, but the fact that they were here now—perhaps even working with Hayn—gave him his first taste of hope that they might not hate him.

He hadn't realized the Academy was starting to feel like home until he'd realized that he could never go back.

But he'd known before that moment that these were his friends.

His heart was beating fast as he made his way out of the alley and darted through the adults who were funneling down the street toward the gate, keeping the hood on his cloak up. Both his friends saw him straight away—and the always-smiling Sakarias wasn't smiling at all. Viktoria wore suspicion like a mask, hiding her thoughts.

The three of them wordlessly stepped to the edge of the street, and as Sakarias moved, Anders saw for the first time that under his Ulfar cloak, his arm was in a sling. His wiry form looked a little smaller than usual.

For a long moment, nobody spoke. Anders knew he was the one who had to break the silence.

"I'm sorry," he said quietly.

"Don't," said Viktoria quickly, her voice hard. "We're not here to talk about it."

Sakarias simply looked away, studying the crowd.

Anders's heart hurt. "You don't understand," he said softly. "If you'd killed their leader, the battle—"

Viktoria held her hand up to stop him. "We were there for *you*, Anders. You and Lisabet. Because you were our friends. We were terrified, we thought they'd be torturing you. We were so scared of going up into Drekhelm, but for you, we—everyone in the class found the bravery to do it. And when we arrived, you fought with *them*."

Anders felt the words like a punch in the gut.

And then Sakarias spoke, still not looking at him. "Why did you go there, Anders?"

Anders fought the urge to look up at the rooftops. He didn't want to give away where his sister was—didn't know how much he should tell his friends. Hated that he had to wonder. "It's complicated," he said weakly. "I promise it wasn't to betray you. Did Hayn send you?"

"He's been arrested," Sakarias said softly.

Anders reeled. *Had Sigrid found out what Hayn was doing? Did she know about their connection?*

"He's been confined to his workshop," Viktoria said. "We don't know what's going on, but Hayn asked one of his guards to pass on a library book to Sakarias, said he'd promised it to him for class."

"And I didn't need it for class," Sakarias said. "And we all know I've never borrowed a library book in my life, unless someone made me. So we figured something strange was happening."

"So we went through it," Viktoria continued. "And we found a map inside, and a note, asking us to find a way to get out and bring it to you."

"He was counting on us still being your friends," said Sakarias, pulling a folded piece of cloth from inside his sling and holding it out to Anders.

Anders took it, mouth dry, tucking it inside his jacket. "And are you?" he asked quietly. "Still my friends?"

Nobody spoke, but the others exchanged a glance.

"How's Lisabet?" Viktoria said eventually.

"She's fine," Anders said, heart sinking. "I promise she's safe."

They were quiet again. He waited, hoping against hope they might have something more to say.

"We want to be," said Sakarias eventually. "Your friends, I mean. We care about both of you, and so do the others—Jai, Mateo, Det. But it's hard."

Viktoria nodded. "Right now, we're in the middle. We'll carry Hayn's message—"

"And miss dinner," Sakarias reminded them, sounding more like himself for a moment.

"And get in all kinds of trouble if we can't sneak back in," Viktoria continued. "But we're doing it because Hayn asked us to. We're trying to trust you, Anders, but . . ."

She trailed off and shrugged, and Sakarias didn't contradict her.

Anders had a lump in his throat that made it hard to swallow. He knew that even this was more than he deserved—his friends still felt exactly like he used to about dragons, and as far as they knew, he'd betrayed them.

And they were *right*, that was the worst part of it. Even if it was to avoid a greater, much worse battle, he *had* fought against them.

Even if he'd been fighting to keep everyone safe, they were the ones who'd fled, injured and afraid. It was a lot that they were even here.

"Thank you for trying," he said quietly. "I'll prove you can trust me. Please just keep trying to believe. You should go, though, before it gets even later."

"Good luck," said Sakarias. "I hope you're not doing something we'll regret helping with."

"Tell Lisabet to be careful," said Viktoria. She moved around to Sakarias's injured side to shield him from being jostled by the crowd, and after a moment, the two of them slipped into the sea of people. Soon, they were just two more shadows in the dim lanterns hanging outside the shops and houses.

Anders hurried back into the alleyway to help the others down, and together they slipped outside the gate, keeping their heads bowed in the dark to avoid the notice of the guards who still stood watch there, calling out to draw attention to their wanted posters.

"We can take off much closer to the city," Ellukka said, once they were clear and making their way along the road outside the walls. "Nobody will see, there's not much moonlight. I can't wait to be in the air, this place is freezing." She looked much weaker than she had that morning, after a long day exposed to the cold of the city, and away from the underground lava of Drekhelm.

"We should look at the map first," Lisabet said. "Just in case there's anything we need from the city before we go. We're so late, we're bound to be in trouble anyway, five more minutes won't be the worst of it."

They walked a little ways along the road that led to the distant ford, but with the crowd thinning as the night drew on, it was easy enough to find a gap in the people and slip off the path. They found a spot behind a large rock, and Anders pulled out the piece of cloth, unfolding it and setting it on the ground.

It was a map of Vallen, almost exactly like those he'd seen in class, or on the wall in the map room at Drekhelm, with a compass rose in the top right corner, and intricate knotwork drawn all around the edges. It had been inked directly onto the cloth.

The cloth itself was shot through with silvery thread, the metal Drifa had forged woven straight into the fabric. That must be how its magic worked—all artifacts required metal, and the magical fire of a dragonsmith, and Anders could only imagine that the wolf-designed runes must be engraved on the thread itself, unimaginably small.

"Well, it's a map all right," said Rayna, poking at it with one fingertip. "Nothing happens when I touch it. How do we let it know we're Drifa's family?"

It still felt so odd, to hear it out loud. Anders studied the map in the pale moonlight. Apart from being made of cloth, rather than paper, it looked perfectly ordinary.

"Blood," said Anders. "That's what worked with the purse. Perhaps after such a long time without anyone touching it, it needs help waking up."

"Good idea," said Rayna, unpinning the brooch that held her cloak shut and pricking her finger without hesitation. She held her fingertip over the compass rose and gently squeezed it until a drop of blood fell onto the circle at the dead center of it. "I want to find the location of the Sun Scepter," she said clearly.

At first, nothing happened.

"There!" said Ellukka after half a minute, pointing at the knotwork around the map's edges. And sure enough, when Anders looked more closely, the beautifully drawn border was writhing, changing, rearranging itself.

"It's making letters," Lisabet whispered, leaning in to study the words that now made up the map's border. Slowly, she began to read them aloud.

"Where the sun greets herself at every dawn,
And the stars admire themselves at night,
Where blue meets blue the whole day long,
The scepter's head is wedged in tight."

A shiver went down Anders's spine. "Well," he said slowly. "I don't know what it means yet, but this is it. This is how we find the Sun Scepter."

"This is how we stop the Snowstone weakening the dragons," Rayna whispered.

Anders nodded slowly. "This is how we keep the peace."

CHAPTER EIGHT

As Anders folded up the map and tucked it inside his coat, Ellukka spoke. "The Sun Scepter could change everything," she said intently. "This is how we could end the feud forever. We dragons have never tried to start fights—it's only ever been the wolves. This could be a way to weaken them so much we can take charge for good. *That* could be how we keep peace."

Anders froze. "Ellukka, no," he said, stumbling over the words in horror. "No, that's not what this is for. It's not what we agreed. We agreed we were going to find a balance, a way to make sure neither the wolves *nor* the dragons were strong enough to beat each other."

She turned to him, hands on her hips. "Why are you defending them? The wolves have wanted posters up for you, you should be on our side!"

"I'm not on your side," Anders began, "I'm—"

"Well, you can't be on *their* side!" she interrupted.

"I'm not on anyone's side!"

Suddenly all three of the girls were staring at him, and he realized he'd shouted. He *never* shouted.

"I think we're on both sides," Rayna said, for once the voice of reason. "I think we have to be, because we *are* both, Ellukka." She didn't sound completely certain—and Anders had never seen her show the slightest concern for wolves before. But the idea of an uncle was a powerful draw. Especially one who cared about them as much as Hayn seemed to.

"Let's talk about it when we get back," Lisabet suggested. "Mikkel and Theo must be covering for us by now."

They walked a little farther from the city gates in silence, until they were in a dark gully where the dragons could transform and take off without being seen. Anders and Lisabet wrapped all their layers of clothing around themselves tightly, preparing for the freezing cold of the night air.

This time there was no landscape to see below them— just black beneath and the stars above, and the feeling of flying endlessly through the night. Occasionally Anders saw the moonlight glint off a river or lake, but after a time he was too cold to really look for anything below. He retreated inside his own thoughts, going over everything that had happened that day, and everything that would happen next.

The girls landed a little ways around the mountain from the doors to the Great Hall, scrambling for purchase on the loose scree and the snow, and once they were securely in place, Anders and Lisabet slid down to the ground. Rayna and Ellukka transformed back into humans, and the four of them made their way up the mountainside together. The dragons were already looking stronger with the mountainside beneath their feet, and even Lisabet, strengthened by a day in Holbard's cold air, looked all right.

They were hoping that they'd be able to slip through the little human-size doors unnoticed, and hurry away into the passageways of Drekhelm, with nobody the wiser that they'd been out at all.

But they weren't that lucky. Ellukka walked carefully through the door with the others behind her. Anders was right on her heels, unbuttoning his coat, which meant that when she suddenly stopped, Anders, Rayna, and Lisabet piled up behind her—Anders got a faceful of blond plait and nearly inhaled it.

When he stepped out to see what had made her stop, his heart sank. There were her father, Valerius, and the bushy-bearded member of the Dragonmeet, Torsten, who had been so suspicious of him when he'd first met the council. The two big men were sitting together at one of the small tables around the edge of the Great Hall—the center was left clear for dragons to land in—and the remains of their dinner were lying before them. They must have come here for a chance to talk.

"Ellukka?" Valerius said, rising to his feet. "What were you doing outside at this time of night?"

Ellukka opened her mouth and closed it again, but Rayna didn't miss a beat.

"Stargazing," she said, from behind her friend. "It's a beautifully clear night."

"What?" Valerius looked from Rayna to Ellukka and back again, and beside him, Torsten snorted.

"We just stepped outside," said Rayna.

Belatedly, Ellukka came to life. "Stargazing," she said, nodding vigorously. She was doing a terrible job of pretending, and if Valerius couldn't tell, Torsten clearly could.

"And why were you stargazing?" he asked, frowning behind his beard.

"Why not?" Rayna said breezily—Anders knew she knew full well what Torsten thought of at least two of them, but she'd faced down scarier people on the streets of Holbard. "It's a beautiful night."

"You're not supposed to be outside after dark," Torsten said with a scowl. "Particularly the wolves. How do we know you weren't signaling someone?"

"Signaling?" Anders spoke up for that. "Who would we signal?"

"And we could just as easily do that during the day," Lisabet pointed out. "With a mirror or something."

Torsten looked very thoughtful. Anders could have kicked her.

"So you've thought about that?" the big man asked.

"No!" Lisabet replied. "I'm just saying—"

"How long have you been out there?"

Just then Mikkel came running into the Great Hall, using an entrance behind the two Dragonmeet members. He skidded to a halt, and Theo slid through the door, coming to a stop up against his roommate.

"Hey, there you are!" Mikkel said, with exaggerated cheer. He could clearly tell they were in the middle of an alibi, and just as clearly didn't know how to back them up. "How was—"

"Stargazing!" Anders and Rayna said together, before he could finish.

"Stargazing," he agreed, nodding hard. Torsten turned and looked over his shoulder at him for a long moment, and Mikkel stopped nodding.

"We were just outside," Ellukka said. "We'd have heard you if you called for us. And we weren't long."

"That's right," Mikkel agreed. "They had dinner with us just before."

"Are you sure?" Valerius asked, looking at the red-headed boy and then back at his daughter.

"Father!" said Ellukka, indignant.

Anders flicked a glance to Torsten. The big man was staring at Anders's chest. *Was the map visible? Had it somehow edged out of his pocket?* He looked down and saw that the bright pink-and-gold waistcoat he'd been wearing as part of his disguise in Holbard was there on show, looking nothing like the clothes he'd been taking from the drag-ons' store cupboards. Torsten had to be wondering where it had come from. Anders realized with a chill that Rayna still had a green-and-gold shawl tied over her skirts.

"Time we started getting ready for bed," Rayna said, with a polite bow to first Valerius and then Torsten. "Good night!"

"Listen, I—" Torsten began.

But Rayna grabbed Ellukka's hand, hurrying off down the nearest hallway, and a moment later the others were all piling in after her. Nobody called them back.

"Let's talk in our room," said Anders.

"With food," Rayna added.

"I'll get it," Theo volunteered. "But don't start without me!"

Anders, Lisabet, and Mikkel settled in on his bed, Rayna and Ellukka side by side on Lisabet's.

Mikkel shook his head sadly as the others shed some layers, warmed up, and waited for Theo. "Leif asked if you were back," he reported. "I said yes, and last time I saw you, you were eating dinner, so he went off to look for you. Then I saw him again later, and he hadn't found you, of course, so I sent him to the classroom. It was kind of a mess."

Theo showed up then with a tray piled high with thickly buttered slices of brown bread, two big bowls of stew—one for each bed—with six spoons, and a bag of apples tucked under his arm. "Okay," he said, distributing the food. "Go."

As they hurriedly ate, they told Theo and Mikkel everything that had happened that day. Anders could tell almost straight away that, like Ellukka, Mikkel could see in the Sun Scepter the possibilities for beating the wolves once and for all. Theo didn't look as enthusiastic about that idea. Dragon he might be, but he'd only left his family in Holbard a few weeks ago, and of course he still loved them.

When they were all done with the story, Anders spoke

into the silence that followed. He knew what he said next was going to be very important, and he'd chosen his words carefully on the way back from Holbard.

Now he felt as if he were leaping out into the air, trusting Rayna to soar out beneath him and catch him. Trusting her to back him, as the two of them had always backed each other, no matter what. He hoped she'd meant what she'd said before, about being both wolf and dragon born.

"There's only one way we're going to use the scepter," he said, making his voice firm.

"What's that?" asked Mikkel.

"We're not going to use it to help either side win," Anders said. "If we can find it at all, we're going to use it to keep things equal between the wolves and the dragons. There can't be more battles, no matter who has the advantage. We're lucky nobody was killed last time."

To his intense relief, Rayna nodded. "Anders and I are the only ones who can use the map to find it," she said. "So that's the deal."

Everyone considered this in silence.

"And we're not going to tell the adults," Lisabet said eventually. It wasn't really a question. It was a statement.

One by one, the other five nodded.

"They'll just discuss it forever," said Ellukka.

"Or use it to win," Lisabet said. "You're our friends, you listen to us—"

"And we understand why you want to use it to keep things even," Ellukka said with a sigh.

"But the Dragonmeet won't understand wanting to keep things even," Lisabet said. "Any more than the Fyrstulf would." Her voice was perfectly even as she spoke of her mother, though her gaze was down.

"Okay," said Anders. "So if we're going to find it and use it, it's going to be all up to us."

"I think maybe that's what Leif means us to do," Rayna said. "To come up with a new, creative way to solve the problem that neither the wolves nor the dragons would think of. They're always looking for ways to win. We're looking for a way to make sure neither side can try to fight the other."

"Are you all in?" Anders asked.

"Yes," said Lisabet and Rayna at the same time.

"Yes," said Theo, nodding his head.

"I'm in," said Ellukka.

Mikkel sighed, looking down and away, his shoulders rounding. But just as Anders's heart was starting to thump, the other boy looked up and grinned. "Kidding," he said.

"I'm in. We have to do something, and this is the best we have."

"Then we don't have a lot of time to waste," said Lisabet. "But for now we should get to bed. Let's meet at breakfast, and we can start figuring out the map's riddle, and work out where to find the scepter."

Anders read out the riddle one more time, so everyone could think about it overnight, and then one by one the others trooped out to bed.

Anders and Lisabet got ready for bed, their movements slow. It had been a long day, and for Lisabet, spending so much time next to the warmth of a dragon had been difficult.

"It feels good to be doing something," she said, as they snuggled down underneath their quilts.

"It does," Anders agreed. "I hope it's enough."

"You've done a lot already," she said. "More than anyone could have imagined."

"Me?" He felt like laughing—he'd been worried and confused for weeks now. He didn't feel much like someone who got things done.

"Sure, you," she said. "You figured out how to see Ulfar with the mirror, made contact with Hayn, met him, got the map, and now you've assembled a team. We're going to do this, Anders. Somehow, we're going to do it."

Anders wasn't sure what to say to that, but as he drifted off, he felt more hopeful than he had in a long time.

Tomorrow, they'd have to work out where *blue meets blue the whole day long*.

But for now, they'd sleep.

* * *

They met again for breakfast the next day, all itching to discuss the puzzle. But as if they knew exactly when they weren't wanted, Nico and Krissin, their least favorite Finskólars, sat down at the next table, eating in silence, perfectly able to hear everything that Anders and his friends might say. They pretended to pay no attention, but Nico was glowering at his porridge from beneath his floppy black fringe, and Krissin sat with her head up, like a wolf scenting the breeze.

So Anders silently recited the riddle in his head, and tried to think over it on his own, and joined the others in casting frustrated glances at their two neighbors. There wasn't room to move far enough from them to speak, so they were stuck waiting for another chance.

When everyone was finished with their breakfast, they rose as one to put away their bowls and plates and head to the classroom. Anders's frustration bubbled up, and he checked over his shoulder before he whispered to his companions. "Why are Nico and Krissin even in the Finskól? They're horrible to everyone. Leif could choose anyone, and there are things that matter more than brains."

Mikkel answered, keeping his voice down. "Leif chooses whoever he wants, and he never explains why. There are all kinds of reasons, though. I've read about it in my history studies. Doesn't mean everyone he chooses is a nice person."

"We have theories on Nico and Krissin," Ellukka added. "They might not be nice, but they're really smart. Perhaps Leif would rather he knew where they were all the time, and what they were doing."

"And then there are people like Ferdie," Mikkel said, grinning.

"He's studying medicine," Ellukka said, "so he could just be learning in the infirmary. He does go there a lot, in fact."

"Right," Anders said remembering what Bryn had said the first time he'd been introduced to the Finskólars. "But everyone who meets him, they like him. Ferdie could end up accidentally ruling the world, he's so charming, so maybe Leif wants to make sure he turns out to be a good person, just in case."

"Exactly," Mikkel said. "In Ellukka's case, she's such a good storyteller that I think Leif wants to be sure she turns out to be a good person, too. Stories are powerful, they can sway people to believe all kinds of things, to *do* all kinds of things."

"Of course I'm a good person," Ellukka said, with a huff. "The best."

"Well, whether they belong with us or not, Nico and Krissin are making this very difficult," Lisabet said.

"Agreed," Anders said. "We've already got the Dragonmeet looking over our shoulders, we don't need more watchers."

Anders had hoped they'd be studying independently that morning, so he could work on the riddle with at least some of the others, but yet again, luck was against him.

"Good morning," said Leif, as soon as they entered. He had the two youngest members of the Dragonmeet with him—Saphira and Mylestom. Anders saw now what he'd missed when the Dragonmeet was gathered around the table in the Great Hall—Saphira used a wheeled chair like others he'd seen in Holbard. There was a knob on each wheel, so she could grab it and turn it, and she wore brown fingerless gloves to protect her palms. She and Mylestom— she round-cheeked and smiling, he lanky, straight-backed, and serious—had taken up places by Leif's desk.

"This morning," said Leif, "we are going to have an unusual lesson. Although it's not often discussed, we're going to talk through the events that led up to the last great battle." A small murmur went through the classroom, and he inclined his head to acknowledge their surprise. "With all that's currently happening, I feel you should know more. Even the oldest of you were children then, and the reasons for it were not simple. Ellukka, can you tell the class the first and most important rule of historical stories?"

Ellukka nodded. "There are at least two sides to every story, and usually a lot more than that. So you should look for the sides you don't know, and then ask yourself why you didn't hear them."

"Exactly," said Leif. "So we will tell you our version of this story, but as we do, I want you to remember Ellukka's rule. If you see another way the story might be told, speak up."

They all nodded, and Anders glanced over at Nico and Krissin, who were already glaring at him, as if they were preparing to hold him personally responsible for everything the wolves were about to do wrong in this story. But he was curious as well—he'd always been told the dragons simply attacked one day, and Leif was making it sound like there was more to it than that.

"Ten years ago," Leif began, "the youngest of you—Anders, Rayna, Mikkel, Theo—were only two years old. And the oldest, Patrik and Isabina, were only eight. Back then, the city of Holbard was growing very quickly. The wind arches at the harbor were being repaired. Lisabet, can you tell everyone about the arches?"

"They're the biggest artifacts on Vallen," Lisabet said. "They stretch all the way across the harbor mouth, and they make sure that no matter how windy or stormy it is outside, inside the harbor it's always calm. They're the reason so many people from all over the world come to Vallen to trade."

"Just so," Leif agreed. "A pair of wolf designers called Hayn and Felix had been working with one of our dragonsmiths, Drifa, and her team, to repair the arches."

Ferdie raised his hand. "You mean dragons were there in Holbard, working *with* the wolves?"

"Exactly," said Leif. "There were disagreements, and we were two very different groups, but this is not just the story of the last great battle. It's the story of how we dragons stopped working in Holbard. How we stopped working together with the wolves." He paused, to let the murmurs around the classroom die down, then continued. "The arches were already very old, and had begun to let in gusts sometimes, endangering ships. Repairing them was a very difficult job, and it required a great deal of fine detail. We had to pause regularly to research, to discuss the best next steps, and to consider our work."

"I can think of a different way to tell that," Rayna said, raising her hand. Leif nodded, and she continued. "The wind arches are important," she said. "If they're not working, food doesn't get into Holbard. And ships don't. People need what's on those ships to make a living, and just to survive. To dragons, it's important to discuss everything forever and ever—" She paused as Saphira laughed, and even Mylestom covered his mouth with one hand. "Sorry, but it's true."

"It's true," Saphira agreed. "We're the newest members of the Dragonmeet, and we're learning all about long discussions."

"Well," said Rayna. "Maybe dragons felt like they were doing it the best way they could. But maybe the wolves, and the people in Holbard, felt like the dragons were deliberately taking their time. Sometimes it's hard to understand what the delay is."

Anders fiddled with the stack of papers on the desk in front of him—some of Isabina's mechanical drawings—and straightened them one by one, though there was no need to do it. These were his and Rayna's parents they were talking about. Felix and Drifa. Working together on the arch.

"Very good, Rayna," said Leif. "Whether you're right or wrong, I do not know, but this is a perfectly valid point of view. I wish we could think so clearly about what happened next. Somebody, we don't know who, murdered one of the wolf designers, Felix."

A gasp went around the room, and Anders bowed his head. It was so hard to hear it said so simply, and pretend it was only a story to him too. Hayn had said that he, Anders, looked like Felix, but he wondered what he had been like. If he had been loud and confident like Rayna, or quiet and thoughtful like Anders. What kinds of things he'd have shown the twins if he'd had a chance to raise them.

If Anders had a chance to speak to Hayn again, he'd ask him.

"That's sad," Bryn said, "that he was killed. But what does it have to do with the battle?"

"Ah," said Leif, his usually friendly face turning grim. "The same day Felix was killed, the dragonsmith Drifa was seen flying away from where his body was found."

"She killed him," said Bryn slowly.

"Or," said Lisabet, "she was running away from the person who killed him."

Every head in the room turned toward her, but Anders glanced up at Leif and found the Drekleid gazing thoughtfully back.

"Perhaps," Leif said. "That is certainly another way to interpret the facts. Unfortunately, and not without reason, the wolves believed Drifa to be the culprit. They demanded she stand trial, but we could not find her."

Mylestom spoke up from the front of the room. "Or we refused to send her to Holbard, from the wolves' point of view."

"Just so," said Leif with a sigh. "As one of the dragons who hunted for her, I can tell you that I, at least, truly could not find her. But the wolves and the citizens of Holbard were not placated. Rumors flew, and every day citizens of Holbard became warier of dragons than they had ever been."

"For all they knew, dragons were murderers," Ellukka said slowly.

Leif nodded. "They told us dragons we had to wear red coats when we were in Holbard in human form, so they knew who we were. And then they told us we were only allowed to move through certain parts of the city."

"They thought you were that dangerous?" Theo asked quietly.

"That *we* were that dangerous," said Mikkel. "Or I bet they could have said it was because people were angry about the murder, and nobody wanted a dragon to be hurt by angry people in Holbard. So better to stay in safe, designated parts of the city."

"Very good, Mikkel," said Leif. "That was exactly the excuse. Every time a dragon flew overhead, coming in to work in Holbard, humans would run for cover, and the Wolf Guard would watch us."

"Who'd want to go to Holbard at all, with things like that?" Rayna asked.

Leif sighed. "As it turns out, almost nobody. Fewer and fewer dragonsmiths agreed to work in Holbard, and projects began to pile up. We were worried for our own safety."

"Or," said Ellukka, "you were refusing to help people in Holbard. I mean, that's what they might have said."

Leif looked across at Saphira and Mylestom. "You see?" he said.

"They're doing more than the Dragonmeet ever manages," said Mylestom. "Usually the 'Meet members are all talking over each other by this stage, or hopelessly off-topic. At least your students are listening to one another."

"That's what being a Finskólar will do for you,"

Saphira replied, with her easy smile.

"This is why I am telling you this story today," Leif said to the students. "We do not speak of it often, but you are young, and your minds are open. Sometimes you see possibilities where we adults do not."

Was Leif telling them again to take action? Anders wasn't sure, but he suspected the Drekleid was. Then again, he had no idea they already had Drifa's map.

Leif continued. "Fewer and fewer dragons were willing to work in Holbard, no matter what the reward. The wolves were demanding Drifa stand trial. Some of us felt she should, and some felt no dragon should subject herself to wolf justice. But in any case, nobody could find her."

Anders's hands made fists under the desk. Nobody had been able to find her, he knew, because she had been hiding. Waiting to have her babies and conceal them with some ally in Holbard. But where had she gone then? *Had* someone found her, and done the justice the wolves thought she deserved? *Or,* a tiny voice in the back of his mind whispered, *was there a chance she was hiding still?*

"What happened next?" Krissin asked softly.

"The wolves took dragons prisoner," Leif said, "refusing to allow them to leave the city, forcing them to work on the wind arches and other projects."

"Hold on," said Lisabet, holding up her hand. "The

wolves are a pack, and we make decisions differently from dragons, but I don't know if you can say 'the wolves' all did something, any more than you can say 'the dragons' all did something. The wolves' *leaders* took dragons prisoner."

"And maybe they were desperate," Ellukka said reluctantly. "If they thought a dragon killed a wolf—"

"And maybe she did," said Bryn. "She hid afterward, that doesn't look good."

Rayna drew a quick breath—Anders knew she wanted to defend their mother—then looked down. He was pretty sure Ellukka had stood on her foot under the table.

"Perhaps they were desperate," Leif agreed. "With little reason to trust dragons, and no help with projects they thought were vital."

"That still doesn't mean you can just take prisoners," Nico said. "Even if everything they thought was true, and we don't know that it was, they were following a wrong with a wrong."

"Many dragons thought that way," Leif said. "A rescue mission was mounted. A raid to free the dragons being held prisoner and made to work in Holbard. But how else might such a mission be described?"

"An attack," Anders said softly. He hadn't spoken yet, taken up with images of his parents, and everyone in the room turned to look at him.

"Just so," said Leif, just as soft. "An attack. Which led to a battle. And a break in what little trust there was, which has led to a separation that has lasted until this day. Many members of the Dragonmeet fought in that battle. The current Fyrstulf was a squad commander back then, one of the loudest voices against us."

"We were never taught this," Lisabet said, her voice shaking. Anders realized with a pang that it was her mother they were discussing. "The older wolves must know, but nobody our age has any idea."

"The older wolves are living their own story," Ellukka said. "Just like the older dragons. Stories about murders, and refusals to care about justice, and red jackets and threats."

"But it's not meant to be that way," Lisabet pressed. "Neither side can make artifacts without the other. The arches in Holbard, they must never have finished repairing them. They're failing even now. Sometimes huge gusts come through, and it's happening more often."

"The arches are the least of our problems," Leif replied. "For now, we of the Dragonmeet are dealing with a wolf raid on Drekhelm, and the theft of the Snowstone. The wolves no doubt have stories about our equinox kidnappings"—and here he looked at Theo, who blushed—"and about our spies in their cities. We have stories about their raids, their attacks, their intentions. The way these things build up and explode is complicated."

"And the Dragonmeet's been talking about it without getting anywhere for ten days now," Ellukka said. "No offense to you three."

"None taken," Leif said. "You're right."

"Leif," said Nico, frowning, "I don't think we should be discussing how to respond to this with wolves right here in the classroom."

"I agree," said Krissin straight away. "They shouldn't even *be* in class. They could be spies."

"They are not!" Ellukka said immediately.

"Go back to your equations," Mikkel said to them from beside her. "You're both better at things with simple answers anyway."

"There's nothing wrong with the fact that an equation has a right answer and a wrong answer," Nico snapped. "So do some of the things we're talking about here."

Krissin scowled. "I thought you were meant to be listening to other points of view. That's what Leif was just saying. Our point of view is that we shouldn't talk about this in front of wolves. You know what his name is?" She was pointing at Anders. "Anders *Bardasen*."

There was a long silence—it seemed that the dragons knew where the name had come from, even though none of them were from Holbard. After the last great battle, orphans whose parents and names weren't known were named after the battle itself.

"His family died, and he's supposed to be friends with dragons now?" Nico asked, one brow raised.

"You didn't see what they did in the battle," Ellukka said, rising to her feet and pointing to Anders and Lisabet. "I did. If you want them gone, would you prefer Leif was dead?"

"I have questions about Theo too," Krissin added. "He only came from Holbard six months ago, his family is still there. How do we know who he's loyal to?"

Anders glanced up at Leif, who had bowed his head and was rubbing his face with both hands. Why wasn't he saying something, defending them? Anders and Lisabet had given up *everything* to come here—their friends, her mother, and his uncle, it turned out. They'd given up their life at Ulfar, everything they were used to. And though they'd found good friends here, that didn't stop him desperately missing Sakarias and Viktoria, Jai and Det and Mateo, or feeling like there was a hole in his heart when he imagined them thinking he'd betrayed them.

"The whole thing could have been a setup," Krissin said, speaking slowly, as if she was explaining something simple. "It was their own class. Who says they didn't make a plan that someone would attack Leif, and Lisabet would defend him, and then we'd all trust them?"

"It wasn't!" The words burst out of Anders. "You think we wanted to be stuck here?"

And then everyone was shouting, fingers pointing and children coming to their feet, yelling accusations and snapping defenses. Anders couldn't even make out what anyone was saying anymore, and he didn't care—what he cared about was that the way *he* felt was pouring out of him, and it felt so, so *good* to raise his voice and shout at Nico and Krissin.

Eventually Leif raised his hands, and then his voice. "Enough," he called, and then when nobody was listening, he shouted louder: "*ENOUGH!*"

One by one the young wolves and dragons went silent, and everybody turned to look at Leif.

"Well," he said quietly. "I see you are not that much ahead of the Dragonmeet after all. And after you started out so well. I'd hoped for more from my chosen students."

Anders could hear Rayna muttering under her breath, and even calm Lisabet sounded like she was growling in the back of her throat. He felt like doing exactly the same.

Leif shook his head. "We will do independent study for the rest of the day," he said. "Usually I would end your lessons here, but frankly, I don't trust you not to continue the fight without me. It's time you all had a day off, so tomorrow will be a rest day. I will expect to see you all calmer when you return the day after."

There was a round of muttered apologies, not one of which sounded like the speaker really meant it, and one by one the students found their work on the long tables and turned their attention to it. As Anders found the booklet that contained his reading and writing exercises, he could feel the room bristling with unspoken arguments.

More than ever, it felt like there was no solution to the bad blood between the wolves and the dragons, except to make it impossible for each to attack the other.

As the class had talked through the beginning of the fight, it had been so easy to see where things had gone wrong. But though it had all started with suspicions and wrong beliefs, the truth was that in the end, wolves and dragons had *died*.

It wasn't just a case of everyone understanding the other side of the story—his class couldn't even do it with the Drekleid's help, and none of them had even been involved. Real harm had been done in the last great battle, and he wasn't sure it could be undone.

Real harm was done, said a small voice in his head, *in the battle ten days ago as well.*

That was the thought that had been preying on his

mind ever since, no matter how he tried to hide from it. He couldn't just explain to his friends that dragons weren't what they'd always believed them to be. They had suffered real injuries—they had run for their lives.

Just like the larger battle, it had begun with myths and lies, but now there were real hurts to be forgiven. And though he hoped against hope they could be, in his heart, he wondered if it could ever happen.

* * *

At lunch, Anders and the others took no chance that Nico and Krissin could sit next to them again and stop them from working on the riddle. Mikkel and Rayna ran to fetch food, and they met the others in the big map room that Anders and Lisabet had discovered the first day they'd broken out of their locked bedroom.

The huge map of Holbard was still there, taking up one whole wall, and as he looked at the markings on it, identifying Ulfar Academy, the site of the port fire, and other places besides, Anders felt the chill of an impending battle looming over him. He forced his mind back to the riddle and took his place with the others around one end of the long table.

"Let's hear it again," said Lisabet, who was helping Theo unload the stack of books he'd brought with him.

He was still trying to figure out exactly what the Sun Scepter did, besides something that presumably had to do with heat—after all, it was named for the sun—and he was not having much luck with his research.

Anders swallowed his bite of his sandwich and recited the words.

"Where the sun greets herself at every dawn,
And the stars admire themselves at night,
Where blue meets blue the whole day long,
The scepter's head is wedged in tight."

Everyone was quiet. "Um," said Ellukka eventually. "Where do you start with one of these things?"

"First line," said Lisabet practically. "The sun at dawn."

"So somewhere in the east," Anders said. "That's where the sun comes up. She can't be greeting herself anywhere else, except where she is."

Everyone turned to look at the big map of Vallen, which illustrated all the details of the island, from pools and lakes all the way up to mountaintops, with almost perfect accuracy.

"I wonder what it means by 'greets herself,'" Rayna mused.

"Some kind of mirror?" Mikkel tried. "There have to

be two of you for you to greet yourself."

"I think it has to be," Lisabet agreed slowly. "In the next line, it says it's somewhere the stars can admire themselves. You admire yourself in a mirror, don't you? Theo, is there . . . ?"

Theo was already standing up with a sigh. "I'll find a book on famous artifact mirrors," he said, trotting out of the room.

Everyone sat in silence while he was gone, eating their lunch and staring at either Drifa's map or the map on the wall, occasionally breaking the quiet to murmur one of the lines of the riddle to themselves. Theo returned and started leafing through the pages of his newest book, frowning.

"What does 'blue meets blue' mean?" Anders said eventually. "I'm trying to think of—I mean, I suppose it's two blue things."

"What kind of things are blue?" Lisabet asked quietly, seeing the thoughtful frown on his face.

"The sea, the sky," he said. "Maybe it's somewhere along the east coast?"

Ellukka dropped her sandwich. "I know the place!" she said, shoving her chair back and hurrying around to the big map of Vallen. "There *is* a place where the sea meets the sky, and it's over here in the east! I've been there with my father, and I was practicing a story about it a few months ago in school!"

She snatched up a pointer that was clipped into a rack beside the map, and used it to point at a spot near the very top of the eastern coast. Just off the coast, a string of islands looked like it had been dropped into the sea, and below, where her pointer was tapping, was a patch of blue named the Skylake.

"It's a huge lake," she said. "It sits at the top of very high, very sheer black cliffs—that's why it's called the Skylake. Because it's so high up compared to the sea. And if you're there on the right kind of day, the water is so perfectly still, it acts like a mirror."

"Good," said Theo, closing the book on mirrors and reaching for his sandwich with visible relief. "Because I was getting nowhere."

"You could see the sunrise in it," she said. "Or the stars at night, if you flew over the top."

"Do you think we need to go there on a perfectly calm day?" Mikkel asked.

"No," said Anders. "It doesn't say 'when,' it says 'where.' So we just have to go to the place where it happens, not on the day it does."

"This has to be it," said Rayna. "We should go on our rest day tomorrow."

Mikkel groaned, lowering his head to thump it gently on the table. "Please get home before dark this time," he said. "Seriously, we're begging. Theo and I are going to completely run out of excuses."

"We'll do our best," Ellukka promised.

Anders barely heard her. He was too busy staring up at the map. *The Skylake.*

Solving the riddle hadn't been as hard as Hayn had warned it would be, but then again, they'd had wolf and dragon friends to help them. And perhaps in some ways, the hardest part was having Drifa's blood—after all, that was something you couldn't pretend.

Tomorrow, they'd find out if they were right. And if they were, they'd find the Sun Scepter.

CHAPTER NINE

THEY SNUCK OUT EARLY THE NEXT MORNING, leaving behind a not-particularly-hopeful Mikkel and Theo—though the two boys were less worried about the success of the mission and more worried about their grilling at the hands of Valerius and Torsten, if anyone worked out that the other four were missing. Theo planned to try and speak to Hayn and let him know what they'd figured out, if he could find a time when the archives were quiet enough to slip into the little room where the mirror lay hidden.

For now, he and Mikkel were determined to do their best, and they waved the others farewell, then ran inside to set up the first of their diversions—a study session in Rayna and Ellukka's room. If anyone came looking for the girls, they planned to say they'd only just gone to find a snack. After all, they must be around if their friends were in their room, right?

Anders kept his scarf pulled up around his face as Rayna soared between mountain peaks. She and Ellukka planned to travel east, flying low across the Sudrain River until they reached the Seacliff Mountains on the coast. From there they would make their way up to the Skylake. The journey would take longer than if they'd flown in a straight line, but there was also less chance they'd be seen from the ground.

The mists of the night before hadn't yet cleared, and as Anders looked down over Rayna's shoulder, he saw they were pooled at the base of the mountains like water, nestled in every gully. The Sudrain ran between tall fir trees like a gray-and-white thrashing beast, and eventually the trees thinned out as the Seacliff Mountains rose toward the sky. To his left he could see the Uplands, the broad, grassy plains that nestled between the two mountain ranges, but Rayna never went high enough for him to see the sea beyond them to the north.

It was a crisp, sunny day, with barely a cloud above them—the sky was a pale silvery-blue, the sun slowly rising from the direction they were flying. It grew colder and colder as the mountain peaks rose, and after a couple of long hours, when Anders had tucked himself down inside his layers—even for him this was getting seriously nippy—he felt Rayna start to descend.

He peeked out again and immediately spotted the Skylake.

It was *enormous*.

Just as Ellukka had said, sheer black cliffs fell straight to the sea below, and the lake itself somehow nudged all the way up to the edge of the cliff, the silvery-blue waters reflecting the sky, broken only by the occasional gust of wind.

The two dragons circled out to sea, and Anders leaned out far enough to spot the waves dashing themselves against the base of the cliffs in flurries of white foam, before Rayna's rib cage shook with a rumble beneath him, and he took it as a sign to stop moving his weight around.

Side by side, wingtips almost touching, Rayna and Ellukka wheeled in from the sea to soar the length of the lake toward the hills at the other end. Anders tried to soak up every detail—the rocks along the shoreline, the green-gold grass that ran up to the edges—knowing the scepter might be hidden anywhere around the edge of this huge lake. Or worse, somewhere under the water.

The girls flared their wings and slowed to land, set-tling on a patch of springy grass at the western end of the lake, farthest from the sea. The rocks that ran all along the edges made this end the obvious place to land, and Rayna and Ellukka picked out spots side by side.

Anders and Lisabet climbed down stiffly, arching their backs to stretch and stumbling until their legs worked again. Lisabet looked a little green around the gills, as she had after the flights to and from Holbard. Anders set down the bag he was carrying so he could properly coax his limbs back to life.

Once they were far enough away, first Ellukka and then Rayna transformed, sinking down almost too fast for the eye to follow, shrinking and shifting until they were humans once more, holding the three-point crouch dragons always seemed to start and end their transformations in.

"It's been nearly two weeks since we transformed," Lisabet said, wistful. "We can't do it at Drekhelm—it's so hard for me, and if the dragons saw either of us . . . but I'm starting to feel like I need to. Like an itch, you know?"

And as soon as she said it, Anders felt it too. "Maybe we can today," he said. "Just for a little."

"But first," said Lisabet wryly, "I think we're having lunch."

Rayna and Ellukka had already reached Anders's bag, and were digging inside it for the supplies they'd packed at breakfast. "I'm starving," Rayna said, pulling the wrapping off a sandwich and shoving half in her mouth.

"Dying," Ellukka agreed. "Always happens after a long flight. Anders, Lisabet, we'll be with you in a minute."

Anders turned to study the lake as the two dragons ate, and Lisabet pulled off her boots and socks, rolled up her trousers to her knees, and waded out into the lake, letting the cold soak into her bones with a happy sigh.

"It has to be the right place," Anders said. "There's blue in the sky and in the lake, and you can see what a perfect mirror it makes."

"Food first," Rayna said from behind him. "Then quest."

He laughed, walking back to sink down onto the grass beside his twin as she devoured the second half of her sandwich. He leaned back on his hands, studying the lake. Anders and Rayna had never really left Holbard before their transformations, and everything he'd seen when aloft with her these past few days—the mountains, the plains, Vallen's jagged coastline—seemed impossibly beautiful.

And, a tiny part of him remembered, *not just impossibly beautiful. Also, just plain impossible.* The lake was huge, and there was no hint in the riddle about where they were supposed to look for the Sun Scepter. The whole Wolf

Guard could search this lake without finding it. With that thought, his good mood vanished like the sun hiding behind the clouds.

He looked up at the silvery-blue sky and squinted against the sun as he mentally traced a path down to the lake itself. From here, you couldn't even see the jagged rocks at the edge. It just looked as though the water ended in the sky, the two of them melding perfectly together.

Suddenly he sat bolt upright. *Where blue meets blue.* They *did* have the clue they needed after all! He didn't need the whole of the Wolf Guard, he just needed to pay attention to the words of the riddle.

"It's at the other end of the lake!" he said, scrambling to his feet. "Look, blue meets blue, right there!"

He threw himself into wolf form, running the moment his feet hit the ground, excitement coursing through him. It felt amazing to have the grass beneath his paws once again, his nose suddenly picking up the sharp scents of the trees all around them, the delicious salty tang of the sea far below, the hint of wood smoke from some nearby cottage.

He heard Lisabet howl behind him as the two tore along the shore of the lake, and he answered her, joyful. It felt *right* to be running with her, stretching his legs and leaping past rocks, swallowing up the distance in no time.

They reached the far end of the lake too soon, and he reluctantly pushed himself back into human form.

Lisabet hadn't bothered putting her boots back on before she followed him, and now she hopped impatiently from one bare foot to the other as he pulled off his own boots and socks.

"Blue meets blue," he said, rolling up his trousers and wading out into the water. "It has to be somewhere here along this edge, where the lake meets the sky. It's obvious from the other end, and that's the best place for a dragon to land. It's where Drifa would have landed. The riddle says it's wedged in tight. That has to mean these rocks."

Rayna and Ellukka were still running along the edge of the lake in human form, and by the time they reached Anders and Lisabet, the two wolves were well out along the edge of the lake. It was shallow along the rocky shoreline, so it wasn't hard to wade, but Anders's spine was tingling with the knowledge that just a few feet to one side of him was an endlessly sheer drop down to the sea.

The two dragons splashed out to join them, both shrieking at the coldness of the water.

For a time, they hunted in different spots along the lake's edge, and then suddenly Ellukka shouted, "Something's here!"

Anders hurried to join her, the water surging around

his legs with every step. She was bent over a craggy bit of rock that seemed to be part of the cliff face itself, tugging at something fastened beneath it.

"It's in here," she said, giving another pull. "But it won't move."

Lisabet leaned down to try and get a look at it, but it was underwater. "Maybe it needs to be Anders or Rayna?" she suggested. "You know, her blood?"

"Worth a try," Ellukka said, panting as she abandoned the attempt.

Anders took her place, pushing his sleeve a little higher up his arm and reaching in to feel underneath the ledge of rock with his fingertips. It only took him a few moments to feel what Ellukka had—a kind of long tube wrapped in what felt like waxed canvas.

He gave it a tug, and with no effort at all, it came free from the place where it was fastened. When he pulled it from beneath the water, the cloth wrapped around it was green and slimy, tied up with string that had threads of silver woven through it, just like the map.

They didn't even bother wading back to the shore— Rayna helped Anders unpick all the knots, and Ellukka and Lisabet leaned in to see the fabric come apart.

Carefully, Anders and Rayna worked together to peel the package open. The piece of worn wood inside was about as thick as Anders's forearm, and about the same length. Thin strips of what looked like iron crisscrossed it, set into the wood, and at one end of it was fixed an iron orb, cradled by wooden claws and engraved with intricate runes.

They all stared down at it.

"It's not very big," said Ellukka eventually, sounding uncertain.

"I thought a scepter was long," Rayna said. "Like a staff. This is more like the Sun Stick than the Sun Scepter."

Anders was underwhelmed as well. He pushed away the feeling that something about this wasn't right. He handed Rayna the cloth and string, then turned the scepter over in his hands, studying it from every angle. "Anyone have any idea how to use it?" he asked.

"Maybe touch it to the map?" Lisabet suggested, not sounding very hopeful. "There might be instructions? I mean, the map is for finding Drifa's artifacts, not using them, but . . ."

They waded ashore and found their shoes (except for Lisabet), and walked up to the other end of the lake in silence. Anders knew he wasn't the only one feeling uneasy about this. He dug the map out of his bag and set it down on the ground. Ellukka and Lisabet held down the corners with their fingertips to stop the breeze from carrying it away.

Anders crouched down with Rayna by his side and carefully touched the tip of the scepter to the map.

For a long moment, nothing happened. Then the knotwork around the edge began to writhe and change, just as it had before. Relief sang through him, the tension in his shoulders easing. The map *did* have instructions.

Lisabet leaned down, squinting, to carefully read out the words that now made up the border of the map.

"From deep within and light on the air,
You'll find this hiding place straight through
The ice-cold veil of a mountain fair,
Where rót meets rock, as it was taught to do."

"Pack and paws," whispered Lisabet.

"Sparks and scales," Ellukka replied, just as quiet. "This is why it was easy to solve the riddle."

Rayna groaned. "It's not the only piece of the scepter."

CHAPTER TEN

EVERYONE WAS SUBDUED AS THEY FLEW BACK TO Drekhelm. At least they had one piece, Anders told himself. Even if the next riddle was even less clear than the first.

Rayna and Ellukka were both tired when they landed, transforming out on the mountainside in the setting sun, so the foursome could make their way up to the doors of the Great Hall and check that the coast was clear for them to creep inside.

"It wasn't just wading through the cold water," Ellukka said. "The weather was cold today as well."

"I feel like I can't think properly," Rayna agreed. "Though it's getting better since we got back here."

Anders bit his lip as he climbed up to the doors. This had to be the effect of the Snowstone. Had Hayn run out of excuses? Had Sigrid gotten her hands on an augmenter?

Once she had, she might be able to easily spread the cold they'd felt in Holbard as far as Drekhelm.

He stopped by the door, which was slightly ajar, and put his eye to the crack. He froze at what he saw, and held his hand up to bid the others keep quiet behind him. The Dragonmeet was assembled at the table at the top of the hall, clearly in the middle of one of their endless debates.

Saphira, one of the young members who'd come to their class yesterday, was speaking. "Well somebody lit those fires in Holbard, even if we don't know who it was."

Torsten snorted behind his big, bushy beard. "I'd congratulate them, if I could."

Valerius shot him a quelling look, which surprised Anders—he'd thought Valerius and Torsten agreed on everything. Perhaps it was only most things. "We have reports from our spies," he said. "They witnessed the fire at the port, and they say it was white and gold. It was dragonsfire."

Mylestom leaned forward from his place beside Saphira. "Are we completely sure the spies didn't light it?"

Leif answered, raising a sheaf of paper he held in one hand. "I trust them. There's more bad news, though. I have here a new report of a small fire three days ago. It broke out in the warehouses of a mercher who supplies Ulfar Barracks and Academy with most of their vegetables. He stores his goods near the city, and the word here is that a white-and-gold fire was lit there three nights ago."

"And our spies have nothing?" Valerius demanded. "No idea how this happened?"

"What matters more is that it did," Torsten growled, sounding as fierce as an angry wolf. "The wolves need reminding that we're not defenseless."

Voices rose all around the table, as everyone began to speak at once.

"You can't possibly—"

"We have to remember—"

"The wolves will—"

Leif raised both hands, and eventually it all died down. "Let's adjourn for dinner," he said. "We will hear everyone's voice, but one at a time."

The Dragonmeet left the hall in twos and threes, all twenty-five of them continuing the conversation.

As soon as they were gone, the children crept inside, Rayna last of all and pulling the door shut behind her.

"I'd better go find my father," Ellukka said. "I'll pretend I've been around all day, and I've been waiting for him for dinner."

"We should eat too," Lisabet said.

As she, Rayna, and Anders fetched food and went in search of Mikkel and Theo, Anders wondered if he should speak to Leif about his theory on faking dragonsfire. But he wasn't even sure if it was possible on such a large scale, let alone whether it had happened.

They found the boys and filled them in on the day's events while waiting for Ellukka in Anders and Lisabet's room. Mikkel and Theo were more enthused than overwhelmed—they reminded Anders that the second riddle might be difficult, but that they'd already solved the first one, and that it hadn't even taken them that long.

"I'm pretty sure Leif was suspicious today," Mikkel said. "We both thought he knew we were covering for *something*, but he didn't ask what."

"We also think maybe he wanted us to keep covering," Theo said. "Better than Torsten and Valerius finding out."

"It must be hard for Ellukka to keep secrets from her father," Rayna said.

"Better that than what'd happen to all of us if he found out," Lisabet said, and nobody could disagree with that.

By the time Ellukka came to join them, they were trying to solve the riddle.

"He's frustrated," she reported. "They all are. Dragons might like to talk everything to death, but even the Dragonmeet knows it can't go on forever. But nobody's listening to anyone else. Where are we with the riddle?"

"Here," said Mikkel. "It says through a mountain's

veil. A veil is something that covers you, right? So could it be clouds? It says as well that the veil is ice cold, and clouds are freezing."

"So we have to fly straight through the clouds?" Lisabet asked, doubtful. "'You'll find this hiding place straight through,' it says."

"Sounds like it," Theo agreed. "Hopefully without crashing into the mountain."

"'Light on the air,'" Anders said, running through the riddle in his head. "That sounds like clouds as well. Do you think it's too obvious?"

"I'm not going to complain if it is," Rayna said. "I wonder what this word, *rót*, means. I haven't seen it before."

"I think it's another language," Ellukka said. "Bryn will know. We can ask her in class tomorrow."

Anders thought of the Finskól's language specialist, who had always been friendly to him. If she knew what the word meant, perhaps its origin would give them another clue.

They made no further progress that night, though Anders lay awake later, turning the riddle over in his mind until he eventually fell asleep. He suspected the others were all doing the same.

* * *

The next morning, he copied the word *rót* onto a scrap of paper and sat down next to Bryn as soon as he arrived in class. But before he opened his mouth to ask her about the clue, he realized something wasn't right. Her shoulders were rounded, her hands were tucked beneath her arms as she worked, and her light-brown skin was paler than usual. Usually she looked strong, but just now she was curled in on herself.

"Bryn, are you all right?" he asked.

His voice seemed to startle her, and she looked up with a blink, then tried for a smile. "I'm fine," she said. "It's just the cold, it's bothering me this morning."

A shiver went through Anders that had nothing to do with the temperature. "Is there anything I can do to help?" he asked. "I could get you a hot drink?"

She shook her head. "It doesn't seem to make a difference. Truly, I'll be all right." She paused, though, and bit her lip. "I'm not worried about me, but my mother's in the infirmary," she admitted. "She came over all faint last night."

"Pack and paws," he murmured. "I'm sorry, I hope she feels better soon."

The silence stretched between them, awkward—he hadn't meant he was apologizing, but in a way, he was the one who'd let the wolves steal the Snowstone. And it was his kind who were doing this to hers. And though he knew Bryn didn't hold him responsible, he still wasn't sure what to say.

She was the one who broke the silence. "Did you come over to ask me something?"

He dug in his pocket for the scrap of paper. "I don't suppose you can tell me what this word means?" he asked, showing it to her.

She leaned in to examine it, frowning thoughtfully. "It depends," she said.

"On what?"

"On which language it's in," she said. "This word exists in more than one."

"Oh." Anders was crestfallen. "I have no idea."

"Well," she said, tapping her finger against the letter *r*. "In Allemhaüten, it means 'red.' Usually you'd have two dots over the letter *o*, instead of an accent, but that can just come down to handwriting, and sometimes in old-fashioned texts they use an accent."

Anders couldn't see how the word *red* helped solve the riddle, but more, he couldn't see why his mother would have used a word from Allemhaüt. She was rumored to be from Vallen and Mositala. Then again, all Anders really knew about Allemhaüt was that Sakarias liked to buy pencils that were made there. "Do you know what it means in the other languages?" he asked Bryn.

"Hmm." She paused so long he wondered if she'd forgotten he was there, and he fought the urge to fidget impatiently. If Bryn didn't know, where could he possibly find the answer to this? "Yes," she said suddenly, just when he was about to give up. "It could be a word in Old Vallenite. That's what we spoke centuries ago."

"Really?" Anders's excitement jumped back to life. He only knew one word in Old Vallenite—*barda*, which meant battle, the word that had given him his name.

"Yes," said Bryn. "I think it would mean root, like the root of a tree or a plant." She frowned. "Or maybe a tooth? Maybe. But . . ."

"Thank you!" said Anders, trying not to hurry as he pocketed the scrap of paper. "You're the best, Bryn."

"You're welcome," she said, looking mildly surprised at his enthusiasm. "Old Vallenite's really interesting, because the verbs . . . actually, that reminds me of something I wanted to look up." A moment later she'd forgotten about him, shivering and turning up the collar of her coat, then pulling one of her books closer with an absentminded expression.

"Thank you," Anders said quickly, hurrying back to the table where his friends were sitting.

He knew the answer to the riddle. He'd heard it on only his second day at Drekhelm.

They'd gone to the gardens in the cave that opened onto the mountainside, after he'd spoken to the Dragon-meet. Mikkel had said they were created by a dragon called Flic more than five hundred years before. A genius, who could make plants grow in the most unlikely of places.

Ellukka had said that Leif had taken her to see a waterfall once, with plants growing everywhere.

Everything in the riddle made sense.

From deep within and light on the air—the river feeding the waterfall could come from deep within the mountain, and the spray itself would be light on the air, wouldn't it?

You'll find this hiding place straight through / The ice-cold veil of a mountain fair—so the piece of the scepter would be hidden behind the waterfall itself, the white, watery veil falling down the side of the mountain. That was going to be cold. And wet.

Where rót meets rock, as it was taught to do—now he knew a *rót* was a root, it all came together. Where roots—plants—met rock, as Flic had taught them to do five hundred years before, planting them in unlikely places and keeping them alive.

He sat down with the others and started to whisper what he'd figured out—he was most of the way through when Nico and Krissin came to sit at their end of the table, forcing him to stop abruptly.

They *never* sat so close. Were they trying to overhear?

Everyone arrived except for Theo, who was in the archives pulling some books he needed, and the class settled into work. There was no lesson from Leif today, and no wonder, after the way the last one had ended.

Anders pretended to practice his reading, while turning over his newest problem in his head. How were they going to get to the Flic Waterfall? It was even farther from Drekhelm than Holbard or the Skylake had been, and they couldn't keep sneaking out. Sooner or later, they were going to be caught.

But Rayna had always been there with a quick story when they needed it, and she didn't fail him now. The class had been working for only a few minutes when she pushed back her chair with a scrape that gained everyone's attention and stood up.

"Leif," she said. "On behalf of the class, I'd like to apologize for our argument the day before yesterday. You were right to show us there are better ways to discuss our problems. It's been a little difficult lately, but we shouldn't have let that get the best of us."

There was a round of blinking from most of the class, who had never heard Rayna speak about anything so humbly, and even Anders—who knew from her terribly sincere tone that she was up to something—wasn't sure what was coming next.

"The apology is appreciated," said Leif, in his usual calm manner. "And accepted. I understand the cool weather and recent events have made things difficult for all of you. Is there something I could do that would help?"

Rayna was ready and waiting.

"Flic Waterfall would be the perfect solution," she said, without missing a beat. Anders had to stop himself from flinching—it felt like telling a secret, having their next destination mentioned out loud like that. But of course, nobody else knew that, which was what Rayna was counting on.

"Flic Waterfall?" Leif repeated, brows lifted in surprise.

"We need a break," said Rayna. "Ellukka said you took her once, and that it was a wonderful, memorable experience."

Easy, Rayna, Anders thought. *Don't lay it on too thick.*

She was still going. "It's also a place of historical significance. It has stories associated with it, it offers opportunities for science and art—there's something for everyone there."

At the next table over Bryn started to shift in her seat,

ready to point out that there wasn't really anything to do with languages that could be studied there, but Ferdie—who was in the same boat with medicine but clearly sensed the opportunity for some time off—discreetly elbowed her in the ribs.

Leif looked around the classroom, examining the students' faces. Anders was pretty sure pleading was written all over his and his friends'. And as he snuck a quick look around, he realized almost everyone was giving Leif some version of big eyes and innocent expressions, even those who didn't know the reason for Rayna's request.

Leif nodded slowly. "All right," he said. "It is a point well made. We will go as a class tomorrow and stay there overnight. If we bring a communications mirror, we can be contacted if we're needed."

Theo chose that moment to arrive from the archives, and he was startled to find himself walking into a room full of cheering Finskólars. He set down his books to join in the celebration willingly enough, letting Ellukka whirl him in a circle.

Once they all sat down again to work, though, with warnings from Leif about paying attention to their work ringing a little too cheerfully in their ears to be serious, Theo was quick to lean in and impart the news he'd brought back with him. "I saw Hayn," he whispered.

Anders immediately leaned in closer. Theo hadn't been able to get hold of Hayn the night before to tell him of their success—he'd found a quiet time in the archives, but Anders and Rayna's uncle hadn't been in his workshop so late.

"What did he say?" Anders asked.

"He says to hurry," Theo whispered. "He thinks the Fyrstulf has other wolves looking for augmenters too, and no matter how much Hayn stalls, if one of the others finds one, the Snowstone could end up much more powerful."

That dampened Anders's spirits, and, as if to prove Hayn's point, another wave of cold came through the classroom that day after lunch.

Everyone was weakened except for Anders and Lisabet, and Bryn was taken away to the infirmary by a worried Ferdie.

Anders could see from their expressions that they wanted to snap at one another or stop working and complain about the cold. But everyone behaved, because they wanted tomorrow's class trip more than they wanted to vent their feelings.

After class Theo disappeared to the archives again, taking Mikkel, the Finskólar historian, with him, to look up as much as he could about Flic, her inventions, and her history, in case any of it was useful in locating the hiding place Drifa had chosen once they arrived at the waterfall. Lisabet would have been useful too, but as a wolf she was banned from the archives, so she did her best with a couple of books in their bedroom.

And Anders himself carried around the knowledge like a light in the dark: tomorrow they'd have the rest of the scepter.

CHAPTER ELEVEN

THE NEXT MORNING THEY GATHERED RIGHT after breakfast in the Great Hall, where Leif was waiting with piles of supplies—food and bedding packed into big bags that were easy for a dragon to lift.

Isabina, the Finskól's resident mechanical genius, was standing and talking to the Drekleid. Her slender frame was nearly hidden beneath the long coils of rope she was carrying, slung crosswise over her body, her tangle of curly brown hair sticking out the top, and her legs out the bottom. It wasn't until Anders got closer that he saw it wasn't rope, but long strips of leather, some parts padded with what looked like fleece.

"Oh, there you are," Isabina said, craning her head to see over the top of the leather rope. She had her usual smudge of grease on her nose. "Ellukka mentioned that you and Lisabet thought harnesses might be a good idea,

so you have something to hold on to when you and Lisabet are riding Ellukka and Rayna."

Anders blinked. The first time Lisabet had raised that
particular idea, Ellukka had nearly gone through the roof.
And now she'd been asking Isabina about it? "Is . . . is that
what that is?" he asked, holding his hands out in an offer
to relieve Isabina of some of her burden.

"Yes, I thought we might as well trial them today,"
she said. "It's not really my field, because there aren't any
mechanics involved, but it's still an interesting design
challenge. Oh, good morning, Ellukka! I've got the harnesses ready."

Lisabet was just arriving with Ellukka, and she joined
Anders in shooting the blond dragon a surprised look.

"No need to make a big deal out of it," Ellukka muttered, crossing over to an empty space where she could
transform. "It would be inconvenient if you fell off, is all."
She dropped to a crouch, changing before either of the
wolves had a chance to reply. Or worse, Anders suspected,
to thank her for being so considerate.

He and Lisabet helped Isabina wrap the first harness
around Ellukka—they both knew they'd better learn how
to do it, in case they wanted to make any trips without
adult permission—and then the second around Rayna.
It was a simple but clever design, crisscrossing under the

dragons' forearms and across their chests.

Anders and Lisabet had leather belts to wear, which had straps that clipped into the harnesses, meaning they couldn't fall off even if they let go. They also had proper handholds now, which Anders much preferred to grabbing hold of Rayna's neck ridges and hoping he didn't hurt her.

"There," said Isabina, tightening a buckle for Ellukka. "Nod once if it feels comfortable, and twice if it doesn't."

Ellukka nodded once and crouched a little, inviting Lisabet to use her front leg as a stepladder to climb up onto her back, and Isabina turned her attention to Rayna.

Rayna and Ellukka launched once they had their passengers aboard, and they circled in the crisp air outside Drekhelm, waiting as one by one the rest of the class launched themselves out the huge, dragon-size double doors. Ferdie was gliding along near Bryn, who had been allowed to come despite her trip to the infirmary before, but as the Finskólar medic, it was clear he wasn't sure it was a good idea. Nearer, Anders could see that Ellukka and Lisabet were testing out the straps, taking some sharp turns, working together to see just how secure they were.

A couple of weeks ago, Ellukka had been ready to spit-roast him and Lisabet on the side of the mountain below them. Now, they were . . . there was only one word for it. They were friends. They weren't just working together—they liked and trusted one another. Ellukka had wanted to make sure Lisabet could fly with her safely.

It was the first time Anders had really thought about it, and though it didn't stop him aching for his friends at Ulfar Academy, he knew now that he had added Ellukka and Mikkel and Theo to his list of friends. Bryn and Isabina and Ferdie as well. He wasn't just doing all this to try and stop a battle. He was doing it to keep the people he cared about safe.

Eventually everyone was aloft, some with the big bags of supplies dangling from one foot, and they formed up behind Leif to wheel away toward the northwest. It was to be a long flight to Flic Waterfall, made a little longer by the need to detour and avoid any populated areas.

To their right rose the highest mountain he'd ever seen—the top of it was completely shrouded in mist. This must be Cloudhaven, the legendary, forbidden home of the first dragonsmiths.

Eventually they left its hidden peak behind, and beyond it Anders caught a glimpse of the red roofs of the village of High Rikkel, nestled on a plateau almost as high as some of the mountain peaks. Tiny spires of smoke rose from faraway chimneys, and he wondered what the people living there were doing at the start of their day, whether they were thinking about the wolves or the dragons, or the battle that might come. Whether anyone from the village would make the long trek to Holbard for the Trial of the Staff this month, to test their wolf blood. Whether any of them carefully hid their dragon blood or had secret dragon family members. They seemed so isolated out here, but though he wasn't even sure if they'd know if a battle took place in Drekhelm or in Holbard, the fight between the dragons and the wolves touched everyone in Vallen.

They flew over golden-green valleys, long rivers snaking through them with twists and turns, the water dashing itself on rocks in some places, so deep and fast in others that it looked still from the air.

And eventually, the wild Westlands Mountains rose up ahead of them. The Westlands were famous for being the fiercest, the most remote, and the most dangerous mountains in Vallen. Storms whipped through them all winter long, and sometimes during the summer as well. On the far side of them lay the inhospitable northwest coast of Vallen, where few ships dared pass.

Today, though, the sky above was a clear blue, and the snow on the mountains looked soft and gentle, as if it would be a comfortable place to rest. Leif tilted one wing and began to angle in on a valley at the edge of the mountains, and Anders looked over Rayna's shoulder to try and make out where they were heading.

At first, the waterfall was so huge that he didn't realize that's what it was. When he understood what he was seeing, he gasped. The wide river surfaced from the mouth of an underground cave and ran along the top of a long plateau like a ribbon laid out in a gently winding path. Then it abruptly reached the edge of the mountain and tumbled hundreds of yards, landing on a series of ledges and pouring off each one in turn, so that the white, frothing mass looked like a layer cake, each section a little larger and more spread out than the one before.

At its base, it spread down to a huge pool, almost the size of the harbor in Holbard—a lake, really. Three great rivers branched away from it, as well as dozens of small silvery streams. It was incredibly beautiful but intimidatingly large, considering the size of the scepter they were hunting for.

Leif headed unerringly for a spot at the base of the cliffs, to the left of the waterfall, where a meadow provided a perfect landing place. The dragons wheeled in as a group to land, and as soon as Rayna and Ellukka hit the ground, Anders and Lisabet set to work pulling off their harnesses, so they could transform back to girls without finding themselves tangled up in anything.

It was only once Rayna was free of all the leather straps that Anders had a chance to step back and really look around. And from the ground, the view was even more extraordinary than it had been from the air.

All around the edge of the lake bloomed the most incredible collection of flowers—he saw the usual white, yellow, and red blooms he was used to finding on the rooftops of Holbard, but as he made his way along the water's edge, he found plant after plant he'd never seen before.

There was a tree with huge, drooping limbs wreathed in purple blossoms, hanging down so low that they dipped in the edge of the water. There were smaller trees with sharp, green, spiky leaves, and red . . . he supposed they were flowers, though really, they looked like red-bristled scrubbing brushes, bundles of hundreds of red strands protruding from the stems in every direction, each ending with a small, yellow pod the size of a pin's head.

This must be the genius of the dragonsmith Flic, who had found ways to make this place hospitable for plants from all over the world, using both mechanical creations and cleverly designed artifacts, bringing them warmth or water or whatever else they needed.

When he looked back, some of the class were still in dragon form, basking in the sun on the grass and rebuilding a little strength after the taxing flight. Deep underneath them there must be lava. Other students had already transformed and were digging through their packs in search of lunch.

They all spent the rest of the afternoon doing as they pleased. Anders would have liked to start exploring for the scepter right away, but there was never a chance to do anything without being watched—Krissin or Nico seemed to find a way to be near them more often than not, and whenever he did shake them, someone else would show up. Ferdie, with his infectious smile and easy manner, wanting to check that everyone was having a good time. Patrik, wanting help carrying his art supplies to the place he'd chosen to paint.

Ellukka and Mikkel had stories and history to share, and Anders and Lisabet sat and listened to all of it, allowing themselves a rest, enjoying their friends' cleverness. It was a welcome reprieve from their constant attempts to solve riddles and stay one step ahead of the looming conflict. It was good to just be friends for an hour or two.

Eventually, before bed, the two of them slipped into wolf form, stretching their legs for a long run across the open meadow around the base of the waterfall.

Just as it had at the Skylake, tearing across the grass felt glorious. They bounded together to the far end of the meadow, matching strides, and when they reached the point where they had to turn around and return, Lisabet leaped on Anders, sending him rolling over and over, then running away before he could retaliate. But even in wolf form he was lankier than her, and he howled as he chased her down to return the favor.

There was a joy in running that he yearned for when he wasn't doing it, and he reveled in when he could. It was the most perfect way to be, he thought.

But when they returned to the camp, he was abruptly reminded that they were two wolves in the company of eleven dragons. Their friends didn't seem to notice that they'd transformed, but some of the others—Ferdie, Isabina, Patrik, Bryn—had never seen them transform before, and they were all openly staring. Perhaps they'd never seen *any* wolf transform before. Nico and Krissin had their arms folded, making their disapproval clear.

Anders pushed himself back into human form, Lisabet a moment behind, and the silence dragged out.

Then Ellukka looked up, rolled her eyes, and stood up. "It's just a different kind of transformation," she said, speaking slowly and carefully, as if everyone needed an explanation. "It's not like you haven't seen someone change shape before."

Ferdie's manners kicked in first, and he shook himself. "Right," he said, though he was still looking at Anders and Lisabet. "Sorry, of course. Shall we find some wood to make a fire?"

Everyone broke up after that and set to work, but there was a lingering sense of unease that took a long time to dissipate. It was a reminder for Anders that even if he forgot it from time to time, he was still a wolf among dragons, and most of them never lost sight of that even for a moment.

***

Dinner dragged on, and it seemed to take hours for everyone to finally be ready for bed. The moon was high, and the sky was clear, which meant it was a crisp, cold night. By the time the dragons finally bedded down around the fire, the stars were twinkling overhead.

Most of the class transformed to dragons to sleep—it was warmer and easier than bringing blankets to wrap up in as humans—but Rayna stayed in human shape, curling up under a blanket between Ellukka's forearms. She wanted to be ready to creep away with Anders and Lisabet, and it would be easier to go unnoticed if she was smaller. Anders and Lisabet changed to their wolf forms under cover of darkness and curled up in furry balls just outside the firelight's edge.

Eventually, when nobody had said anything for what

felt like at least an hour, and Patrik and Leif were both softly snoring, Anders made his move. He whined almost inaudibly to let Lisabet know he was moving and rose silently to his feet. Rayna must have been watching, because as the two wolves padded away from the class, she crawled free of her blanket and stood to hurry quietly after them.

It didn't take long until they were at the edge of the lake, looking up at the waterfall. The sound of the water crashing on the rock would easily drown out the sound of conversation, and invigorated by the cold of the water, Anders pushed himself back into human form, Lisabet following a moment later.

"It's freezing," Rayna said, wrapping her arms around herself.

"Lovely, isn't it?" said Lisabet, drawing in a lungful of cold air, her head tipped back in pleasure, just like a wolf sniffing the breeze.

"I can think of other words," Rayna told her. "Right, where do we hunt?"

"I think it's behind the waterfall," said Anders.

Her eyes widened in horror. "Are you certain? I'm not sure I can walk through water that cold."

"The riddle makes it sound that way," he said. "It says 'straight through the ice-cold veil,' that sounds like it's through the water. And then it says 'where rót meets rock,' so perhaps if there are plants with roots behind the waterfall . . ."

Rayna shivered. "Ugh. This is going to be horrible. The waterfall's so wide, and there are so many layers leading up. Drifa could have hidden it anywhere."

"She probably thought you'd know what she knew about the waterfall," Lisabet said. "Remember, the Sun Scepter isn't the only artifact the map can locate. It would have taken her a long time to hide all her artifacts around Vallen. Perhaps she sensed a battle was coming, but she must also have done it before . . ." She trailed off, then continued, soft and apologetic. "Before your father was killed. So she didn't know yet that she wasn't going to raise you. She might not even have known you existed yet."

It was a sad, sobering thought, and all three of them were quiet as they walked in closer to the waterfall.

"I think we should try it in wolf form," Anders said, making himself sound businesslike. "It'll be too cold for us if we're humans, we won't last very long. And we'll see better as wolves, anyway."

Rayna's teeth were already chattering, and she held out one hand to test the water, then yanked it back. "Snow-melt," she said, shivering. "Anders, I don't think I can go in there. I already feel like I'm thinking at half speed, and if I get soaked to the bone going through the water . . ."

Her voice was a mix of upset and apology, and she turned away, walking a few steps, then swinging abruptly back toward them. "I could do it if I could breathe ice-fire," she said through gritted teeth.

"You'll figure it out," he said, aware of just how unhelpful he'd found those words, when he'd been the one who couldn't throw an ice spear.

"I'm trying so hard!" Rayna's frustration burst to the surface. "I've tried so many times, before you came and since. And it just doesn't happen, nothing comes! If I could throw it I'd be some use if there's a fight, and I'd be able to walk through the waterfall with you right now, and . . ."

She trailed off, and he wrapped his arms around her without thinking, squeezing her in a hug. He couldn't remember Rayna *ever* saying this before—that she couldn't do something. *And I'd probably have panicked if she had*, he admitted to himself. But now, he felt surer.

"It will show up," he promised, hoping he was right.

"What if it doesn't? What if I can't do it?" she whispered.

Lisabet answered, her tone as matter-of-fact as if she was reading from a book. "Of course you can," she said.

Anders and Rayna both looked across at her, Rayna sniffing inside the circle of his arms.

Lisabet shrugged. "You inherited the ability to transform," she said. "If you were going to be a regular human, that's what you'd be. But you're a dragon. And a dragon who coincidentally can't breathe fire, the same way Anders couldn't throw ice? Your gift is in there, Rayna. It's just taking its time to show."

Rayna was quiet, and then she nodded. "I guess it'll show," she murmured, sounding a little more certain than she had before. "I just wish it would hurry up. We don't have time to waste." Then, as she always did, she turned purposeful. "You should both go," she said.

Anders gave her a squeeze and stepped back. "If anyone wakes up and wonders where we are, just say we went running. Wolves prefer to be awake at night anyway, Leif will know that."

She nodded. "Good luck," she said, stepping back into the dark and turning for camp.

Anders and Lisabet watched her go, then turned back toward the waterfall, staring up at it. "This is going to be cold, even for us," Lisabet said. "How *does* your new thing with the heat and cold work?"

"The heat doesn't bother me the way it used to," he said. "I still get hot, but it doesn't make me feel slow and awful. Sometimes it even feels nice. The cold always feels good."

"Well, even we can still get too cold," Lisabet said. "So let's be quick. We'll have to hope there's some kind of ledge behind the water, somewhere we can walk along. If we have to walk *through* the water for long, we'll be swept down into the lake."

"Let's try the lowest level first," Anders said. "Then we can try the next one up if we have to."

They slipped into wolf form, both full of energy, brought alive by the freezing-cold spray on the air—it felt like breathing in cold itself, and aches and pains and slowness Anders hadn't even known he was feeling slipped delightfully away.

He was a little taller than Lisabet in wolf form, just as he was in human form, so he went first. He approached the edge of the waterfall slowly, peering through the torrent to try and see if there was anything behind it. He needed a ledge, or even a cave, so the waterfall didn't knock him down into the lake. If they were right, and this was where the next piece of the scepter was hidden, then there had to be *something* behind the water. The riddle said he had to go through. He couldn't tell, and after a long moment's hesitation he simply plunged in.

There was no ledge behind it.

His claws scraped against slippery, mossy stone, and the water landed on him like a pile of rocks, shoving him straight down into the lake. He banged his side against the steep, jagged stone on the way down, and then the force of the water falling from above was pushing him down, down, down. Icy water was wrapping around his lungs, and without the sun above him, he had no way of knowing which way was up and which was down.

He desperately held his breath, lungs burning, and swam as hard as he could, hoping against hope he was heading for the surface. Then his throat clamped and closed, forcing his mouth open to drag in a lungful that was half water, half air. He coughed and spluttered, but his next breath was more air and less water, and as he blinked his eyes, treading water with flailing limbs, he realized he'd found the surface.

Lisabet had jumped in after him and was just swimming up, ears pricked forward, worry all over her face. She lifted her muzzle in a gesture he instantly understood. *Swim for the other side.*

He wasn't sure why she wanted him to head over there, but he obediently turned and struck out for the far shore—it wasn't so far to swim, just a little way from the base of the waterfall. Farther out, the lake got much wider. He was still coughing as he dragged himself up onto the rocky shore, water streaming from his sodden coat, tail clamped between his legs.

Lisabet climbed up beside him and they each gave themselves a shake, shedding a little of the water. *No ledge?* she asked.

No ledge, he confirmed. *Maybe from this side?*

That's what I was hoping, she agreed.

They were both considerably slower and more careful as they explored this side, but this time they didn't have to poke their heads through the water to be sure there was no space behind the waterfall. They'd have to try farther up.

The incline next to the waterfall was so steep as to be nearly a cliff, rough and rocky, tufts of determined grass clinging to it. But as Anders scrambled up the first few feet, sinking his claws into every available handhold, he found a thick, glossy green vine hanging down from somewhere above. He didn't remember seeing it during the day—it must have blended into the cliff. He grabbed a mouthful of it to help pull himself up, and then nearly let go in surprise. All up and down the vine, tiny lights had come alive in response to his touch—little white flowers no larger than a pea, unfurling their petals and seeming to reflect the moonlight back at the sky, undulating slowly, as if they were underwater.

He climbed very carefully past them and heard Lisabet

whine her surprise as she came up behind him. They followed the path of moonflowers up two tall layers of rock, and Anders felt his excitement building. He'd never seen these moonflowers before, or even heard a whisper of something like them. Could this be something Flic had taught to live here?

His legs were trembling with effort when he reached the second ledge, the water thundering down just past his nose, the moonflowers still gently glowing by his tail. They went no higher, though—the vine seemed to disappear behind the curtain of water.

If there wasn't room back there, and Anders was swept off by the waterfall again, it would be a brutal fall. The kind of fall that could kill a wolf. But he had to take the risk. He growled a low warning to Lisabet to stay well clear, took a deep breath, and plunged in.

And he came out the other side into a perfect garden.

To his left, the torrent of water was still pouring down, filling the air with crisp, cool spray that danced before him. And hidden behind the curtain was a large, round cave. It should have been completely dark, but the moonflower vines snaked all around the walls, softly illuminating the room. Some of them seemed to be growing on some sort of metal lattice, and he shook the water from his coat, then padded over to stand up on his hind legs, pressing his front paws against the wall. There were runes engraved all along the lattice, and it was slightly warm to the touch. These artifacts must have lasted the five centuries or more since Flic had first made this place. They must be why such incredible plants grew here.

He heard a soft whine behind him and turned to see Lisabet, who had followed him through the waterfall after he didn't emerge and was staring slack-jawed at the cave. She walked over to join him, standing up to look at the artifacts. *I've never seen anything so old*, she said without words, but with a tilt of her ears, soft whines, and intakes of breath. Every move was tiny in wolf form, but he'd never seen her so excited.

He dropped down, nosing through the flowers at the base of the vines. They must get some light through the waterfall during the day, for they were all facing that way, their dark petals closed against the night just now. *How did it last?* he asked her, following the edge of the cave around, finding a small bush with berries that glowed a deep red, and then a pale moss that lit up when his paws touched it.

Perhaps Drifa came here to make sure it did, Lisabet replied, when he turned back to look at her.

Anders's breath caught. He imagined his mother—who he couldn't picture at all, except as a dragon, and he didn't even know what color her scales had been—coming here, one in a long line of dragonsmiths who had come to maintain the work of Flic, who had gone before. This place was worth that kind of effort. And being here, somewhere she had been, made him feel connected to her. It made him miss her, even though he'd only just found out who she was.

Let's look for the scepter, said Lisabet, picking the other direction to the one Anders had taken and hunting around the edge of the cave. He mentally shook himself and returned to his own search, using his nose to try and sniff out anything that didn't smell like a plant, anything that didn't quite fit. He soon caught a whiff of oiled wood, and pushed himself hurriedly back into human form, brushing aside the vines at that section of the wall. "Lisabet, look!"

It was a huge, stout wooden door, banded across with metal—engraved with more runes—and most definitely locked.

Lisabet shifted back to a girl beside him. "I really hope she wasn't expecting you to have the key," she said.

Anders hoped so too, feeling all around the edge of the door and going up on his toes to feel along the top of the rim. He had an inkling Drifa wouldn't have left it quite that much to chance. After all, she wouldn't have left a map that gave them clues if she didn't want them to be able to find what they were looking for.

"I wonder how she got in here," Lisabet mused as she watched him. "It would be difficult to climb the waterfall in human form. She and Flic must have wanted to very badly."

Anders's fingers closed over a cylinder at the top of the doorway's arch, and he tugged it loose from where it was woven into the vines. It was wrapped in the same waxed canvas as the first half of the scepter had been, and his hands were shaking in excitement as he pulled the string away. A moment later, the dim light of the moonflowers revealed a second section of the Sun Scepter, dark wood wrapped with engraved metal bands. "Got it," he said, squeezing it tight. "But," he continued, as realization sank in, "it's not big enough to be the rest of it."

"Two pieces down," Lisabet agreed. "I was sort of hoping there'd only be two pieces, but I think we'll have to keep searching. Looking at the size of what we have so far, comparing it to the Staff of Hadda, I'll bet my tail there are two more pieces to go."

Anders thought of the tall, worn wooden staff used to test whether those with wolf blood could make their transformation and join Ulfar. She was right—it had been taller than he was.

"We'll find the others," he said confidently, buoyed by success. "All we need is time. Let's get back to Rayna, and see if the map has another clue for us."

There was no real way down except to jump from the waterfall, and though Anders would have preferred to do it in human form to hold on tight to the piece of the scepter, he couldn't afford to soak all his clothes. So he transformed back into his wolf form and picked the piece up, gripping it experimentally in his jaws. It tingled a tiny bit, just the way his amulet had the first time he'd put it on, or the purse had when he'd held it, as if the essence inside was tickling his skin, and then it subsided.

He and Lisabet exchanged a nervous glance. They'd have to take the waterfall at a run, to be sure they could jump all the way through it and come as far as possible out the other side, landing clear of the tumbling water at the bottom. It went against all his common sense to charge a waterfall and leap out into the air, but he backed up as far as he could and readied himself.

Lisabet looked back at the wooden door. *We'll come back one day*, she said with a soft, determined growl. *And see all the amazing things behind that door.*

And then, side by side, they ran toward the waterfall as fast as they could, leaping from the edge of the rock.

The waterfall pummeled Anders breathless as he flew through it, and he closed his eyes tight as he arced out toward the water, landing with a splash at the bottom and sinking down, down, down. His mouth was forced open by the piece of the scepter, and water wanted to pour in, but this time he was sure which way was up, and he used all four legs to propel himself. Lisabet, being lighter, had surfaced quicker, and she was treading water and waiting for him. Together, they struck out for shore.

They were careful returning to camp—they rolled in the grass until their coats were dry, and Lisabet signaled with a flick of her ears that she'd creep ahead of Anders to make sure the coast was clear. If anyone saw her, she would shift to her human form and speak loudly to give him warning.

He lay still as she slunk forward, her belly close to the ground. Her fur was so dark it was almost black, and she was nearly invisible in the night. When all was silent after a minute, he crept in after her. She was sitting with Rayna between Ellukka's forelegs, the dragon looming over the pair of them and looking down at Anders with interest. It was a bit intimidating, what with the size of her eyes.

Rayna had the map ready, and Anders quickly transformed back into human form, then crouched down to touch the piece of the scepter to it. By the firelight, they all saw the knotwork around the edge of the map shift and wriggle and form the words they were expecting.

Lisabet leaned in and read them in a whisper.

"They might be crumbs, or scattered jewels,
For wolves they're home to mighty strength.
Through spray so high and wind so cruel,
Go search along the shortest length."

Everyone stared down at the map. Eventually Rayna spoke. "What?"

"Couldn't have said it better myself," Lisabet admitted.

"It sounds like somewhere wolves like," Anders whispered. "Somewhere on a coastline, if there's spray, maybe? Does that sound familiar, Lisabet?"

With an apologetic expression, she shook her head. "Maybe Hayn can help. Or if he can't, he has the whole library, he can research it for us."

"Right." Anders relaxed. Their uncle would know how to find out where wolves felt strong, or found strength, or . . . whatever the riddle meant.

"Let's get some sleep," Rayna said quietly. "Long flight in the morning." And then, after a pause: "Good work, you two."

Above them, Ellukka rumbled soft agreement.

251

"Thanks," said Anders, smiling at Lisabet. "It was pretty amazing. We'll all go back someday, when the sun's out and the weather's warmer."

"But for now," Lisabet said, "Rayna's right, we should rest."

They all settled down in the firelight, Anders with the map and the scepter piece tucked inside his cloak. He curled up beside Rayna, just as they had all their lives, tangled together beneath a blanket, as if they were once more hiding in an attic or stable, rather than sleeping beside a waterfall between a dragon's forelegs.

And as the stars twinkled gently above them, one by one they each fell asleep.

CHAPTER TWELVE

IT WAS NEARLY DINNERTIME THE NEXT DAY BY the time they reached Drekhelm. Rayna and Ellukka each took their turn landing in the Great Hall, and Anders was so relieved to climb down and stretch his cramped legs that at first he didn't register the group of dragons at the other end of the hall, too busy pulling off his twin's harness.

Both the girls transformed, and they hadn't missed the gathering—Anders followed their gazes and realized all the members of the Dragonmeet were gathered around their customary long table. All of the Dragonmeet, except for Leif.

Mylestom came immediately to his feet, and several others rose as well. Saphira wasn't wearing anything like her usual smile.

Leif, who had arrived and transformed first, walked

forward to address the Dragonmeet. "I was not aware we have a meeting scheduled," he said. "Has something happened?"

It was clear from the looks most of the dragons exchanged that they had not meant him to return while they were still speaking. When Leif turned his attention back to the Finskólars, his expression was grave. "Thank you for your company on our trip," he said, with all his usual courtesy. "We will resume classes in the morning."

Nobody felt easy as Anders and the others made their way from the Great Hall, leaving Leif and the Dragonmeet behind them. Theo peeled away almost immediately to head for the archives—he was hoping to find Hayn before the big wolf left his workshop for the night and ask him whether he could cast any light on the next riddle. Whether he could think of or knew how to find any places the wolves traditionally said gave them great strength.

Anders was dying to go with him, but though the guards on the archives were now used to Theo visiting— Leif had given him permission, as part of his research—if a wolf tried to go inside, even a Finskólar, they would insist someone ask the Dragonmeet for permission. He couldn't afford to risk drawing their attention just now, especially the way they'd looked when Leif and his students had landed.

So he went with the others as they collected food and retired to his and Lisabet's room, taking up their usual positions while they waited for Theo.

"I don't know what was happening in the hall," Mikkel said, "but it wasn't good."

"My father wouldn't meet my eyes," Ellukka said. "That's not normal."

"I have a horrible feeling," Lisabet said, "that they were talking about Leif."

It was the same feeling they all shared, and they lapsed into uneasy silence. Leif was the voice of reason on the council, the one who had stopped the dragons from throwing out Anders and Lisabet right after the wolves attacked. If his power was slipping, what would that mean for them and all the rest of the Finskólars? For the fragile truce between the wolves and dragons?

Anders didn't know about the others, but he was focused on silently willing Hayn to be in his workshop, to know the answers, to help them hurry toward the third piece of the scepter. More and more, it felt like time was running out.

As if to emphasize his point, Rayna shivered and stole one of the blankets from the end of his bed to wrap around her shoulders. He'd never seen her need so much extra warmth in the dragons' own stronghold before.

Everyone looked up when the door opened to admit Theo. Straight away, his face told them he had not been successful.

"Hayn wasn't there?" Lisabet asked.

Theo shook his head. "Worse," he said. "He was there, and he wasn't alone."

Anders sucked in a quick breath. "Did they see you?" he asked.

"No," said Theo. "But I think they know he's been talking to us. Or to someone, anyway. I only got there at the end of it, but four of the Wolf Guard were marching him out of his office, and right before they made it to the door, another one threw a blanket over the mirror."

"They wouldn't do that unless they thought he'd been using it," Lisabet said.

"This is bad," said Ellukka.

"This is really bad," agreed Mikkel.

"We have to assume he won't be back," said Lisabet. "If they sent four guards to take him wherever he's going, they don't think he's on their side. They won't give him another chance to speak to whoever they think he's speaking to."

"Then we have to find some other wolves to help us," Anders said. "We're not going to find what we're looking for here at Drekhelm. If it's anywhere, it will be in the library at Ulfar."

"Agreed," said Lisabet. "But it's getting harder and harder to get away from here without anyone noticing."

"And . . ." It was hard to say, but Anders made himself. "I don't know if our friends at Ulfar will help us. They barely, barely trust us."

"We don't have any choice but to ask them," Rayna said, but she slipped her hand into his, squeezing for comfort.

"I don't think we can talk Leif into leading a class trip to Holbard," Ellukka said with a dark smile, her concern for the Drekleid showing through.

"Then we have to find a way to get to Holbard ourselves," Lisabet said. "And convince Viktoria and Sak to help us. Without Hayn we're on our own, and the Dragonmeet's undermining Leif. It's up to us to do something, and it has to be soon. It has to be tomorrow."

"Can it wait even that long?" Mikkel asked, biting his lip.

"I think it has to," Lisabet replied. "You've just flown all the way from the waterfall. You can't fly on to Holbard tonight, you need to rest." Reluctantly, the dragons all nodded. "And we're going to have to find a way to speak to our friends," she said. "It's difficult to get in and out of Ulfar. When Anders and I were trying to find Rayna, we had to wait until our rest day to get outside. You can't just come and go like dragons do here at Drekhelm. Sakarias and Viktoria got out to see us the day we got the map, and they probably got in a lot of trouble for it. We'll have to hope they can do it again. But first, they'll have to know we're looking for them. Let's all get some rest, and Anders and I will try and think of a way to get in contact with them."

They parted ways, the four dragons leaving to take their plates back to the kitchen and head for bed.

Anders and Lisabet talked long into the night, pulling together worse and worse plans, and discarding each one in turn. The memory of their last visit to Holbard weighed heavily on them—the extra guards, the chill in the air, the sense of a city so wrapped up in tension that anything could happen. The walls of Ulfar had never seemed so high as now, when they were outside them.

*　*　*

By the next morning they had the beginnings of a plan, but no chance to share it with the others at breakfast. Nico and Krissin had taken up their place right beside the group's table again, and this time they had company. Among the adults in the breakfast room was Torsten, and he eyeballed Anders and Lisabet for a long moment as he walked over to join Nico and Krissin.

"They're not even pretending to support Leif," Mikkel whispered, fuming. "And they're Finskólars!"

"We're not even pretending we like Torsten," Ellukka pointed out.

"But Torsten's against their own classmates," Mikkel replied, his voice low and fierce. "Finskólars stick together."

"Don't be overheard," was all Lisabet said, spooning up her porridge as if nothing was out of the ordinary. Anders tried to follow her example, though his stomach was turning flip-flops even thinking about the day ahead.

They had no chance to tell the others what they had in mind once they got to class either. This time the disruption wasn't Nico and Krissin, but rather almost every member of the Dragonmeet, filing in the door in ones and twos to interrupt Leif every time he began to work with any of the students. Clearly there had been important discussions while he was away—and just as clearly, going away had been a miscalculation. *It would be just their luck,* Anders thought, *if the Dragonmeet finally managed to make a decision right when it was least convenient.*

At lunchtime, Leif simply gave up. "I think our work has been disrupted enough today," he said, with a sigh. "There's no need to return after you've eaten. If you wish to take your lessons elsewhere, please do so. If you would like the afternoon off, then please enjoy the time. We will attempt to resume classes tomorrow."

Everyone filed out in worried silence, and Anders and his friends grabbed sandwiches and retired to the map room, gathering together on the far side of it and keeping their voices down, in case Nico and Krissin had managed to work out where they were and were listening at the door.

"We have an idea about how to get a message inside to our friends," Lisabet said. "Ellukka can pretend she's come from Sakarias's family's village and deliver a letter to him. We'll have to hope they're willing to answer and to help us."

"If we go now, do you think there's a chance we could get back before dinner?" Rayna asked, not sounding very hopeful.

"Not really," Anders admitted. "We don't know how quickly he'll send his reply. And then, if he and the others will help us, it will take time to find the information we need, though Lisabet has some ideas on where they could look in the library."

"It's going to take a *lot* longer sending people in instead of doing it myself," Lisabet said with a grimace.

"Lisabet's kind of our library expert," Anders explained. "Anyway, by the time we get a note in and out, and meet them, explain what we want, they find it, and they tell us the answer . . . someone here at Drekhelm is going to have missed us. Maybe everyone. So we think that if we can find the answer in Holbard, we need to go straight to where the piece of the scepter is hidden. And maybe even the place after that, if there's a fourth piece. Once the Dragonmeet knows we're gone, it might not be safe to come back until we've found the Sun Scepter *and* used it."

Everyone's faces were grim. But it was clear nobody had a better idea.

"It'll be dangerous in Holbard, spending all that time there," Ellukka said. "They have posters up with your faces on them, so we'll have to stay almost completely on the rooftops."

"It's a risk," Anders agreed. "The wolves are on edge— the whole city is. But it's all we can do."

Theo nodded slowly. "Mikkel and I will cover as long as we possibly can," he said. "We might make it through to breakfast tomorrow, you never know."

"We'll try," Mikkel promised. "The longer we can buy you, the longer before anyone tries to come after you, or they alert their spies in the city to look for you."

"Are we agreed?" Lisabet asked. One by one, everyone nodded. "Then let's not waste any time," she said. "Sooner there, sooner we can get started."

"Can't be that much colder in Holbard than it is here," Ellukka said, trying to sound cheerful. But everyone was feeling it, even the wolves. Despite Hayn's stalling, the Snowstone was in full effect now—one of the other wolves Hayn had told them about must have found the augmenter she needed. Which meant Sigrid's attack was only a matter of time.

Anders couldn't help wondering if Sigrid wanted to get Lisabet back when she eventually attacked the dragons, or whether she wanted to exile her. He was sure Lisabet was wondering the same thing, but her expression was resolute as they gathered up what they needed and crept out of Drekhelm, and farther down the mountain. This time they used the harnesses, which meant they could afford to pack warm cloaks for all four of them to sleep in, food, and better disguises. Still, it was a risky business.

Rayna launched off the side of the mountain, and Anders barely noticed the view beneath them as he pulled his cloak around him to keep away the wind, staying down low to her body for shelter. He went over every scenario he could imagine as they flew, turning each one over and over, trying to plan for different disasters. In the end, he knew something would still happen that they hadn't expected.

* * *

The sun was setting by the time they neared Holbard, but there was still enough light that they needed to land a fair ways outside the city and go in on foot. They stowed the harnesses and some of their supplies in a clump of bushes that would mostly keep any rain off, and they were on their way.

If anything, there were even more guards around the edge of Holbard than there had been before. This time, at least, the children were prepared. They had good cloaks and hoods, Lisabet had a staff for her old-lady act, Anders had a bag wrapped around his front that looked like he had a baby in a sling—since everyone knew the wanted children didn't have any babies with them—and Rayna had joined Lisabet, streaking her black curls gray with a handful of flour.

They all kept their heads down as they made their way past the wolves up on the boxes and the wanted posters with their faces on them, then ducked into the same alleyway they had used last time. One at a time Anders helped boost the others up onto the familiar rooftops, then climbed up after them, and they set off. Their goal this time was Ulfar Academy.

Ulfar was a little north of the center of the city, and they'd come in through the west gate again, so there was quite a lot of ground to cover, but they made excellent time. They had to climb down only a few times, when they couldn't find planks to cross from one set of buildings to another. Each time they hurried across the street, heads down, and Anders realized they were matching everyone around them. The cold weather and the guards on every street corner had subdued all the citizens of Holbard.

Dark was falling rapidly, and Lisabet shifted to wolf form to listen better—and smell carefully—for any of the Wolf Guard that might be patrolling the rooftops. She was sure there were still some at the Wily Wolf, which was the highest point in the city, and they spotted a few other patrols in the distance, carefully detouring around them.

Eventually they reached Ulfar, and Anders carefully helped Ellukka climb down into an alleyway across the street from the Academy and the barracks' huge gates. "Ready?" he said quietly.

"Ready," she said, her nerves showing. It was one thing to make friends with two wolves. It was quite another to march up to the gates of their headquarters and ask to be let in. "Wish me luck."

He watched from the shadows as she flipped her plaits over her shoulders and walked across to the gate like she owned the place. She spoke with the two guards at length, occasionally pointing to the northwest, in the direction of Sakarias's family's village. There was a lot of emphatic nodding, and quite a lot of gesturing. And eventually one of them held out his hand.

Ellukka gave him the letter—Lisabet had sealed it with wax, which was a little too fancy for a village like Sakarias's, but worth the risk, they thought, as the adult wolves probably wouldn't break a private seal before giving it to him. And then she turned and left, one of the wolves tucking the letter inside his coat behind her.

"Done," she said as she reached Anders, far enough into the shadows that the guards couldn't see them. They climbed up to the rooftop where the others were waiting. "I tried to get them to fetch him," Ellukka said, "but they seemed kind of paranoid right now."

"Wonder why," Lisabet said, with a faint smile. "They'll give it to him?"

Ellukka nodded. "And they said if there's a return letter, come back after breakfast tomorrow and they'll have it for me. He's not allowed out since it's not a rest day. Security's tight."

"Then I guess we settle in for the night," said Rayna. "Can't sleep at the Wily Wolf, so let's find a stable or something and get warm, have something to eat. We'll know if they're going to help us tomorrow morning."

They picked their way across the rooftops to one of Anders and Rayna's old haunts, though they'd never stayed the night there when they could go to the Wolf instead. The four of them climbed in through the window of a loft belonging to another inn and made themselves comfortable among the piles of hay.

"Nobody will find us here?" Ellukka asked, passing out cheese sandwiches she'd stolen from lunch.

"Not as long as we're out early in the morning," said Rayna. "I checked downstairs, they have plenty of hay if any guests with hungry horses show up during the night."

They ate and lay down to sleep, but nobody had much luck drifting off. Anders lay awake for a while, his mind racing with all the things that could go wrong, and listened to the others' breathing.

Eventually Rayna spoke. "Do you think they'll help you?"

"Do you think they *can*?" Ellukka added.

That was the question, Anders realized, that they had to answer on a much larger scale. So much had happened on both sides—so many years and layers of misunderstandings, and of truly harmful words and deeds. Even before the deaths of his parents, things had been tense between Drekhelm and Ulfar.

Ultimately, could either side forgive a grudge they could barely remember the start of?

"They're our friends," Lisabet said quietly. "I'd always

have said nothing could come between us, but . . . it was a very big thing."

Anders was about to reply, though he hardly knew what he was going to say, when Rayna cut him off. "Anders," she whispered, suddenly very still. "Do you see that up there in the window? Don't move."

Everyone froze, and Anders kept his head still as he turned his eyes to look over at the window. It was so dark outside now that only the stars told him where the gap was. And the longer he looked, the more he saw—until he realized there was a small silhouette in the window.

It was a cat. And as its ears pricked up and its head tilted in a particular way, he realized it was a cat he knew very well.

Kess had often slept with him and Rayna for warmth, and one of the worst moments since Anders's transformation had been the morning he'd found her again, only to have her hiss and spit, and run from him in fear, smelling the wolf on him. He'd told Rayna about it at Drekhelm, and they'd both worried about her since.

But now, somehow, Kess had found them.

"There's some ham in that bag by your hand," Rayna whispered.

Anders groped for it without looking and found a bit to hold between two fingertips. Then, very slowly, he sat up. He could make out Kess's eyes gleaming faintly in the dark now, and he knew her little nose would be twitching as she smelled the ham. "Kessie girl," he whispered, holding it out to her. "It's just us. I know we smell funny, but we're safe."

"Come on, Kess," Rayna crooned behind him, pushing up on her elbows.

They all held their breath, and slowly, slowly, Kess leaned forward. Then in a sudden movement she jumped down from the window, scampering across the hay to plant her paws on Anders's outstretched arm, and nip the ham from between his fingers. Waiting for the sharp sting of her claws, he gently stroked her back as she chewed. Instead, he got the low rumble of her purr. "Hey, Kess," he whispered, happiness brimming up inside him. "Rayna, she's so skinny, I can feel her ribs."

"Kess," Rayna scolded, leaning in to offer the cat another piece of ham. "Did we feed you so much you forgot how to hunt? Or are you just a lazy cat?"

Kess meowed, as if to say she was nothing of the sort, but simply deserved to be fed, and Rayna giggled.

"Are you going to introduce us?" Ellukka asked, her smile audible in her voice.

"Ellukka, Lisabet, this is our cat, Kess," Rayna said, in the most formal of tones. "Kess, Ellukka is a dragon and

Lisabet is a wolf, but try not to hold it against them."

They took turns feeding pieces of their food to the little black cat, who had clearly decided that although she'd prefer they smelled the way they used to, she was pleased to see her friends again, and to make new acquaintances. After all, she lived in Holbard—it wasn't as though she'd never smelled a wolf before. She just hadn't been expecting Anders to smell like one.

When Anders finally lay down again, Kess in a purring ball between him and Rayna, he found he could get some sleep after all.

* * *

His nerves came back in full force the next morning, as he watched Ellukka walk up to the Ulfar gates again. She'd looked a little ragged when they'd woken—even he and Lisabet could tell the city was cold, and wind had gotten into every possible crack in the stable overnight, as if it was seeking them out.

He watched from his position in the shadows as she spoke to the guards, who stood alert and unfriendly, watching everyone who passed by as though they might be a threat. They looked so much taller than Ellukka, and the conversation seemed to take far too long, stretching his nerves thin. But eventually she accepted something from them and walked back the way she'd come. It was a return letter, also sealed in wax.

"Sakarias went along with it," Ellukka reported, as Anders unsealed the letter. "The guards said to let his mother know that Ulfar was thinking of her."

Lisabet and Rayna were already climbing down from the roof, and their feet hit the ground just as Anders opened the letter. He passed it to Lisabet, who would read it quicker, but that didn't prove very important—the note turned out to be short.

"*Come to the northwest corner of the Academy wall,*" Lisabet read. "*Hurry.*" She looked up, grinning. "They're going to get us inside, I'll bet my tail. You'll have to come too, Anders, just in case your family bloodline's somehow needed."

"What do we do if it's a trick?" Ellukka asked, though the four were already drawing up their hoods and joining the early morning bustle, making their way around the Academy walls, which towered above their heads. Rayna had Kess tucked inside her coat, which she'd buttoned up to make a sling for the cat. Kess seemed happy with this arrangement.

"It won't be a trick," Anders said, confident. "If they didn't want to help us, they just wouldn't answer. But they wouldn't trick us. I can't imagine Sak and Viktoria doing that."

"I hope you're right," muttered Rayna, as they arrived at the corner. "Now what?"

A whisper came from overhead. "Up here!" Their heads all snapped back as one, and there was Sakarias peeking over the wall. "Quick, while everyone's at breakfast," he said, glancing back inside the Ulfar grounds.

Anders wove his fingers together to make a step for Lisabet and boosted her up. Sakarias helped drag her the rest of the way, and then passed her over the wall to someone. Ellukka boosted Anders, hefting him up until Sakarias could grab his hands. Anders clambered over the wall, dropping down to the other side, where he found Viktoria, Jai, and Mateo waiting. Jai was white as a sheet with worry, running their hand through messy red hair as they glanced up at the corner where Det could be seen keeping watch over the main courtyard, ready to signal trouble. Mateo looked much as he always had, tall and broad and placid, but he was watching for a signal from Det as well.

"Thank you," whispered Lisabet.

"You better be telling the truth," Sakarias said, as sternly as Anders had ever heard him, outside of a discussion ranking the Academy's desserts. And he took dessert *very* seriously. "We're trying to do what we think Hayn would want. He's locked up, but Professor Ennar won't hear anyone say anything bad about him, and we think if we're going to trust anyone, it's her. And your letter promised . . ."

Jai finished for him. "You're our friends, we're trusting you won't hurt us."

"We won't," Anders promised. "We only want to keep the balance."

"Let's go," said Viktoria. "It won't be long until everyone's coming out of breakfast and going to class. We need you gone by then."

Jai took off their cloak and wrapped it around Anders's shoulders, and Viktoria was doing the same thing with hers for Lisabet, hiding their clothes underneath, since they weren't in Ulfar gray anymore. It was another uncomfortable reminder of the distance between them and their friends.

"Keep in the middle of the group," said Viktoria, as the six of them moved off. "Try to blend."

Det joined them as they passed him, white teeth flashing against his dark-brown skin as he shot Anders one of his easy grins. "If Sak was snoring that loud, you could have just switched rooms," he said in his easy Mositalan accent, putting himself between Anders and the gate guards. "I know he was a messy roommate, but you didn't have to run away over it."

"Hey!" Sakarias protested, but there wasn't any heart in it. Det's words were the first any of the wolves had offered without an edge of suspicion, and Anders was more grateful for the trust than he knew how to say. Perhaps Det could see things differently than the others because he'd grown up outside Vallen, without stories of wolves and dragons from the day he was born. In the end Anders didn't say anything, but he tried to find a smile for Det, even though he knew it was weak.

Lisabet was whispering with Viktoria and Mateo about which aisle she wanted to try first, and when the group entered the library, Mateo peeled off to walk straight over to the librarian. She looked up, surprised to see students at this hour. "Did you all forget to do your homework?" she asked, amused.

"Something like that," Mateo said. Anders could hear him as they hurried toward the back of the library. Mateo was big and strong and always looked calm, and some people thought he wasn't clever just because he was quiet. Anders knew better than that, but the other boy was using that impression to his advantage with the librarian, talking in circles, pretending not to understand her answers, and keeping her completely diverted from the rest of the group.

When they reached the aisle they wanted, Det and Viktoria took up guard positions at each end of it, and Lisabet, Sakarias, Anders, and Jai made their way down the shelves. Lisabet issued quiet orders, and they all pulled down the books she wanted, laying them out in a row on the ground so she could crawl along it, opening each in turn and flicking through it.

Anders had always known Lisabet was clever, but now she was moving at the speed of lightning, flicking through pages, darting back and forth between books, comparing paragraphs, murmuring to herself under her breath. Looking for the places the wolves considered their greatest sources of power.

"Almost all of them are in the north," she said, focusing on one book, which had a map of the top part of Vallen. "Makes sense, that's where it's coldest."

Anders kneeled down beside her, laying out Drifa's map so they could compare it to the one in the book. Sakarias and Jai joined in, helping point out the places that showed up on both.

"It has to be one of these," Lisabet said. "It wouldn't be hidden in a place that isn't even marked on the map."

"What wouldn't be hidden?" Sakarias whispered.

"An artifact that will help keep the weather even, we hope," Anders said quietly. "Not too hot, not too cold. Safe for everyone. We don't want to help anyone win, we just want to keep us all safe."

Sakarias looked like he wanted to argue, but Lisabet leaned down to the page. "The riddle says 'through spray so high and wind so cruel,' so one of these places on the coast . . ."

"Here." Suddenly, Anders saw it. "Look, the Chelle Islands, off the coast in the very northeast. The riddle says 'they might be crumbs, or scattered jewels,' we haven't been paying enough attention to that bit. That's exactly what the islands look like. And they have lots of coast, lots of spray, and they'd be windy, out there in the middle of the sea. Is there anything in the book?"

Lisabet was already flicking through the pages. In a soft, excited voice, she read out the entry when she found it: "It says, *The Chelle Islands, also historically known as the Sainelle Islands, from the Old Vallenite word for "wayfarer," "adventurer," or possibly "discoverer," were home to colonies of wolf scholars in centuries past. They located their bases in the islands because of the high natural concentration of essence there. Essence is the natural force channeled into artifacts to imbue them with magic, and—'*

Yes, yes, we know this bit, what else? *'Although the islands have been abandoned for centuries due to their unreliable weather and difficult living conditions, they are considered an important and powerful part of the Ulfar pack's history.'*"

"'Home to mighty strength,'" Anders said, echoing the riddle. "That's the place."

"You're making absolutely no sense," Jai told them, peering down at the book. "But this is what you need?"

"This is it," said Lisabet, standing to start putting the books back on the shelves. "Let's go."

They were quiet as they walked past Mateo and the librarian, who barely spared them a glance—she was busy drawing Mateo a diagram now, a hint of desperation in her tone, as he nodded slowly. Out in the hallway they could hear the distant sounds of the dining hall emptying, and they hurried in the other direction. Sakarias had chosen their meeting place well—they were around the back of the Academy buildings, hidden from almost everyone, and if they made good time they'd get over the wall without anyone spotting them.

Anders spoke quietly as they made their way outside, and around the building. "Is my—" He bit his tongue. He'd almost said "my uncle." That was how he thought of Hayn now. "Is Hayn okay?"

"We don't know," said Det, soft and worried. "We

heard he's shut in his rooms, but you know he doesn't teach our year, so we're just getting rumors. We tried asking Professor Ennar, and she said we should keep our noses out of trouble, but she looked really worried."

"Speaking of rumors," said Jai, just as soft, "they're saying the artifact we stole from Drekhelm is making it colder. That Sigrid has a plan."

Anders and Lisabet exchanged a long look. "She does," Anders said. "And we think her plan is an attack. If that happens, wolves will die too."

Mateo jogged up to join them, adding his bulk to their protection. "Well, that's going to take a while to live down," he muttered. "Get what you needed?"

Anders nodded, but Det was speaking. "Perhaps we would be in danger if Sigrid had us attack the dragons. But if we don't, they'll attack us first."

"No!" Lisabet insisted. "That's exactly what we're trying to prevent."

"Lisabet . . . ," said Sakarias, doubtful.

"She's right," said Anders. "Whatever you think about Lisabet's ideas about dragons, it's a lot more complicated than we thought. A *lot*."

Lisabet's lips were pressed together in a thin line, and she looked down. "You'd think that of everyone, I'd be the one who could figure out where she'd hide it," she said quietly. "But I have no idea. I don't know her as well as I thought I did."

Before anyone could reply, Jai grabbed Anders's arm, and the seven of them slowed to a stop as two adult guards rounded the edge of the building, making their patrol. Anders kept his head down, hoping his gray cloak would mask him in the middle of the group.

"About time you were all in class, isn't it?" asked the senior of the two, a broad-shouldered woman with a slightly crooked nose, as if it had been broken sometime in the past.

"Just on our way," said Jai brightly.

"It's in the other direction," the woman said, raising one eyebrow, and everyone hesitated.

"We just have to check the results of our science experiment first," said Sakarias, as Anders silently urged him on, unable to speak himself for fear he'd draw their notice. "It's really very interesting, we're studying the moss on the northern wall, and whether it—"

The guard held up her hand, to save herself from the rambling science explanation that was clearly coming, and then she simply waved them on.

Anders didn't speak again until they were safely past, but Sakarias's words had jogged something in Anders's mind. "Will you do one more thing for me?" he asked.

"What is it?" said Viktoria.

"It's not a small thing," he admitted. "Have you ever seen the puppet shows of the last great battle? They put them on in the streets sometimes, you pay a copper to watch."

"Sure," said Viktoria, her brows drawing together.

"They make fake dragonsfire in those," he said. "It's white and gold, like the real thing. I think they use salt to do it, and iron. Would you look it up, find out exactly how they do it?"

"You want us to make fake dragonsfire?" Mateo asked, blinking. "I thought we were trying to stop a war, not start one."

"I don't want you to make it," Anders said. "I want you to see if it leaves any traces, the salt. And then check where the big fire at the port was, and see if you can find anything."

The others gasped or slowly shook their heads.

"Anders," said Jai, their voice a whisper. "You can't possibly think . . ."

"I don't think," said Anders. "I just wonder. And it doesn't hurt to know."

They'd reached the wall then, and Mateo was preparing to boost Lisabet up, as Jai and Det looked over their shoulders to see if they were being observed.

"Be careful," said Viktoria, suddenly slinging her arms around Lisabet and squeezing her old roommate tight.

Lisabet squeezed just as tight. "We promise," she whispered. "And whatever we learn next, we won't let it be used to hurt you."

Mateo pushed Lisabet up the wall, and she disappeared over to the other side, to where Ellukka and Rayna were hopefully waiting to help with her landing.

Viktoria had the same hug for Anders, and then Sakarias was joining in, and then Jai. Det was keeping watch, but he reached back to rest a hand on Anders's shoulder, and Mateo nearly squished everyone when he wrapped his arms around the whole group.

And then Anders was up and over the wall and lowering himself down to his sister and friends on the other side, before he could find the words to tell his friends what their trust meant. What it was worth, that they could set aside what had happened even a little—something generations of wolves and dragons had failed to do.

But he knew the best way to repay them was to keep them safe.

It was time to head for the Chelle Islands.

CHAPTER THIRTEEN

A NDERS AND LISABET TOLD THE TWO DRAGONS what they'd learned as they made their way across the rooftops, hurrying toward the city wall. The morning crowds were still all abustle, which meant now would be the perfect time to get through the gate without the guards noticing them.

"Should we bring Kess?" Rayna asked, cuddling the cat close—Kess had her little black head sticking out of the top of Rayna's jacket, and looked perfectly content.

"She got so thin while we were away," Anders said. "It won't be that safe with us, but I think it's where she wants to be, and she might not be that safe here either."

They climbed down from the rooftops and made it out through the gate without incident, letting the crowd on the road slowly carry them away from the city. Ellukka's usually suntanned skin looked sallow, and even Rayna's warm brown skin was dull, both the dragons clearly affected by the cold. Anders was so busy worrying about that, that when someone fell into step with him, he didn't notice straight away.

"Anders."

Anders nearly jumped out of his skin, whipping around, and then remembering an instant too late that he should have pretended he didn't know who that was. *Mikkel* was walking beside him, dressed in a coat and cloak as well—Mikkel, who they'd left to cover for them back at Drekhelm, along with Theo. An instant later, he realized Theo was on Mikkel's other side.

"What are you doing here?" Anders whispered.

"They know," said Mikkel, without a trace of his usual smirk. "We ran out of excuses. They know you're up to something, and they know that we know what it is. It was either run for it and hope we could find you and help you, or let ourselves be locked up somewhere."

They all fell silent until they reached the bend in the road where it was time to peel away from the crowd and strike out across the countryside. Those who saw them go no doubt thought they were heading for some little farm or village. Soon they were far enough away to speak.

"They wanted to lock you up?" asked Ellukka, who looked sick at the thought.

"Torsten did," Theo said. "And some of the others were starting to agree. Don't worry, your father wasn't one of them. He wasn't happy, though."

"Do they have any idea what we're up to?" Lisabet asked.

"Not yet," Theo said. "Except that you two wolves are involved, and you wouldn't be keeping it a secret if it was good news for the dragons."

The silence was grim. Rayna was the one who broke it. "How did you get away, if they suspected you?"

"Some of the Finskólars helped us get out," Mikkel said. "Bryn and Ferdie. And maybe Isabina, though to be honest we weren't sure if she was trying to help us or was just so distracted by her mechanics that she got in everyone's way."

"It's good to have you with us," Ellukka said.

"Good to be here," Mikkel agreed. "Sparks and scales, Holbard's *huge*, I had no idea. We figured you'd have gone in the western gate, coming from Drekhelm, so we just waited outside it. Nobody knows our faces, after all. What are we doing next?"

Eventually they reached the spot where they'd hidden the harnesses and the rest of their supplies, and they all sat down to breakfast, catching Mikkel and Theo up on what they'd missed. Anders looked around at the group as he ate, feeling a strange mix of amazement that he'd found such friends and allies, and worry about the wolves and dragons at Ulfar and Drekhelm who were all now looking for them.

They seemed such a small group, to keep so many people safe.

They rolled out the map and leaned in to study it carefully. It wasn't very clear, but it seemed as though the smallest island was up in the very north of the chain.

"Farthest to fly, of course," said Rayna. "Assuming they're all marked on it, anyway."

"We'll be able to tell from the air," said Mikkel.

"It says to search along the shortest length," Lisabet mused. "So we find the smallest one and then . . . ?"

"Walk the length of it?" Anders suggested. "There are six of us. If we all stay in a row, we should find the piece of the scepter—assuming it's hidden there—even if we have to go back and forth more than once."

"And then we hope like anything that the final riddle is one we can understand without going to Drekhelm," Rayna said. "Or anywhere, really."

"Um," said Theo. "Is that a cat?"

They introduced Kess to Mikkel and Theo, finished their breakfast, and then packed up their things. Anders took Kess from Rayna before she transformed, and he wrapped a scarf around his body in a sling, tucking the cat inside. She seemed to like it there.

They all knew there was a chance that they'd be seen from Holbard if they took off—it might be early morning, but the sun was most definitely up. Still, the dragons all insisted they couldn't wait the whole day feeling this cold, and they were all worried that either the wolves or the dragons might find them if they didn't keep moving. They'd just have to take off as low as they could, fly as fast as they could, and hope.

They took to the air and followed the same route that Anders and Lisabet had with their class a few weeks before, on their way to the fateful campsite where they'd stolen Fylkir's chalice and made their run for Drekhelm. Anders saw the Trondain River pass underneath them, and after a few hours the green gold of the rippling plains gave way to the steep, sharp, black slopes of the Seacliff Mountains, snow blanketing their upper slopes. They plunged straight down into the sea on the dragons' right, and the air currents around them were perilous, one moment pushing them up, the next buffeting them sideways.

Ellukka was the strongest of all the dragons and was out in front carrying Lisabet. It was when they reached the familiar shores of the Skylake that she angled down, gently descending until she could land at the water's edge, flaring her wings to help her stop, and then folding them back as Lisabet jumped down and began removing her harness.

"Time for a rest," Lisabet called back, as Anders and Rayna landed and began to do the same. "And lunch!"

Anders looked back over his shoulder as Mikkel and Theo landed, then shifted quickly to boys crouching on the grass. Theo looked tired, but his spirits lifted when he saw the Skylake, and they all gathered together on its edge to eat a quick lunch. Mikkel even lit a small fire, heating up water to mix with cocoa powder and passing mugs around. Kess raced across the meadow in pursuit of a butterfly, not seeming to mind in the slightest that she'd been flying only a few minutes before.

They couldn't afford to break for long, though—they needed to reach the Chelle Islands by early afternoon, so they'd have time to seek out somewhere sheltered to sleep before dark.

"And," Mikkel said with a grimace as they packed up their things, put out the fire, and retrieved Kess, "by now the Dragonmeet is doing everything they can think of to look for us. So we'd better keep moving whenever we can. They could have some kind of locator artifact we don't know about."

Soon they were aloft once more. Anders saw the

coastal town of Port Tylerd pass beneath them, with its tall, white lighthouse sitting atop a thick stone base, painted so brightly it seemed almost to shine in the afternoon sun without the lamp even being lit. Anders didn't have much chance to admire it, though—by now they were over the northern coast of Vallen, and the winds were fierce.

He tucked himself down against Rayna's back, arching his body over where Kess was nestled inside her sling. As the young dragons followed Ellukka out across the sea, freezing-cold winds buffeted them, tearing at their wings, at Anders and Lisabet, roaring around them. Anders tried to lift his head a few times to check on how the others were doing, but he couldn't manage it for long. He could only look straight ahead, to where Ellukka was scrambling through the wind like she was swimming.

He could also drop his gaze and look downward, to where the islands were laid out in the deep, rich, dark blue of the sea just like jewels, or the crumbs the riddle had made them. Their sage-green shapes were jagged around the edges, each one as different from the others as a snowflake from its fellows. He saw one green shape like a huge letter C, fishing boats huddled inside its harbor, waiting out what was clearly now a burgeoning storm.

He saw others that were longer, or flatter, some with a single high peak that seemed to plunge straight from its top down into the sea, as if the mountain continued underwater.

As the sky turned gray, he began to wonder if they should turn back before the storm caught them, but he had no way to tell anyone what he was thinking.

And then, after what felt like a lifetime—with the sun already dipping toward the horizon—they reached the top of the chain of islands. The final two lay side by side, and beyond them, nothing but ocean, all the way to the great ice of the north. The island to the left was large, hills rising and falling, trees nestled between them.

But the little island to the right was tiny. The smallest, without a doubt. It had steep, rocky cliffs on every side, leaving not one spot where a boat could safely dock. The only way to approach this island was from the air. *Had the dragons brought the wolves here, to their place of power?*

The top of it wasn't rocky at all, though. It was shaped like the inside of a bowl, one end higher than the other. The ground was perfectly smooth and green, marred by not one tree, not one shrub, not one stone. Just perfect grass.

But tucked into the higher side of the bowl was one thing to disrupt the flawless stretch of green—a small white house with a green grass roof. It was recessed into the slope, so only the front wall, the front door, and the windows were visible, the glass glinting for an instant as a hint of sun made it through the clouds.

The dragons started to descend toward it, the wind only growing worse as they lost altitude, twisting around the islands and the coastline behind them, vicious and unpredictable. Mikkel and Theo shot past Anders and Rayna, Theo veering dangerously off course, Mikkel forced to throw himself to one side at the last minute to avoid a collision.

Rayna was arrowing too fast, far too fast, toward the ground, and Anders wrapped himself around Kess and ducked his head, every muscle tense. At the very last instant, just as he was sure they were about to smash into the grass, he felt the shift of muscles in her back as she flared her wings and managed to slow them down. They landed with several tripping, bumpy steps, and then they were still.

The wind seemed to swirl around inside the cauldron of the island, nipping at them from every direction, and Anders uncurled cramped arms and legs, jumping down from Rayna's side to drag off her harness as quickly as he could, so she could transform. Kess stuck her head out of her sling once, yowled her disapproval, then stuck it straight back inside again. Anders couldn't blame her.

Mikkel and Theo had already changed, and Mikkel

staggered over to help Anders with the harness. Anders felt incredible, invigorated by the cold, as if he could run the length of the island, but his friend was clearly feeling just the opposite, his face white, his hands fumbling.

They dragged the leather straps clear, and Rayna shifted back to human form, staying crouched on the ground. Anders hurried over and pulled his cloak off, wrapping it around her shoulders for extra warmth, and helped her to her feet. She was suffering as badly as the other dragons, and the twins hurried toward the house after the rest of the group.

They arrived just as Ellukka and Lisabet were pulling on the door—it was swollen with damp and wedged shut, but as they both tugged, suddenly it gave way, sending both girls stumbling back in surprise. All six children bundled inside, and Anders hauled the door closed behind them and then turned to see what kind of place they had found.

They were in a large room, lit only by what gray sunlight made it in through the salt-encrusted front windows. To their right was a large fireplace, surrounded by thick, squashy chairs that were covered in cushions, some of them losing their stuffing. To their left was a long-abandoned kitchen, dull pots and pans hanging from the ceiling above a long counter, an empty wood-burning stove behind it, with a pipe that led up to the ceiling and disappeared through the hill.

Down the middle of the room ran a long table, still strewn with books and papers, as if whoever had left here had intended on coming back to resume their work. The books were everywhere, stacked on the ground and crammed into shelves lining the walls, and a series of doors suggested the house led farther back into the hill.

"We need a fire," Lisabet said, stepping away from the dragons, who were huddled in a small group, almost too cold to think. "The wind's freezing, we're surrounded by cold water, this place is terrible for anyone who needs to be warm. I'll start one in the fireplace. Anders, you try the stove."

Anders set down Kess, who scampered away to explore, then hurried over to the stove, crouching in front of it and pulling open the black iron door. There was a basket of kindling stored beside it, and blocky brown squares of peat. He raised his voice to call to Lisabet as he found two pieces of flint connected by a piece of string, hanging on a hook beside the stove. "The wolves might have used this place centuries ago, but I don't think it was abandoned that long ago. More like ten years than a hundred. There's not enough dust, and there's still fuel here."

Theo called out from where he was standing by the table, his voice shaking as he shivered. "And th-there are dates on some of these p-papers. Someone was coming here."

"Our mother, hopefully," said Rayna, tugging both her cloaks tighter around her. "And hopefully she left something behind."

Anders had the feeling Drifa could have left all kinds of things behind—after all, the map was showing them where to find the pieces of the Sun Scepter because that's what they'd asked about, but Hayn had said she'd hidden many of her most valuable artifacts. He wondered what else might be tucked around the house, if only they knew to look for it.

Soon enough, he and Lisabet had the two fires going, and the room was beginning to warm up. The water pump in the kitchen still worked, so they had water boiling on the stove, and Lisabet and Mikkel made toasted cheese sandwiches out of some of the extra supplies the boys had brought when they joined the others.

It had fallen dark outside, but the fires and lamps inside the hidden cottage cast a glow over the room, and everyone began to cheer up as the temperature rose—even Lisabet didn't mind a little more warmth. A little exploration yielded a bathroom with plumbing that seemed to still be working. There was even hot water—pipes ran through the wall behind the stove to heat the water up, then poured it out of a spout and into the bath. They found a room set up like a scientific laboratory and finally three bedrooms, though Ellukka and Anders dragged the mattresses out to the living room, so they could all sleep together in front of the fire, where it was warmest.

"Well," said Theo, sometime later. They were all sitting on the mattresses or in the squashy chairs in front of the fire, drinking cocoa and eating toasted cheese sandwiches, except for Kess, who had some roast beef in hers. "This place was once used for research, I'm sure of it. There are books on all kinds of things. It's so cold up here, it feels like wolves could think faster and sharper here than anywhere else in the world. Maybe that's why they came."

"If they did, dragons must have flown them in," Anders said, echoing his earlier thought. "There's no way a ship could dock. Perhaps Drifa brought wolves here, and that's how she knew about it."

"There are artifacts here," Lisabet said. "Odd ones, I can't tell what most of them do."

"I'd like it," Mikkel said, "if it wasn't so cold. We'll need to keep warm tonight, so we're well enough to fly out in the morning, assuming we can find the next piece of the scepter."

"I wish I knew exactly what the scepter did," Theo said, looking around at the piles of books. "I mean, it'll make it warmer, but I don't know how. Changing the weather is a big thing to do."

"Whatever you do, it can affect somewhere else," Anders said, remembering the artifacts he'd seen in the Skraboks back at Ulfar, when he'd first been searching for a way to find Rayna. "If you make it rain in one place, you might cause a drought somewhere else."

"I wish we knew what heat would do," Theo replied.

"We have to risk using it, even if we're not quite sure what will happen," Lisabet said. "Hopefully, it's just like the Snowstone—the temperature around where it is changes. So if we set them against each other, they should cancel each other out. Hopefully."

After they'd eaten, the dragons stayed gathered around the fire, each taking a turn to use the bath, their smiles growing as they got the heat all the way into their bones. Meanwhile, Anders and Lisabet took a lamp each and started hunting for the next piece of the scepter, hoping it might be inside the house itself. Now that they'd seen the island, it didn't seem possible Drifa would have risked hiding anything on the smooth expanse of grass outside. After two discoveries, they knew what they were searching for—a cylinder about the length of their forearms, wrapped in waxed canvas, tied with string.

"I'm hoping the main trial was getting here," Lisabet said, as she looked under the bed frame in one of the bedrooms, while Anders searched the high shelves. "And now it'll just be a matter of looking."

"I think so," he agreed. "She wasn't trying to make it impossible for us to find them. Just difficult for anyone who didn't have a clue. It should be somewhere in here."

They were nearly ready to give up when finally they reached the laboratory at the back of the house. It had a fireplace, but it hadn't been lit, and they could see their breath in the air. Lisabet started going through the equipment on a square table, and Anders held up his lamp, studying the shelves, trying to put himself into the mindset of a dragon. Where would his mother think was a good place to hide something?

Then he took a closer look at the fireplace. It wasn't just a fireplace—it had metal hooks set into the wall around it, ready to swing pots of different sizes out over the flame, to heat or melt whatever was inside. That was as close to a forge as Anders had seen so far inside the house. And Drifa had been a dragonsmith.

He tried to picture her at work here, but he didn't know what she'd looked like. Judging by how he and Rayna looked, and the stories that she'd been half Mositalan, she'd probably had about the same brown skin as they did, and black hair too.

She would have been strong if she was a smith. If he'd gotten his tallness from their father, perhaps Rayna had gotten her shortness from their mother.

He wondered if his father had ever been here, or if Hayn had visited this place. Would a dragon have brought them there? Maybe even Drifa?

He pulled the biggest pot away from the wall, easing its hook around so the pot swung back and forth. What kind of thing went in it? Metal? He held up his lantern to take a look inside, and he stared as he realized something was still in the pot.

It was a very familiar shape.

"Lisabet, I've got it!"

He reached inside, closing his fingers around the wrapped-up piece of the scepter, and pulled it out triumphantly. His mother had left it just where she'd worked, of course.

He and Lisabet ran through to the main room where the others were waiting, and they greeted him with cheers when he held it up. Quickly they untied the string and revealed another piece of the wooden scepter, wrapped in bands of metal as the others had been, engraved with runes.

They unfolded the cloth map and laid it out on the floor, the silvery threads glinting in the firelight. Anders touched the newest piece of the scepter to the map, and they watched as the knotwork drawn around the edge wriggled and twisted and formed new words.

As always, Lisabet leaned down to read them out.

"The final piece is hidden high,
Concealed in the forbidden sky.
By name it is the safest place,
But know you well that danger waits."

"The final piece! We were right!" Rayna said, scooping up Kess and holding her aloft like a trophy until the cat meowed indignantly to be let down.

"We're nearly there!" Ellukka agreed, leaning down to read the words for herself.

But Anders was quiet, and eventually the others noticed, one by one turning to him with questioning eyes.

"I know where it is," he said. "It's somewhere high up, in the sky. Somewhere we're forbidden to go. We've heard its name plenty of times—somewhere that sounds like it should be safe. A haven. Cloudhaven."

They all stared at him in silence. *Cloudhaven. The legendary home of the first dragonsmiths, the highest point in Vallen.*

A place all dragons were forbidden to go, though nobody knew why.

"'But know you well,'" Rayna whispered, "'that danger waits.'"

CHAPTER FOURTEEN

THE NEXT MORNING THEY WERE ALL UP EARLY, preparing to leave. Anders had the same feeling as he'd had when they'd left Flic Waterfall—that there was so much here they could still discover, so many more stories that could be told. But they'd have to come back another time. Now there was no time to waste in getting to Cloudhaven.

"It's a dangerous route," Ellukka said. "We'll fly across the Uplands—that part's all right, it's mostly just shepherds out there, and I'm pretty sure they're used to seeing dragons from time to time—but then we have to cross the Icespire Mountains. We'll have to go high. It'll be long, windy, and cold."

"And north of Drekhelm," Mikkel said, with a grimace. "If they're keeping a lookout, there's a chance they'll spot us."

"We can't afford to take a longer path," Rayna said. "Not when we know they're probably already looking for us."

"Agreed," said Anders. Rayna had always been good at assessing risks, whether they were pickpocketing on the streets or trying to avoid the wrath of the Dragonmeet. Hopefully once they reached Cloudhaven itself, they'd be protected by the clouds that gave the mysterious peak its name. First, though, there was something he had to say to the others.

"Anders?" said Rayna, reading the look on his face.

"Before we go," he said, "there's something I've been thinking about. To do with what happens next, when we go after the final piece of the scepter."

They were all silent, gathering around, waiting for him to continue.

"I suppose what I want to say," he began, "is that once we start out, we can't go back. I mean, I know we can't go back already, the Dragonmeet's after us. But . . . what we're doing is more important than anything. To be honest, when I began, I was thinking about Rayna, about Lisabet, and then about the rest of you as I got to know you. I wasn't trying to do anything to change the world. I felt too small to do that. I just wanted to keep my part of it safe."

Small nods told him he wasn't alone in feeling that way.

"But now it's bigger than that," he continued. "Hayn's been arrested, Leif's being undermined by the Dragonmeet. Dragons are sick, and so are the people of Holbard. If the cold continues the wolves will attack eventually, and terrible things will happen to people on both sides—but things will get much worse even before then. It's not about how we keep ourselves safe anymore. It's about how we keep everyone safe."

"It has to be," Rayna said quietly, and the others made soft noises of agreement.

"So I think that means," said Anders, "that no matter what happens at Cloudhaven, we have to put getting the scepter before anything else. And then using it, no matter what happens to us."

"No matter what happens to any of us," Lisabet said softly, "the others have to use it."

"No matter what," echoed Ellukka, making the words a promise. And one by one, the others whispered them too. Quiet, determined, and—Anders knew now—of one mind, ready for whatever lay ahead.

* * *

They finished packing up their supplies, and Mikkel and Theo closed the door of the cottage firmly behind them while Anders and Lisabet helped Rayna and Ellukka with their harnesses.

"We'll be back," said Lisabet, looking at the door, echoing Anders's earlier thoughts. "One day. When this is over."

Anders didn't say what he knew both of them were thinking—that they only hoped that one day it *would* be over, and that they'd all make it out the other side.

The flight away from the island was as treacherous as the approach had been the night before, with icy winds snatching at Anders like so many fingers, determined to drag him from his sister's back and send him tumbling to the dark-blue sea far below. Eventually they reached the coast, and the big white lighthouse and small stone village of Port Tylerd, and they flew out across the Uplands.

Here the clouds cleared a little, and the golden green plains beneath them seemed to glow; silvery, mirrored streams ran across them in endlessly winding patterns, hills cast long shadows, tiny sheep and cows gathered together in flocks far below. But too soon—or perhaps not soon enough, to the tired dragons—the Icespire Mountains loomed up ahead of them, dark stone rising from the grassy plains like huge creatures shaking off their velvet cloaks and reaching for the clouds.

Anders could tell Rayna was weary—she hadn't slowed, but there was a different quality to her wing-strokes, as if she were pulling herself along like a tired swimmer—when they finally reached the far side of the peaks. Whether lookouts at Drekhelm had seen them or not, he didn't know.

Now they were approaching the permanent clouds that surrounded Cloudhaven, and the winds were falling away to a breathless quiet. Anders strained every sense as Rayna flew through the clouds, occasionally calling out in a fraction of her usual roar, and receiving replies from Mikkel, Theo, and Ellukka, though the others were all invisible in the perfect white, except for the occasional flicker of a nearby wingtip or tail.

The four dragons were flying as slowly as they could, the still air strangely dead around them—Anders realized he'd become used to the updrafts and downdrafts, the crosswinds and playful tugs of the weather. Flying was usually like swimming through moving water, but suddenly everything around them was thick and heavy. Everyone was being careful not to fly into one another, or worse, into the rock of Cloudhaven's spires, which must be somewhere inside the mist.

Just as Anders was beginning to wonder if they'd flown

past the spires—if they were about to come out the other side of the clouds having missed Cloudhaven altogether—something dark loomed up in front of them. It wasn't quite a mountaintop—it was an impossibly high pillar instead, at least as big in circumference as Drekhelm's Great Hall, or Ulfar's dining hall—the sides jagged enough to look natural, but far too steep to ever climb.

He thought for an instant he saw something like a staircase carved into one section, and then it was gone again, and he was holding on tight as Rayna angled up, up, up, heading for the top.

And then he saw the buildings.

Crammed on top of the huge natural pillar of rock, clinging to one another like they might fall off if they didn't hold on, were dozens of small buildings, each built from stone slabs, each topped by a domed roof. They looked like a crop of mushrooms all growing close together, except they were far too dignified for such a comparison. A couple were much larger, and the rest all clustered around them, each supporting the next, their windows just little black slits in the smooth stonework.

Rayna wheeled away to their right and followed the edge of what had to be Cloudhaven until the buildings gave way to a landing pad clearly designed for dragons. It was a large, smooth stone courtyard, though there was no wall around the edges to stop the careless from simply tumbling into nothing.

One by one the four dragons landed there, the fog swallowing up the sound of their claws hitting the stonework. Mikkel and Theo shifted back to human form immediately and came over to help with Rayna's and Ellukka's harnesses.

"This place is incredible," Lisabet whispered, dragging the leather straps along Ellukka's side and over her head. "Do the stories say anything about it being . . . like this?"

"The stories just say it's forbidden to come here," Mikkel replied, keeping his voice to a whisper as well. "It's so powerful here, though. The air is cold, but I can feel . . . something, deep under the rock."

Theo nodded beside him. "The Icespire lava is down there somewhere."

"But the air is so cold, and the mist is so strong, I still feel good too," Lisabet said. "This place is unique."

They stepped back, and Rayna and Ellukka both transformed, shrinking in a couple of heartbeats down to a pair of girls crouching, then pushing up to stand.

"We should keep moving," said Ellukka, as soon as she could speak. "If they saw us from Drekhelm, they could be on their way to get us right now. Mikkel, you and I are strongest, so we should fly patrol. If we keep moving, and listen carefully, perhaps we'll get some warning if anyone's coming."

The others agreed, keeping their voices low. The place was affecting all of them—Anders wasn't sure if it was the still, strange atmosphere or the fact that they were walking where every dragon story forbade them to go, but he felt it just as they did.

Ellukka and Mikkel walked over to the edge of the courtyard, preparing to transform and launch, and he watched them go.

Anders, Rayna, Lisabet, and Theo walked over to the huge door that led into the domed building straight off the courtyard. It was a dark, ancient wood, fitted perfectly with black metal hinges into an arch of gray stonework, pale moss clinging here and there to the surface of it.

Squinting up through the swirling mist, Anders could make out a single word carved into the archway above the door, the letters deep and clear:

CLOUDHAVEN

It took Anders and Rayna working together on one side and Theo and Lisabet on the other to pull open the huge metal bolts, but the doors swung open without a sound, as if they had been oiled only yesterday.

The chamber was dark, and as Anders took his first step inside, a faint glow appeared beneath his feet—he was standing on a metal plate, carved in runes. He drew breath to warn the others—of what he did not know—and suddenly the light snaked away from the place where he stood, running as fast as a blink out toward the far walls, tracing metal paths inlaid on the stone floor, each coming to life and glowing brightly.

The lines of light ran straight up the walls and all around the enormous hall, lamps came to life, bathing the place in a warm, golden, welcoming glow. The room was obviously designed to accommodate large numbers of people—there were tables and chairs, and a clear area where several dragons could fit without a squeeze. The place felt abandoned, perfectly empty, but despite being forbidden, not unfriendly.

There was only one door through which they could continue, and that was on the far side of the hall. None of the four spoke as they made their way across, motes of dust dancing in the light of the lamps, the room so large it swallowed up their footsteps rather than echoing them back.

The door was of the same dark wood as the last had been, but this one had no handle anywhere, and no visible means by which to open it. Instead, it had metal letters fixed to it, glinting in the lamplight.

COME NO FARTHER WITHOUT . . .
~ A TOKEN ~
~ TRUE BLOOD ~
~ TRUE PURPOSE ~

"What does any of that mean?" Theo whispered as they all gazed up at it.

"She must have thought we'd know," Rayna said quietly. "We probably would have, if she'd raised us."

Everyone was silent for a long moment, and then Kess mewed from her sling in Anders's chest, breaking the tableau.

"She's right," Rayna said. "We'd better just get on with it. Any ideas?"

"Let's look at it closely, see if there are any more clues," Lisabet suggested. "And think about what the words could mean."

"I wonder what kind of token you use to open the

door," Anders said, stepping forward. "I don't see a key-hole anywhere."

"It might not be a key," Theo said, leaning in to study the letters. "With artifacts, there are all kinds of ways to bring them to life. Usually you need something else that's an artifact, though, or a part of the larger creation. Or it's linked to a person, but that's probably the 'blood' bit, not the 'token' bit."

"So something forged?" Anders asked, looking down at himself as if something might appear.

"Usually," said Theo. "I mean, I'm only a few weeks into researching how dragons classify artifacts. Right now, I'm lucky if I can even work out what shelf they're on. Ideally we'd have ended up on this quest five or six years from now, but I do know that much. It would probably have at least one rune on it as well, the token."

"I can't . . . ," Lisabet started. Anders had never heard her sound so despairing. "I can't think of anything like that. Maybe we were supposed to gather up something from the house on the island. Or you were just meant to own it, because she would have given it to you, if she'd had time. But your mother never gave you anything."

Anders and Rayna both stiffened, their gazes snapping around to find one another.

"She did!" Anders said, as Rayna fumbled in her hair,

gave up with a growl of frustration, and doubled over as if she were bowing, presenting Anders with the top of her head.

"What?" said both Lisabet and Theo at once, staring at this peculiar display.

"Rayna's hairpins!" Anders said, guiltily ignoring his sister's yelps as he pulled first one and then the other out of her hair, being as careful as he could. "We never knew where they came from, but she's always had them. They've got runes on them."

"And they transformed with me that first time," Rayna said, holding her hand out for one. "When I lost all my clothes by ripping out of them, because I didn't have an amulet yet, *I kept the pins.*"

"I *thought* they were artifacts," Theo said excitedly. "I told you so in the archives, the day we found the mirror."

"Perhaps there's somewhere they fit into the door," Lisabet said, bending down to start searching from the bottom. "It wouldn't have to be big."

"Here," said Theo, pointing to a spot underneath the word *token* on the door. "Look, there's these two small slots, like an equals sign. They'd take hairpins."

Anders and Rayna both lifted their hairpins, holding them up to the slots, his on top and hers underneath. They looked like they would fit. "Runes facing in," he suggested.

As one, they pressed them into the shallow trenches in the door.

His fingertips tingled as they always did when an artifact filled with essence activated, and with a click somewhere deep inside it, the door swung soundlessly open, revealing a long hallway. One by one, dusty lamps along its length were coming to life, revealing door after door, and hundreds of strips of metal lining the stone floor and walls, as if turning the whole place into one enormous artifact.

They were in.

"True blood," said Lisabet, interrupting Anders's internal celebration.

"Huh?" He blinked at her. "Oh, the next thing on the list."

"Do you think it means, like, a pure dragon bloodline?" Rayna asked. "This place was built a long time ago, maybe that was possible back then."

"I don't know if any of us has that," Anders said with a frown. "Maybe Ellukka would come closest, she doesn't have any family in Holbard, or even outside the dragons, as far as I know."

"Maybe," said Lisabet, "it wants a descendant of the creator of this place, whoever that was."

"Or someone who worked here?" Theo suggested. "I mean, Drifa got in here to hide the piece of the scepter, and she left you two a way in, so that makes me think you'd have the right blood to get inside."

In the end, they decided the only option they had was to experiment. Theo and Lisabet each took one of Anders's hands, ready to pull him back to safety, and heart thumping, Anders prepared to take a step backward onto the first flagstone inside the tunnel. He had to hope they'd have time if things went wrong.

He took a look at each of the others, then stepped back, holding tight to their hands.

Nothing happened.

Everyone breathed out.

"Right," said Lisabet. "Let's see if Theo or I can make it in, just in case. We'd be helpful in the search." She politely wasn't saying that both she and Theo knew more about artifacts than either Anders or Rayna, she from her years of study, and Theo from his recent work as a researcher. But Anders had to agree.

Anders hovered behind Lisabet as Rayna and Theo took her hands. After a soft, nervous sound, she stepped back.

Instantly the flagstone beneath her foot crumbled to dust, and in less than a heartbeat she was standing on nothing at all. She screamed as Rayna and Theo yanked her back to safety, and Anders struggled to help without stepping into the emptiness, and in two heartbeats the whole thing was over. Anders blinked as the flagstone she'd been standing on started to re-form itself, the dust settling back into place and becoming rock, the metal strips laid into the stone all around it glowing softly.

"So just us two, then," said Rayna, into the silence that followed. They were equally cautious as she stepped in, but after a moment it was clear that the floor would permit her to stand behind Anders.

"Step three is true purpose," said Theo. "Maybe tell it what you want?"

Anders adjusted the satchel he was wearing over one shoulder—it held the map and the three pieces of the Sun Scepter—and raised his voice. "We're seeking the last piece of the Sun Scepter," he said, in what he hoped sounded like a confident tone.

At first, he thought nothing was going to happen. But then the strips of metal in the floor and the runes and lamps along the walls all dimmed, leaving the hall in almost complete darkness, lit only by the glow of the lamps in the entrance hall where Lisabet and Theo stood. Before Anders could voice his disappointment, the glow started to return. This time it was just one long strip of what had looked like iron, laid into the flagstone floor and carved with some of the most intricate runes he'd ever seen.

It had turned a pale blue and was leading away into the distance.

"I guess it's that way," said Rayna, with a nervous laugh.

"I hate to say it," Lisabet said, "but you should hurry. Just because Mikkel and Ellukka haven't sounded the alarm doesn't mean the Dragonmeet isn't on its way."

She was right. Anders carefully adjusted Kess inside her sling—she wanted to climb out, but he wasn't sure whether cats needed the right blood too, so they compromised on letting her stick her head out to see where they were going—and the twins set off following the blue strip of metal.

They walked past a long hallway of closed doors, and Anders couldn't help wondering what was behind them. But this wasn't the day for finding out, and they plunged on into the middle of Cloudhaven, following the path the place had laid out for them.

Eventually it took them up a flight of stairs, and then

another, and when they emerged at the top it was to find a room lit by natural light from the outside. The swirling fog was visible beyond the thick glass windowpanes—the glass was less even than Anders was used to, much older, and he thought perhaps it would be harder to see through. It was impossible to tell, though, with the ever-present clouds outside.

"This looks like someone's study," Rayna said, drawing him back to the room itself. There were piles of books everywhere, sketches and open notebooks, diagrams and pieces of half-finished artifacts hanging from hooks on the walls and from the high, domed ceiling. The glowing strip of metal that had led them here simply ended at the threshold. *This is the room*, it seemed to say. *It's up to you to figure out the rest.*

"Do you think she came here?" Anders asked quietly. "I mean, she must have once, if she was hiding the piece of the scepter, but . . ."

"But maybe this was *her* study," Rayna finished, when he trailed off. "Some of her things were at the cottage, but maybe she worked in lots of different places."

"We could learn so much about her," Anders said, the yearning tugging at his heart. "But let's find the scepter piece first."

They each took one side of the room, beginning a

methodical search through the stacks of books, lifting sheaves of paper to peer underneath them, scanning each pile of artifact parts in the hope of seeing the familiar cylindrical shape, perhaps wrapped in the usual waxed canvas and string. Anders was trying to move as quickly as he could, imagining angry dragons flying through the clouds toward them right now to find their friends waiting outside, but he dared not hurry too much, in case he missed what he was looking for among the clutter.

"Anders," Rayna said after a little while, a shake in her voice.

"Did you find it?" He looked up.

"Anders," she said again, still staring down at a spot on a desk.

He hurried over. The object of her attention wasn't the piece of the scepter. It was a charcoal sketch, executed by someone on a page torn from a notebook. At first, he thought the man in the picture was Hayn—he was big and broad-shouldered, with dark-brown skin indicated by a smudge of charcoal, and a neat black beard along a square jaw. But he was missing the designer's square-rimmed glasses, and there was something a little different about his face. The dimples were the same, though.

He was standing with an arm around a woman who looked a lot like an older version of Rayna. She wore her hair out, the tight ring of curls almost as tall as it was wide and long. She shared Rayna's cheeky, unrepentant grin, which the artist had captured perfectly. She had lighter brown skin than the man, and though she was a full head shorter than him, even with the hair, she looked fit and strong, as if she could do anything. The pair of them wore matching necklaces—discs of metal hanging around their necks on leather straps. Each of the discs was engraved with a tight spiral of runes.

"It's them," Rayna whispered, her voice so wobbly that Kess mewed her concern, wriggling a paw free of her sling. Anders carefully lifted her out, his hands shaking, and let her settle on Rayna's shoulders, where she could keep a closer eye on her girl.

"It's them," he agreed, resting one fingertip on the sketch. "Felix and Drifa."

"They look really happy," Rayna murmured. Then she sniffed and visibly tried to pull herself together. "Put it in your bag," she said. "We'll take it with us, we can look at it later. For now, we have to figure out where she put the scepter."

They both went back to work, and it was only a minute later when Rayna called his name again, this time in delight. "Anders, I've got it!"

She was brandishing the last of the four pieces,

scrambling to pull off the string and canvas. He ran over to her.

"Put it together," she said, passing it to him, her other hand lifted to make sure Kess stayed on her shoulders. The cat didn't know why they were so pleased, but she was celebrating by attacking one of Rayna's curls.

Anders pulled the other three pieces from his satchel. The top was easy, with its iron orb to mark it, and he quickly saw the order in which they'd screw together, from the flow of the metal strips that wrapped all around it. The thrill of assembling such an important artifact, here in the main workshop where its creator—their mother—had worked, ran through him.

As he screwed the last piece into place, he felt the familiar tingle of the essence awakening inside it. All the runes along it briefly glowed, then subsided. "I can feel how to use it," he said after a moment, wondering. "I never thought about how you'd activate it, but now I'm holding it, I can tell that it's . . . listening, I guess, is the best word. All I need to do is tell it what I want."

Rayna held out her hand, and he passed it to her. A moment later, her face lit up. "We're ready to use it," she said. "Let's go."

"One more thing," Anders said, turning back toward the door. "Cloudhaven," he said, as clearly as he could, though the nerves were making his throat feel tight. "We have another true purpose. We want to find out where Drifa the dragonsmith went."

For a moment, nothing happened. And then, just as it had before, the glow out in the hallway faded. When it returned a moment later, the path of runes led down the stairs again. Anders and Rayna hurried down them, and when they reached the base, the new glowing path led in an entirely new direction.

"Pack and paws," Anders whispered. "It's taking us to an answer."

Rayna was just drawing breath to reply when Lisabet's voice rang down the halls in a shout that came all the way from the entrance, raw with panic. "Anders! Rayna! The dragons are coming!"

The twins exchanged a glance that lasted only a heartbeat, and at the same time, lasted forever. Anders asked a question with his eyes. With infinite reluctance, Rayna nodded.

"Cloudhaven," Anders said. "Show us the way back out again."

The path faded before them, and the old one sprang up again. They wasted no time in tearing along it, running back to their friends as quickly as they could.

Lisabet and Theo were waiting at the door, leaning

through it without daring to set a foot on the flagstones inside. "Quick," called Lisabet. "Rayna, transform, we need to get your harness on!"

Ellukka was out on the ledge in dragon form when they ran across the huge hall to burst outside, Mikkel pulling her harness on over her head and buckling it into place. Rayna ran to a clear place to make her own change.

"We've got the scepter," Anders called, as he and Lisabet grabbed Rayna's harness.

"What do we do?" Mikkel called.

"We have to keep it away from the dragons," Lisabet said. "They'll use it to warm up the whole of Vallen, to attack the wolves."

"So do we hide it somewhere?" Theo asked, looking out into the fog, in the direction Mikkel and Ellukka must have seen the dragons coming from. "If they're going to catch us, we can't have it with us."

"We—" Mikkel got no further—a sudden wave of cold swept over the wide landing platform, so strong that even the natural power of Cloudhaven's deep-rooted lava was overwhelmed. His knees sagged, and Theo cried out, and in their dragon form, Ellukka and Rayna groaned.

"No," Anders said. "We have to use it as quickly as we can. If they catch us, they'll make us prisoners and take it for themselves. We can't risk that happening."

"But how?" Theo cried, frantic. "We still don't know what it does, apart from make things warmer. Or how to use it, or where we should use it, or—"

"I can use it," Anders said, cutting him off. "And we're taking it to Holbard."

"Holbard?" Lisabet's eyes went wide. "If you think those dragons chasing us are mad, just wait until we fly right over the capital city! The wolves will bring a whole new meaning to the word *mad*!"

"It's the most likely place for Sigrid to have the Snowstone," said Anders. "If she'd left the city to hide it, someone would know, and there's no way she'd want it where she couldn't control it."

"So either the wolves are going to catch us, or the dragons will," Mikkel said, buckling the final piece of Ellukka's harness into place.

"And we don't even know which is worse," Theo concluded, as the two boys ran back to find room to transform.

"We have to use it," Anders said. "Whatever it costs. Or there'll be war. And we have to keep it away from the dragons . . ."

". . . or there'll be a war," Lisabet finished for him.

Rayna stamped one foot on the ground impatiently,

with a noise that wanted to be a roar, but only dared be a whisper.

"What she said," Anders agreed. "Let's go."

A few seconds later, Mikkel and Theo were dragons, and Anders and Lisabet were scrambling up onto Rayna's and Ellukka's backs, Anders jamming the scepter through the straps for safekeeping, Lisabet tucking Kess inside her jacket.

One after another, the four dragons launched, tipping out into the endless fog and turning for Holbard.

CHAPTER FIFTEEN

RAYNA BURST OUT OF THE CLOUDHAVEN MISTS, hurtling toward Holbard as fast as her wings could carry her.

But the Drekhelm dragons were south of Anders and his friends, and now they lay between them and the city. Their only hope was surprise.

Anders couldn't identify any of the adult dragons—he'd never seen them transformed—but he had an inkling that most of the Dragonmeet, if not all of it, was in the air right now. They were all at least twice as big as the four Finskólar dragons, and they weren't exhausted either.

Anders heard a bellow of defiance off to one side, and he saw Mikkel peeling away to their left, heading into the Icespire Mountains. An answering roar came from the right, and Theo tore off toward the rivers and lakes. Ellukka was hot on Rayna's tail, calling out encouragement.

For a moment Anders had no idea why his friends were abandoning him—and then as their pursuers split, it came to him. Mikkel had seen a chance to lead away some of the Dragonmeet, and Theo had understood his bellowed instructions, though Anders had not. The dragons chasing them had no way of knowing what the foursome were doing, or who might be the threat, so they had to chase all of them.

Now there were only ten or so dragons pursuing Anders, Rayna, Ellukka, and Lisabet, fewer than half those in the air. It would still be a race, but their friends had just improved their odds.

Ellukka was making use of her extra strength, weaving around Rayna, no doubt certain that her father would stop the Dragonmeet harming the twins when there was a chance his daughter might be hit.

Anders hoped she was right.

Did the dragons think the children wanted to betray them to the wolves? Or had they somehow guessed they had the Sun Scepter, or something like it, and wanted to take it for themselves?

Another wave of cold hit them, rippling through the air like a gust of wind, and every dragon he could see dipped for a moment, fighting against its weakening force.

Somewhere ahead, there was no doubt that Sigrid had

found the augmenter she needed. And whether or not she knew there were dragons on the way to Holbard, she was using the Snowstone to generate as much cold as she could.

The cold seemed to hit the adult dragons even harder than the children, and as minutes stretched to an hour, and then two, somehow Ellukka and Rayna stayed just ahead of them. Anders could hear the dragons roaring in pursuit, and he knew Rayna and Ellukka must be understanding the terrible threats coming from behind them, but neither of the girls faltered. The waves of cold told them they had no choice but to get to Holbard and use the Sun Scepter—and everything Torsten and the others had said and done told them that they couldn't let the adult dragons be the ones to do it.

They'd flown over the Great Forest of Mists now, and crossed the Sudrain River, and the walls of Holbard were in sight. They'd been flying since morning, first from the Chelle Islands all the way to Cloudhaven, and now down to the city itself. The sun was starting to dip toward the horizon, and Anders could sense Rayna's exhaustion.

And he knew that if they could see the city, the wolves could see them—a dozen dragons flying as fast as they could toward the walls. The wolves would be scrambling even now, running to their positions, ready to defend Holbard. He could imagine the fear, the determination.

Another wave of cold hit them hard, and two of their pursuers freewheeled toward the ground, out of control, too weakened to stay aloft. Anders held his breath as they spun downward, and despite the threat they posed, he willed them desperately to spread their wings, to somehow slow themselves enough to land safely. He thought they did, but he wasn't sure.

And then they were over Holbard, the familiar green rooftop meadows flashing below them, cold air rising from the city, the tiny figures of the wolves racing along the city walls and taking position, ready to cast ice spears and waves of cold the moment the dragons came within range.

Rayna was floundering beneath him, the cold air sapping her strength, pulling her down toward the city, and he could sense she didn't have much time left before she, too, crashed. And just as bad, now that they'd reached the city, she and Ellukka were forced to slow, giving the Dragonmeet time to close the gap.

Ellukka was still valiantly weaving around Rayna's smaller form, trying to protect them, but when the Dragonmeet caught up, they'd be surrounded.

Anders pulled the Sun Scepter from the straps on the harness, holding on tight with both hands, desperately afraid he'd drop it. He raised it above his head and fumbled for words, his brain suddenly completely empty. *Pack and paws, now wasn't the time to forget how to speak!*

He knew it was listening, but what was he supposed to say to bring it to life? Something grand? Something fancy?

"Heat!" he yelled, giving up on sounding impressive and hoping the scepter could hear him, with the wind ready to whip away his words. It was pummeling him from all directions as Rayna dodged and dove, and only the leather belt he wore clipped to her harness kept him safe.

Ellukka's sunrise scales darted past, and out of the corner of Anders's eye he saw a burst of pure white dragonsfire, golden sparks flying from it, falling to the city below.

The flame had been aimed at them!

Ellukka and Lisabet pulled up just in time, and suddenly there were two more dragons there, adults, bigger than any of the others.

One had scales like a warm sunset, and from its similarity to Ellukka, Anders was sure it was her father, Valerius. The other was a deeper red, and for no reason he could explain, Anders was positive it was Leif, protecting his students. The quiet, calm Drekleid was roaring now, his fury directed at the dragons who had dared threaten the children.

Everything was chaos—the adult dragons circling them as Anders tightened his grip on the Sun Scepter, the wolves racing along the walls below, casting up ice spears that wouldn't fall short of their targets for long, Rayna twisting and turning beneath him, and nothing was happening with the scepter, no heat was . . .

. . . and then suddenly, Anders felt it.

A wave of warmth washed over him like a real wave of water, sending all the dragons scrambling to stay steady, sudden updrafts lifting them unexpectedly, tipping them off balance. Beneath them, wolves howled their discomfort, and the runes on the Sun Scepter glowed so brightly he had to look away.

Theo had been right that the Sun Scepter would bring heat where the Snowstone brought cold—but this wasn't simply heat. This was changing the very air around them, and it was too much for the wolves below.

Rayna was suddenly stronger, surer in her movements.

But what would the adult dragons do now? They'd peeled away, suddenly convinced that the children were on their side after all, and as they soared out over Holbard, bellowing their defiance at the weakened wolves below, Anders's heart shrank.

Had they led an attacking force to the city despite all their efforts to bring peace? Were they about to make themselves the traitors to Ulfar they'd never meant to be?

He'd only just finished the thought when far below, a white cloud—a white explosion—appeared over the roof of the Wily Wolf, the tavern he and Rayna had slept above for so many years. Jagged white frost was ballooning out in every direction.

A few seconds later, a wave of cold hit the dragons midair, and Anders realized it had all come from the Wily Wolf.

Sigrid must have hidden the Snowstone in the roof, the highest point in Holbard!

That was why he'd always seen wolves there on his visits—not because they were using it as a lookout, but because they were guarding something.

Could he and Rayna get there? Could she make it through the waves of cold rolling off the tavern's roof, and if she did, was there a way to pit the Sun Scepter against the Snowstone? A way to protect Holbard from both sun and snow?

A cloud of ice and cold flowed down from the highest

point of the Wily Wolf, barreling along the streets of Holbard in every direction, freezing them over. It reached the harbor, and icy fingers snaked out into the water, freezing the surface solid and squeezing the hulls of the ships until they began to crack with bangs Anders could hear even above the city.

Suddenly ice spears were flying up from the walls, along with huge clouds of cold cast by the most powerful of the wolves, and the dragons were staggering, tossed about by the cold wind.

Anders felt the Sun Scepter tingle in his hands, and as he stared at it, mouth open—not speaking a word—it began to glow again. "No!" he cried, but it was too late—a wave of heat had flowed out from it to crash into the cold air around them, and below, a huge crack was opening up right through the middle of Holbard, running straight through the courtyard and outbuildings of Ulfar Academy itself! Stonework crumbled, walls collapsed, and a jagged trench cut the ground in two.

Was the lava far beneath the city trying to find a way up?

"Stop!" he screamed, shaking the scepter in his hands. "Sun Scepter, enough!"

It was too late to think of somehow counteracting one artifact with another. Both were completely out of control. Now, all Anders could do was try and save as many as he could from the chaos below.

Ice was meeting heat below, sending up great clouds of steam, and Anders could only imagine the pandemonium in Holbard's streets. The dragons were roaring and breathing flame, and the wolves below were casting ice spears, and the city that had always been Anders's home was coming to pieces before his very eyes.

Somewhere below him, almost everyone he'd ever known—his friends from Ulfar, the friendly shopkeepers who'd slipped him and his sister meals, the children of the street, the local traders and the foreign merchers—everyone was caught in this battle of fire and ice.

He shouted again, helpless, as half a dozen dragons swooped down at the wolves on the wall, breathing fire and sending them scattering in every direction.

Leif was still flying near his students, but as a sudden volley of ice spears soared toward Ellukka and Rayna, it was Valerius who threw himself into their path to protect his daughter, roaring his defiance.

Ellukka shrieked as a wave of gray cold started at her father's foreleg, racing along his side. One wing paralyzed, he began to fall, fall, fall toward the ground.

Leif plunged with him, somehow maneuvering himself underneath Valerius. The injured dragon's good wing flared, his tail whipped, and by sheer luck he managed to keep his balance as he landed atop Leif's back. And with an extraordinary show of strength, Leif managed to carry him, winging his way toward the plains beyond the city, and safety.

He had saved Ellukka's father, but he would play no further role in the battle.

As Anders stared after them, a deep red dragon he thought was Torsten soared over the city wall, blasting a long section with white-and-gold flame. He left smoldering ruins behind—Anders couldn't tell if there were any wolves among the detritus or not.

He jammed the scepter back into Rayna's harness and thumped on her back with both hands to get her attention.

"Take me lower," he shouted, the power already welling up inside him in response to the danger and his desperation, threatening to overtake him. He could feel it coming like a rush, and there was no way to slow it, let alone stop it. "Take me closer!"

He had to transform if he was going to do this, and he had to do it while Rayna was arrowing through the air. Without his safety harness. He unbuckled the belt that connected him to the leather straps, grabbing hold with his hands instead. Once he let go, he'd have only a heartbeat to change and grab hold of her harness again.

If we get out of this alive, he told himself, *we're adding extra straps to these things. Some kind of safety system.*

And then he was out of time. Rayna dove, understanding his plan, and Anders hurled himself into wolf form with everything he had, channeling his fear and his determination, making the change more quickly than ever before. He grabbed hold of her harness with his teeth, then let his hind legs slide down until they were jammed between the straps and her body. The bright colors of the world faded out, and he was alive with the sharp scents of acrid smoke and crisp frost.

Rayna took a path that would lead her straight between the attacking Dragonmeet dragons and the wolves assembled atop the walls to fight them. Straight into the path of their flame, of their spears.

Nobody was expecting it.

Nobody could stop themselves in time, even if they'd wanted to.

Anders managed to lift his front paws, and he howled and brought them down on Rayna's back.

And there was *icefire*.

Silver flames billowed out, consuming the dragons' fire and the wolves' ice, swallowing them whole before they could touch the twins. Rayna pulled up, and Anders grabbed the harness with his teeth again as she looped around to see what lay behind them.

Last time Anders had thrown icefire, both the wolves and the dragons had been so confused, so overwhelmed, it had been enough to end the battle.

This time, they were prepared. His heart sank as he realized the wolves were already launching another volley, and the dragons were regrouping, preparing to reply.

This time, his icefire wouldn't be enough.

Everything was moving so quickly around him, images whirling past, the wind whipping at him, steam rising from below, ice cracking buildings and heat sending billowing updrafts to grab at Rayna. He thought he saw Mikkel, and Theo, but could his friends have caught up with them already? Once he saw five wolves racing across the roofs, and his heart wanted to tell him they were his Ulfar friends, but his head told him they were simply more attackers.

His gaze traced back a path the way they'd come—and then he blinked, and looked again. Amid the ruins of Ulfar, the crumbled stonework and the jagged trench running through the Academy, there was a beam of white light shining up from one corner of the debris. It was perfectly straight, spearing up into the sky. His tired brain tried to make sense of what he was seeing, tried to understand which part of the Academy the light was coming from, whether it was some kind of new danger.

But then he realized he knew exactly where it was coming from.

It was Hayn's workshop.

Was their uncle sending them a signal?

He howled to Rayna, throwing his weight in the direction he wanted her to look, and her great head swung around as her wings beat to keep them aloft. Unhesitating—trusting him utterly, even though she had no idea why he was asking her to do it—she made for the pillar of light. She dodged and wove, and he clung to her straps with claws and teeth, flung around like a rag doll as she narrowed in on the signal.

He could see even as they approached that the workshop itself was empty, the whole roof missing, as if it had been blown off. Where Hayn was, he did not know, but the light was shining up like a beacon from a huge sheet of metal, engraved in runes. What had Hayn wanted them to see, or do?

He flung himself from Rayna's back, aware they had only moments before the wolves would be on them, forcing himself back into human shape even as his feet hit the ground. His sister couldn't transform—not without losing her straps, and the only way she had of carrying him safely. She roared a warning—to him, or perhaps to the approaching wolves—as he scrambled over the rubble toward the center of the room.

There, beside the almost blinding light rising from the metal plate, were two pendants, hammered discs of metal engraved all over with intricate spirals of runes.

He had seen these before. He had seen them in the drawing of Felix and Drifa, each of them wearing one around their neck. And now here they were again. Had Hayn found them in his search for augmenters? *Were* they augmenters?

As he snatched them up, he saw they rested on a sheet of paper, a quick note scrawled in his uncle's hand:

> *Use them well.*
>
> *—H*

Anders threw one around his neck, and turning, stared up at Rayna for a heartbeat. He couldn't get the augmenter around Rayna's neck. But perhaps pressing it against her skin would be enough. He ran back to her in three quick steps, shoving the leather necklace through the nearest part of her harness, intending on tying it there, hoping it would stay secure.

But as if it knew its home, before his eyes, the necklace simply melted into her skin, vanishing, perhaps to the same place her clothes and the contents of her pockets had gone when she transformed.

He threw himself onto Rayna's back, and even as he wedged himself into the straps and prepared to transform again—though his icefire, he knew now, would not be enough—she was launching herself back into the safety of the air. They spiraled up, and as another wave of cold air hit them, the Sun Scepter blossomed with heat—a new, burning heat that forced Anders to turn his face away. It seemed hotter than ever. Was it the augmenter around his neck? Could he . . .

He got no further in that thought. The next moment, a huge explosion of ice and frost billowed up from the Wily Wolf below, as if in answer to the challenge of the scepter. As if the Snowstone itself had exploded—and perhaps it had.

And tucked into Rayna's harness, a moment later, the Sun Scepter gave a deadly quiver of warning.

And then the Sun Scepter exploded too.

Rayna went whirling down toward the rooftops, the force of the detonation tossing her end over end in a terrifying cartwheel. She kept trying to spread her wings and stop her fall, only to be thrown around once more.

Anders held on to the harness with teeth and claws,

with everything he had, and together brother and sister tumbled to the ground and skidded across the green of the rooftop meadow. He was flung free of her, arcing through the air, not knowing which way was up or down. His breath was knocked out of him as he connected with the grass, and he and Rayna tumbled over and over until they came to rest against a sloping roof.

Anders staggered to his four feet, forgetting his pain, the heat, the cold, the battle around him, forgetting everything as he scrambled toward his sister.

She wasn't moving.

As he reached her, standing up on his hind legs to press his paws against her side, she groaned and raised her head.

Her straps and her scales were burned out where the Sun Scepter had been, and there was no sign of it. Had it truly exploded, burning out the last of its essence in an attempt to fight the Snowstone? Had the Snowstone done the same?

Dragons were wheeling overhead, the sky orange behind them, and in his daze, Anders wasn't sure if it was the sunset or if the whole world was on fire.

He turned and saw a huge lone wolf racing toward them over the rooftops. He howled at Rayna, willing her to stand up, to be able to fly again.

In a rush of air, Ellukka and Lisabet landed beside

them, Lisabet shouting a warning over the chaos and pointing at something.

He whirled around, and from the other side he saw a group of wolves leaping across the rooftops, running toward them in an arrow formation.

It was his classmates! He saw Sakarias in the lead, with Viktoria, Jai, and Det behind him, and Mateo's hulking form bringing up the rear. They were racing toward them at top speed. For an instant, Anders's heart insisted they were coming to help, and his head told him he had to be careful, but he had no more time to wonder about it than that.

Sakarias yipped a greeting, and then his friends were taking up positions around the twins, facing out, ready to defend them.

On his other side, the lone wolf was drawing near in big, powerful strides, and—his heart swelling to have his friends with him once more—he ran to take his own place in the formation. He *had* to defend his sister, but he didn't want to hurt any members of the Ulfar pack in the process. What was he going to do?

Ellukka bellowed a challenge, standing over the injured Rayna, swinging her head back and forth as if threatening to breathe flame on the first wolf to come near their group. Anders wasn't sure if she'd really—that she'd really kill someone—but he knew the Wolf Guard wouldn't hesitate to throw a spear at her.

Lisabet's voice somehow carried over the howls and snarls and roars, the crashing noises of a breaking city all around them.

"Stop!" she screamed, sliding down Ellukka's side and running to stand between Sakarias and Mateo, facing the lone wolf as it drew closer.

Anders had no idea what she was going to say next, but he didn't get a chance to find out. For suddenly the lone wolf had reached them, and even as she ran, she transformed, pushing herself into human shape.

And then Lisabet and Sigrid were face-to-face.

"Lisabet, what are you doing?" The Fyrstulf's voice was sharp, furious, her soot-stained face white with rage.

"I'm trying to stop the fighting," Lisabet replied, lifting both hands to gesture to the carnage around them. "I'm trying—"

Sigrid cut her off. "You will join the pack this instant. All of you will join the pack."

"We won't," said Lisabet, lifting her chin.

Sigrid stared at her, fury in her pale-blue eyes.

"You're no daughter of mine," she said, the words carrying perfectly clearly over the noise around them.

Even in draconic form, Anders heard Ellukka's gasp, sparks spilling from her mouth as she let out a quick breath, as if someone had punched her in the stomach. He could practically hear her voice: *Daughter? The Fyrstulf's daughter?*

Lisabet's head bowed, her shoulders rounding, as her mother's words went through her like a weapon.

Sigrid simply looked away, dismissing Lisabet completely, to survey the other Ulfar students ranged in front of Rayna and Ellukka. "All of you will come with me," she snapped.

Nobody moved.

With a snarl, Sigrid sank back into her wolf form, baring her teeth.

Anders heard himself give an answering snarl, and then he heard it echoed, louder and deeper, behind him.

With a sound halfway between a groan and a roar, his sister was staggering to her feet, ignoring her burns, to defy the Fyrstulf. And knowing she was there gave Anders the strength to address the furious pack leader directly.

I don't know what the icefire will do if it hits you *instead of your spears*, he said, speaking with a flick of his ears, a snarl that bared his teeth. *And I don't want to find out, but I will if you make me.*

You are cast out, she snarled in reply. *You are exiled from the pack.*

And then she lifted her head and howled, long and loud, summoning the Wolf Guard to join her and take up the fight.

Panic ran through Anders's friends, and they backed up, tails low, heads swinging around as they looked for escape. Mateo howled a warning beside him, and Anders whipped around in time to see Mikkel and Theo swooping low overhead.

Let them down! he howled to his friends, raising his voice above the cacophony of battle.

Lisabet was running back to Ellukka as her mother howled her summons, and she joined Anders in shouting to their friends. "Let's go! Now, all of us!"

Anders saw the moment the realization hit his friends. They'd just lined up to defend him. Sigrid's order of exile had included all of them.

They'd just made themselves traitors. The very deepest part of him was pierced with pain at the knowledge he was forever separated from the pack. But they had not a moment to lose—the Wolf Guard were racing toward them, to join the Fyrstulf and take up arms against them.

Viktoria was the first one to throw herself back into

human form, making the transformation as neatly as ever, despite the chaos. Mikkel and Theo took it as a sign, and each of them landed, buffeting the wolves with wind as they flared their wings.

Anders stayed in wolf form—he had to be ready, in case more icefire was needed, though already he wasn't sure if he could manage it again. He wasn't sure it would help.

Sakarias ran alongside him in human form, his gray Ulfar cloak flapping, and together they scrambled up onto Rayna's back, grabbing hold of the half-burned straps. Surely, any moment now, Sigrid would throw an ice spear—and with her strength, it would be deadly, killing whoever it struck.

But as they ran and scrambled to safety, the spear didn't come.

He could see Viktoria climbing up behind Lisabet, Mateo climbing onto Mikkel's back, and Jai pulling Det up behind them on Theo's back.

The Wolf Guard were seconds away from joining their leader now, at least a dozen of them running up behind Sigrid, and any moment the adult dragons overhead would realize what they were doing. With Mikkel and Theo back in the fray, their pursuers had come as well, and there were more dragons up there than ever.

As the Wolf Guard reached her, finally Sigrid came to life once more, and ice spears flew past on either side of them. Whatever hesitations she'd had about attacking her daughter, about attacking children, were gone, and the Fyrstulf joined the other pack members as they tried to take down the Finskólars and their passengers.

What would the wolves and dragons do if the children fled? Would both sides keep on fighting?

Anders knew he couldn't let that happen.

He reached deep within himself, pulling every ounce of his power to the surface, and howling to Rayna as she launched. He could see what every movement was costing her now, but she made a noise he hoped was a reply and winged her way up once more.

Rayna's movements were jerky and uneven, and Sakarias wrapped both his arms around Anders to keep him in place, taking handfuls of his fur and clinging to him.

Desperately, pulling up every last ounce of his energy, Anders threw his icefire again, hardly seeing what was happening. He hurled it out blindly into the void between the wolves and dragons with everything he had, hoping against hope they'd see that neither side could win. That he'd stand between them, force them back to peace. That they'd believe it, before he completely ran out of energy.

The silver flames bloomed, and then they kept growing—and growing.

And growing.

They blossomed out until they were almost touching the combatants, sending the wolves scurrying back along the wall with howls of alarm, the dragons veering sharply away to escape by a hairsbreadth.

This flame was impossibly large. Impossibly strong.

Because it wasn't just his.

Rayna, who hadn't breathed a single flame, not a spark, since her transformation, had joined him.

His sister had found the same well inside her that he'd discovered in his desperation, the gift of both their mother and their father, and as the augmenters Hayn had left them did their work, he knew that together their silver flames were bigger, stronger, more powerful than his had been alone.

Though she brought a dragon's fire and he brought a wolf's ice to their silver flames, together they would always be stronger. No difference between them—no time apart—could weaken them. The more they grew, the more they learned to know themselves, the stronger they became.

The Snowstone was gone now, and the Sun Scepter,

and together, in this moment, the twins were the most powerful thing in Holbard.

The silver flame rolled out across the city, consuming ice spears and dragonsfire, consuming everything in its path.

It halted the spread of the ice in the streets below.

It calmed the hot wind left behind by the Sun Scepter.

It traveled out and out, enveloping everyone and everything, leaving them standing in its wake, their fire cooled and their ice gone.

And when it finally dissipated at the city walls, everything below them was still and silent.

Anders had nothing left, and he was sure Rayna didn't either, but she gamely circled around, as if to bluff the adult dragons that the twins were ready to do it again, and *again*, until everyone else gave way to them.

What would happen if the wolves somehow rallied for one more attack?

What would happen if Torsten and the dragons swooped in to breathe their white-gold flame again?

Anders howled his warning, and Rayna bugled her challenge, and both of them knew they were lying—that this was their last and only remaining move.

One second passed, and with it a swoop of Rayna's wings, a thump of Anders's heart.

Another second.

Another.

And then, as the children watched, the members of the Dragonmeet turned one by one toward the northwest.

And they flew away from the city, on a course for Drekhelm.

CHAPTER SIXTEEN

DARKNESS WAS FALLING RAPIDLY AS THE DRAG-
ons disappeared into the blue velvet of the night.
Anders could still make out the wolves in the city below,
forming up, ready to defend Holbard if the four dragons
still above them descended.

Rayna and the others were talking about something,
bellowing to one another across the distance between
them, but he had no way of knowing what they were
saying. Some decision must have been made, though—as
one, they turned for the west. They were leaving the city
but picking out a direction that made it clear they weren't
following the adults.

They crossed the Sudrain River by moonlight after
about half an hour, and slowly descended to land near a
clump of trees in the farmland beyond it. The Great Forest

of Mists loomed on the horizon, black trees wreathed in white fog.

One by one the dragons came to ground, and the wolves slid down from them. Anders transformed as soon as his paws hit the earth, and once human, silently pulled off Rayna's harness so she could do the same. Nearby, Lisabet was seeing to Ellukka. Both the harnesses were charred in places, and he wasn't sure Rayna's would hold if they used it again.

One by one the dragons transformed, until the eleven children stood in a circle. Some leaned over to rest their hands on their knees, exhausted, others hugged themselves, staring at their companions in the moonlight.

The tableau was broken when Kess suddenly streaked across the circle, leaping down from Lisabet's arms to run straight for Anders, scaling his body and perching on his shoulders. He was so exhaustedly happy to see her, he didn't even mind the places where she sank her claws in.

As if the cat's movement had woken her up, Viktoria spoke in a whisper. "What have we done?"

"The same thing as us," Ellukka replied. "You can't go home. Neither can we."

"We had to," Lisabet said, sounding just as tired as the others. "If we hadn't brought the Sun Scepter, the wolves would have weakened the dragons until they killed them. If we hadn't kept it from the dragons, they'd have used it against the wolves until they could attack instead. We're the only reason they're not at war right now."

"All we did was destroy half of Holbard instead," said Theo, looking sick.

Rayna sighed. "And they'll still be at war, once they've had the time to think about it. They hate each other. The wolves think the dragons just attacked them, and the dragons know the wolves were getting ready to do the same."

"Then we'll need a plan to stop them," someone said.

Anders blinked, as he realized it had been him. Everyone was looking at him. He took a deep breath and continued. "Viktoria, Sakarias, Det, Mateo, Jai, this is my sister, Rayna," he said, pointing at her.

"But, Anders," Det said carefully, as his wolf friends all blinked. "Um, she's a dragon."

"Wolves, this is Ellukka, Mikkel, and Theo," Anders replied.

"Lisabet," said Ellukka carefully. "Did I hear the Fyrstulf call you her daughter?"

Mikkel's mouth fell open. All the dragons were looking at Lisabet.

"Actually," she said, lifting her chin defiantly, the soot

on her pale skin streaked with the white paths of dried tears, "I think you heard her say I'm not her daughter anymore."

"You could have mentioned that earlier," Ellukka said slowly.

"Would you have?" Rayna asked, with one of her snorts.

"We all have a lot to tell each other," Anders said. "But right now, we need somewhere to hide. And to make a plan. We thought it was enough to try and counter the Snowstone, to push Ulfar and the Dragonmeet back to a stalemate. But we were wrong. *How* we do it matters as much as what we do."

"Anders, the problem is even bigger than you know," Sakarias said. "You asked us to look into the dragonsfire attacks on Holbard. We have to tell you what we found."

Mikkel spoke up. "We have to get to safety first. We can fly again, but we're going to need an hour's rest, something to eat. It feels like I've flown farther today than in all my other times since my first transformation put together."

Anders watched as Viktoria, Sakarias, and the other wolves exchanged a long glance. He knew what they'd been taught about dragons—he'd been taught the same things. He'd felt the same way, even a few weeks ago.

"These are my friends," he said. "They've lost their home for this. We wolves have been exiled, but they have too, whether the Dragonmeet's told them so or not. They can't go back to Drekhelm now, and they gave that up to help us stop the wolves freezing half of Vallen so they could attack the dragons. *And* to stop the dragons taking the Sun Scepter from us to heat up the city and attack in return."

Theo spoke up behind him, hesitant but determined. "I lived in Holbard until not long ago. The dragons kidnapped me. I thought I was going to die, but they knew something I didn't. I needed to transform, and they had to help me do it. They're not what I always thought they were."

"And the eleven of us, wolves and dragons," said Anders, "we're all that's left to stop a war. We *have* to work together."

He watched as the wolves spoke silently—even in human form, they communicated with glances, with twitches of body language that would have been invisible to him before he'd become one of them. It was a lightning-fast conversation—uncertainty from some, decision from others.

Slowly, on behalf of all of them, Viktoria nodded. "We need somewhere to hide," she said, her voice soft but clearly determined not to shake.

"Cloudhaven," said Rayna.

Anders nodded. "It's where the first dragonsmiths worked," he said. "Nobody ever goes there now, it's forbidden." Then, after a moment: "Our mother worked there too."

Sakarias did a double take. "I'm sorry, what?"

"Like I said," Anders replied, with what felt a little like his old smile. "We have a lot to catch you up on." But the mention of his mother had made him think of someone else. "Does anyone know if Hayn's all right?"

Slowly, one at a time, the young wolves shook their heads. "I saw him during the battle," Jai said. "But I don't know what happened to him." They sounded far from certain.

Anders reached up to grasp the augmenter at his neck, his fingers tingling with a hint of its power as its edges pressed into his skin. Wherever Hayn was, somehow he was sure it wouldn't be too long before they saw their uncle again. And Professor Ennar had refused to let anyone speak against Hayn when he'd been locked up. Perhaps there was some hope she'd listen to them.

Beside him, Lisabet started going through her bag, pulling out food and setting it on the ground. "Let's rest," she said. "And then Rayna is right, we should go to Cloudhaven. There's lava deep below it, so the dragons will regain their strength there. And it's permanently sur-rounded by mist and cloud, so the cold of it makes it a perfect place for wolves. Once we're there, we can . . ." But that was where her practical tone of voice ran out, and she trailed off.

Anders didn't know the answer either. He didn't know what they'd do next, or how they'd keep the peace. It couldn't be another act of brute force, another attempt to force the hands of Ulfar and Drekhelm. It would have to be something new.

But as he watched Sakarias break a bread roll in half and pass the other piece to Ellukka with a tentative smile, he knew one thing for sure.

Whatever he did next, he'd do it with *all* his friends at his back.

ACKNOWLEDGMENTS

No book is created by the author alone, and I have a wonderful pack of wolves and dragons to whom I owe many thanks.

I've been to every corner of that map of Vallen with my inspiring editor, Andrew Eliopulos—his navigation is never wrong, and I can't wait for all our future adventures! The wonderful Abby Ranger first handed me the compass, and will always be a part of these stories.

A huge thank-you to the wonderful team at Harper, who have made publishing these books such a joyful experience—I must particularly mention Bria Ragin; Joe Merkel and Levente Szabo (who are jointly responsible for these incredible covers); Virginia Allyn for a map that inspired large parts of this story; Jill Amack and Emily Rader for saving me from myself on many occasions; and Rosemary Brosnan and Ann Dye for all their support. To my team at Harper Oz—I'm having such a blast! Thank you so much for taking such good care of me. A huge thanks as well to the team at Harper Audio and to my incredible narrator Johnathan McClain, who truly brought these books to life.

My agent, Tracey Adams, is a part of all my stories and all my journeys—Tracey, I value your friendship as much as your fierce intelligence. I feel so lucky to have you, Josh, Cathy, and Stephen in my pack.

Many people lent their expertise to this telling of this story—as always, any mistakes remaining after their wonderful advice are mine. Thanks and more thanks to Alex Gino, the staff at the Wolf Conservation Center in South Salem, New York, and many others. Thanks as well to Will Marney (who also lent me his middle name) for all his feedback, and to Meg Spooner for every part she played in making sure both book and author came through in one piece.

Other support came from many wonderful friends: Jay, Marie, Leigh, Michelle, Cat, Kacey, Kiersten, Nic, Kate, Soraya, Ryan, Peta, Eliza, the Roti Boti crew, my retreat-mates at the House of Progress, and the Wordsmiths. I am immeasurably lucky to have all of you in my life.

Many, many thanks to the readers, reviewers, book-sellers, and librarians who help to spread the word about this and many other books—I am so grateful for all your efforts in helping Anders and his friends find their way to new homes and new hearts.

To all my family, both two- and four-legged—thank you so much for all your support, your enthusiasm, and your love. I am so grateful, and so lucky.

And finally, as always, to Brendan: You are endlessly patient, loving, generous, hilarious, and supportive. I couldn't tell my stories without you, and I wouldn't want to. I love you.

Read the full Elementals series by
AMIE KAUFMAN

Book 3 coming soon!